PRAISE FOR

"*NO BODY* is well-fashioned, inventive and entertaining."

—Lawrence Block,
author of the *Burglar series*

"As resourceful Jenny pursues her parallel cases—one involving too many bodies, the other too few—Pickard fashions some of the most fiendishly hilarious scenes this side of Donald Westlake."

—*San Francisco Chronicle*

"In *NO BODY*, Ms. Pickard vividly creates the sense of small town community life . . . . A thoroughly modern heroine, Jennifer Cain is clever and witty. . . . Readers will look forward to her further adventures."

—*Kansas City Star*

"*NO BODY* is fast-moving, sparked by humor and an unusual plot."

—*Publishers Weekly*

"Pickard's satire is scalpel-sharp . . . *NO BODY* is deliciously ironic."

—*Washington Post Book World*

"*NO BODY* is fast, well-constructed, well-written—this is first-class entertainment."

—*Kirkus Reviews*

Books by Nancy Pickard

Bum Steer
Dead Crazy
Generous Death
I.O.U.
Marriage Is Murder
No Body
Say No to Murder

Published by POCKET BOOKS

NANCY PICKARD

A JENNY CAIN MYSTERY

NO BODY

POCKET BOOKS

New York   London   Toronto   Sydney   Tokyo   Singapore

Bruce Springsteen lyrics used by permission of John Landau Management, Inc.

POCKET BOOKS, a division of Simon & Schuster
1230 Avenue of the Americas, New York, NY 10020

ISBN: 0-671-73429-6

First Pocket Books printing November 1987

10 9 8 7 6 5 4

POCKET and colophon are registered trademarks of
Simon & Schuster.

Printed in the U.S.A.

FOR GUY AND NICHOLAS

NO BODY

Prologue

Some days are better than others for walking in graveyards. This first day in April, following a rainy weekend, was less than ideal, thought Lucille Grant as she struck a path among the old slate and marble tombstones in Union Hill Cemetery. Built rather like a tombstone herself, tall and broad and weighty, Lucille sank into the mud with every step. The rain-softened ground pulled at her sensible brown hiking shoes like grasping hands.

Lucille directed a glare, one that only a former schoolteacher could have mastered, at the ground, as if disciplining recalcitrant sixth graders.

"Don't be greedy," she admonished the nineteenth-century ghosts whose remains moldered below her in our town's Civil War–era cemetery. "I'll join you one of these days, but in my own good time, thank you. Don't rush me."

With a hungry, sucking sound, the ground released her left foot. Lucille nodded approvingly. She squished forward to her goal: the grave of her great-great-grandfather who had been a distant cousin to Ulysses S. Grant.

"Good morning, Sarah!" Lucille sang out in a robust contralto to a tipsy gravestone that bore the ambiguous inscription: "Good Wife, Died a Mother, Loved God, None Other. Sarah Clark, b. 1824, d. 1848."

As she marched past the grave, Lucille announced conversationally, "It's a lovely spring day in the late twentieth century, Sarah. Bit of sunshine today, though we've had plenty of rain to nourish the elm trees you planted by the church. My love to your family, dear!"

The sun glanced off Sarah Clark's tombstone in a slow wink.

They were alive to her, these ghosts, in a most friendly way. In her four decades as president of the Union Hill Cemetery Historical Society, eighty-year-old Lucille Grant had come to know well the inhabitants of these modest graves on a stark and lonely flat stretch of cliff overlooking the Atlantic Ocean outside of Port Frederick, Massachusetts. She knew which of them had lost their babies in childbirth and who had died of drowning. She could name the victims of consumption and of measles. She knew whose boys came rattling home from war over the dirt roads in plain pine boxes. Simply by judging the quality and size of a gravestone, Lucille could estimate the net worth and social status of its owner. And she sensed, by their absence among the graves in the old yard, who had stepped beyond the pale of nineteenth-century society into the outcast world of murder, suicide, or penury.

Lucille smiled gently at five little graves all in a row, small victims of a dreadful winter of influenza in Port Frederick in 1872.

"Oh dear, not again." One of the little tombstones had fallen over on its back; worse, the ground had eroded over all five graves during the winter snows and spring rains. Those gullies would have to be filled and resodded, but who would pay for it? Heaven knew, young Stan Pittman over at the Harbor Lights Funeral Home was generous with his backhoe and dump truck, not to mention seed and sod. But as that father of his so often objected, they could hardly be expected to support Union Hill, where the paying customers had long since passed on beyond the reach of cemetery-plot salesmen! And the historical society always had such a time pinching pennies out of that tightwad Town Council, most of whose members she'd had in her classrooms and who should have known better than to talk back to her . . .

Lucille stuck her big rough hands into the pockets of her shapeless corduroy jacket. She frowned behind her horn-rimmed glasses in worried thought. Where to get the money this year?

"Jenny Cain!" she crowed in sudden inspiration. "Of course! The dear child is director of that charitable foundation. I'll remind her of what a sweet, obedient little girl she was in the sixth grade, and then I'll ask her for the money."

That settled, she resumed her purposeful march over the flat, eroded ground toward her great-great-grandparents' graves, which lay on the single, gentle slope after which the cemetery was named. On the first relatively warm day of every spring, she liked to visit with her ancestors. She would stand over their graves and say a little prayer for their souls (even though they would have thought it "popish" and disapproved), then chat a bit about the latest doings in their old hometown, not that they would recognize it now with all the cars and computers. They would be sad to learn of the passing of the great-great-great-nephew of John Rudolph, and so young, too, but they would be pleased to hear she'd had their old cherry-wood table refinished so it looked as good as if Erasmus Pittman had built it yesterday instead of 135 years ago. And they would take joy in the births and marriages, though they would be shocked, as she was, by the recent divorces and separations. . . .

The soft jowls that framed her wide mouth eased from a disapproving pucker into a fond smile as she sighted the tall gravestones that marked the burial ground of Ulysses P. and Lida M. Grant. Obligingly, the sun broke through the remaining clouds to warm her annual visit with her distinguished forebears—distinguished, at least, by the modest standards of Port Frederick, where even a secondhand claim to fame qualifies one for local immortality. Lucille was, however, not so pleased to observe ugly striations in the earth around the two graves. Months of wet weather had washed away the topsoil; in fact, she saw to her dismay, the whole bottom of the slope

11

was cut away a good foot where the rain had carved a new stream. To reach the graves, she stepped wide and carefully over rivulets that still ran several inches deep with cold water.

Lucille walked as lightly as a 192-pound woman could onto the mud atop her great-great-grandfather's grave. She stood for a moment in meditation upon his leaning gravestone: "Fought and Nearly Died in 'Sixty-four, Saved by the Lord for One Fight More." They had loved poetry, the old ones, she mused wryly, although they didn't necessarily discriminate as to quality; death provided one last chance for the telling epigram, the fitting epitaph, not to mention the strained rhyme and the wounded metaphor. She adored the old, crumbling tombstones with their colorful inscriptions and equally loathed the new "memorial parks," which forbade such expressions of the individuality of the human species.

When Lucille awoke from her historical reverie, she was up to her shoelaces in cold, hungry mud.

"Bother." She frowned at the ground where the toes of her shoes had disappeared.

Lucille tried to lift her feet from the mud. But her knees twisted painfully; her feet didn't budge. The grasping hands of the mud held her tight, its soft fingers creeping now toward her ankles. A rumbling alerted her to ominous movement below. Then, with a monstrous shifting and sucking, the mud washed away all around her, carrying her and her ancestors' graves with it down the slope. She pitched backward, tumbling and rolling in the mud like a child at play, but a child who was utterly surprised, and terrified of breathing mud into its lungs. She landed on her back at the bottom of the slope, gasping for breath and in terror. With her head toward the hill and her feet toward the road, Lucille looked backward at the once-lovely site where her great-great-grandparents' graves had lain. Now there was only a cave, a horrible hollow in the hillside that laid bare the innards of the earth to her view. And what she saw, where two disintegrating coffins should have been, where two old skeletons might have been tossed to lie in the mud was . . . nothing.

Five feet below the crest of the hill, with the sun bright

above her head, Lucille Grant wiped mud from her eyes, stared, and concluded to her horror that she was all alone. Great-great-grandfather wasn't there; neither was his coffin. And with the side walls of the grave fallen away to reveal her great-great-grandmother's grave, Lucille discovered that it, too, was empty.

She tried to raise herself from the mud. Excruciating pains shot through her twisted knees.

"Help!" She yelled with all the power of a woman with fifty years of playground duty behind her. "Help me, somebody!"

It took Stan Pittman's grounds crew only a mercifully short time to hoist poor Miss Grant back to her feet, wash her off with a garden hose, wrap her in blankets, and escort her to a doctor. It took a little longer for them to ascertain that all the other graves in Union Hill were empty, too.

1

"Jenny?" Marvin Lastelic said my name with the air of a man who is about to tell a joke. "Guess who's buried in Grant's Tomb."

I looked up from a thick booklet that endeavored to explain the latest refinement of the tax code as it applies to charitable foundations, and gave him the look of a woman who is in no mood for jokes.

"Marv," I said to the kind and conscientious gentleman who serves as the part-time accountant for the Port Frederick Civic Foundation, of which I am director, "that was old when Groucho Marx told it."

"No, really, Jenny, take a guess." He was standing by my desk, nodding his head and arching his eyebrows at me in encouragement. I noticed with interest that his gray hairs were curly, although the rest of his thinning, dark hair was straight. Was this what maturity had in store for me one day: naturally curly hair, at last? I hauled my attention back to the absurd question at hand, as Marv repeated himself: "Who's buried in Grant's Tomb?"

"Oh, Marvin." I groaned, resting my chin in my palm. "All right. I don't know. Who?"

"Nobody!" He grinned. "No body."

I shook my head at my secretary, Faye Basil. Her desk was just on the other side of the wall from mine, and she had wheeled her chair over and craned her neck around so she could see us. Now she was observing us with that amused but long-suffering expression that mothers wear.

"It has happened, Faye," I said in mournful tones. "I knew it would, someday. Leave a man alone in a room with tax forms for too many years, and eventually he cracks up. A man can take a lot, you know, prisoners of war have proved it time and again . . . torture, deprivation, loneliness. But the tax forms of the United States government are beyond the capacity of a sane man to behold and withstand, and every time our representatives, in their wisdom, 'improve' and 'shorten' the damn things, accountants all over the country get that much closer to the precipice that Marv here has obviously just plunged over."

"Coffee, Marvin?" Faye inquired with false and humorous sympathy. "Aspirin?"

"Whiskey?" I suggested more usefully.

His grin grew even more gleeful, and he rubbed his bony hands together as if he were rolling dice. I began to wonder if my normally sane and sober accountant was adding with all his numbers.

"It's true," he insisted. "I heard it on the news as I was driving over here. Yesterday afternoon, the president of some Port Frederick historical society fell into Ulysses S. Grant's grave. And guess what? It's empty!"

"Not Ulysses *S*. Grant." Derek Jones, my administrative assistant, closed the door of the outer office behind him as he came in from lunch. "Ulysses *P*. Grant, her cousin or something."

"Not Ulysses P. Grant!" I exclaimed.

"Yeah," Derek confirmed, nodding his blond head at me. "That's what I just said."

"No!" I shook my head back at him.

"Yes, Jenny."

"No." I held up my hand to still the bobbing heads. "What I mean is, that's terrible news if it's really Ulysses P. Grant, because that's Miss Lucille Grant's great-great-grandfather, of whom she is most inordinately proud. She'll be crushed if he's missing."

"Missing?" Derek looked confused. "I thought he'd been dead for a hundred years."

"She nearly was crushed," Marv Lastelic informed me, and he explained what he had heard about the accident at Union Hill. "They say that all the graves are empty, all 133 of them! Her great-great-grandmother wasn't there, either," he added as an afterthought.

I was shocked. Twenty years after the fact, I still remembered my beloved sixth grade teacher explaining the Civil War by illustrating it through the lives of her own ancestors, the illustrious Grants, who were buried in Union Hill. "But is she all right? She wasn't hurt, was she?"

"Twisted her knees," Marv said.

Derek was beginning to grin. "Hey," he said. "This gives a whole new perspective to that old joke, you know . . ."

"Who's buried in Grant's Tomb?" Faye and Marvin chorused back at him. And then, "No body!"

I grabbed my suit coat and left the office, abandoning them to their hilarity. I was going to pay a long-overdue visit to my sixth grade teacher. I had learned a lot about life and the love of same at her knees; now I wanted to return some of that love to those same, now-hurting knees.

If image always matched reality, Miss Grant should, by all rights, have retired to a charming, vine-covered cottage on a woody acre at the edge of town.

One can't afford much charm on a schoolteacher's salary, however, particularly when most of that salary was paid in the days before teachers' unions. So she lived in the second-floor right-front apartment of a red brick fourplex in one of those neighborhoods where old ladies clutch their purses to their chests when they walk to the grocery store. Flower beds, just beginning to sprout with purple and yellow crocuses, hugged the outside walls. Her doing, I guessed. They had that tended look about them that some gardens and greatly loved

17

children possess. We had all worn that look for a year, all of Miss Grant's sixth graders. I wondered if the owner of the building or the other tenants pitched in to pay for seeds and fertilizer, or if she squeezed that out of her pension as well.

In the unlighted entryway, I rang the small ivory bell beneath the shiniest of the four gold mailboxes. "Luke Grant," the label on the mailbox said. It was, I believed, her brother's name; a stratagem, I supposed, to fool and discourage the monsters who prey on elderly single women who live alone. It made me feel sad and angry. I climbed the creaking stairs to her door. Beside the cheap metal knocker, she had affixed a sheaf of dried flowers and dried grasses, which she'd tied together with a hand-sewn ribbon that looked as if it might once have seen duty as the hem of a bedsheet. Charm, it seemed, like luck and beauty, lay where you found it. Or made it. I knocked.

"Yes?" I wasn't prepared for the age and weariness I heard in the voice on the other side of the door. "Who is it?"

I stood straight, pulled back my shoulders, sucked in my stomach. Smiled when I realized what I was doing. "It's Jennifer Cain, Miss Grant. May I come in?"

"Dear child." The voice dropped years, gained vigor. "Of course."

The three rooms in which she lived—living room, dining room, bedroom, plus kitchen, porch, and tiny bath—were bright with yellows, comfortable with antiques, fragrant with cooking spices. In an ugly apartment building in a depressing neighborhood, Miss Grant had her charming English cottage after all.

After she had hobbled over on aluminum crutches to let me in the door, she allowed me to baby her to the extent of pouring Twining's Gunpowder Green tea from her antique pewter pot into antique cups of translucent china. "In grateful memory of the Boston Tea Party," she instructed me by way of a toast. "December 16, 1773. But of course you remember that, Jenny."

"Of course," I murmured.

18

She further permitted me to lift her bandaged legs onto a footstool—an enormous, heavy wooden Victorian thing with scrolled legs—and to fluff her pillows and to pass her the cream. But then I offered to stir her tea for her.

She lowered me back into an antique country side chair with the force of a stern glance and a frown. I was in the classroom again, caught talking out of turn.

"There is nothing wrong with my wrist, young lady," she informed me. I half expected to be told to write it 100 times on the blackboard. "I can stir my own tea, thank you. I may be old, foolish, and horribly embarrassed, but I am not yet feeble." The stern expression melted and the soft skin of her jowls quivered. "Oh, Jenny, all those years I labored over the archives of that cemetery—not to take all the credit for myself, you understand, but after all, I had the time. All the years I've dedicated to preserving that old graveyard, and there's nobody buried in it!" She told me then all about her aborted stroll in Union Hill Cemetery. "Oh, I am an old and foolish woman, and so horribly embarrassed. Oh my . . ."

She trailed off into the unapproachable misery of the proud. I longed to pat her gardening-roughened hands but didn't dare. Before I could speak words of comfort and denial, the old black telephone on the antique table beside her rang.

"Yes?" she said crisply into the receiver. I watched as she wrote on a pad of paper, "Lewis Riss, *Port Frederick Times.*" Then, in firm block letters, "NO!" which she underlined twice in thick, dark strokes. The tone she used with the reporter was the same one she had employed years before when little boys giggled behind their schoolbooks. "I have made a sufficient exhibition of myself for one day, young man. No, you may not interview me. Good-bye." She set the receiver down as if it were a ruler and the phone were knuckles.

Miss Grant continued our conversation as if the phone had never rung. "If you only knew the irony of your coming here, Jenny." Her smile was rueful. "I planned to approach you for money from that foundation you run! When I saw how badly the graves were eroded, I thought you might give us the money to replace the topsoil . . ."

Abruptly, she broke off. Her lips twitched. The smile grew wide and a merriness that I recalled returned to her eyes. "It will," she admitted, "take quite a bit of dirt, won't it, Jenny?"

We laughed then, until tears appeared in her eyes again. "Where are they, Jenny?" The despair in her voice tugged at my heart. "Where are my great-great-grandfather and my great-great-grandmother? How will I find them if I'm all laid up like this, trussed like a stuck pig! Oh, Jennifer." Her voice went silent.

I heard myself saying, to my own astonishment, "I'll find them, Miss Grant. I'll be your legs. And I'll run them off if I have to, to find your ancestors for you. I know the foundation will be happy to fund my search."

"Jenny." She beamed. I had earned an A. "You always were such a dear child, so pretty and sweet."

Stupid, too, I thought, as an awful comprehension of my promise struck me; I have always had a real strong streak of stupid. I had tax laws to learn, reports to make, meetings to attend; I didn't have time to go chasing all over the county after 133 dead bodies! As for my bosses, the foundation trustees, agreeing to fund this wild ghost chase, well. . . .

Besides, there was no telling how many times I would have to endure having some joker ask me who was buried in Grant's Tomb. By the time I was through, I might well wish it were I.

2

"If you find those damn bodies," Stanley "Spitt" Pittman, Sr., swore to me the next day in his office at the Harbor Lights Funeral Home, "I will bury you, your next of kin, and your dog. Free."

"Not anytime soon, I hope," I said.

"When the time comes," he promised in a sonorous rumble.

His son, Stan, Jr., murmured from a far corner of the office, "I guess you'll have to get a dog then, Jenny." I smiled down at my coffee cup. His father glared at him.

Luckily, the phone on Spitt's massive Victorian desk interrupted us as it had continually since I had arrived for my appointment at 1:30 that afternoon. My trustees, it turned out, had not only okayed my mission, but had blessed it enthusiastically since some of their ancestors were among the missing. Stan, who looked rather unfortunately like Stan Laurel to his father's Oliver Hardy, leapt up to grab the receiver. Spitt continued to glare at him as if the whole fiasco were his son's fault. I waited as Stan listened to the now-familiar plaint of a burial-plot owner.

"Yes, ma'am," he said in his reedy, hesitant voice. "I understand your concern, but I assure you, your Uncle Talbot

21

still lies where we buried him. We don't even own Union Hill Cemetery anymore, ma'am . . ." He listened to a voice whose dismay I sensed though I couldn't hear the words. Suddenly Stan had the look of a man in a pain-reliever commercial. He sighed. He raised a finger to the narrow space between his eyes and pressed it there. "No, ma'am, there's no need for you to sue us. If you wish us to dig up your uncle to make sure he's still there, we'll certainly do that for you." Because he was listening intently, he failed to notice his father's grimace. "A minimal charge, that's all, ma'am, for the labor. Yes. Thank you. Good-bye."

His father detonated. "That's twenty-five of those nuts this morning alone!" Spittle flew from his mouth like sparks, lending a whole new meaning to the childhood nickname that had originated as a combination of the first letter of his first name and the first syllable of his last. "We're gonna have to disinter the whole damn place to prove nobody's stolen our stiffs! And what do you mean, minimal charge? What about the wear and tear to our equipment, what about oil and gasoline, what about soil and sod replacement? What about that, Mr. Minimal Charge?"

"We won't have to dig up the whole place, Dad." Stan returned to his chair and sat down with his hands under his thighs, his fingers grasping the front of the seat. He leaned forward like a small, earnest boy in the principal's office, though this small boy was over thirty years old and nearly six feet tall. "After we dig up a couple, people will see that our park's intact, and they'll calm down. I'll just dig up a few, Dad. You'll see how quickly it all smooths over, honestly."

"Dig up." His father looked to the ceiling and spread his arms wide as if in appeal to a greater force, possibly one lodged within the acoustic tiles above him. "Ten years in business the boy's got. Eight generations of funeral directors in the family. A degree from the best mortuary-science college in the country he's got. And he still says, 'dig up.' The word is *disinter*, you dumb bunny. When are you going to learn that vocabulary is very important in this business." Spitt appealed to me. "Wouldn't you rather have your great-great-granddaddy disinterred than dug up?"

"I'd be happy just to find him," I said to the man who had just called my late loved ones "stiffs." "Some of my relatives are among the missing of Union Hill. May we talk about that?"

"Talk to Stan here." He waved toward his heir. "He's the damn historical buff around here, he's the one got us involved with all those damn freeloaders in that historical society." Spitt let out a great bark of ironic laughter. "Trim the shrubs, cut the grass, prop up the tombstones . . . and all the time, there's nobody there! Pouring money down a damn hole, that's what we've been doing! One hundred and thirty-three empty holes!"

With a discreet nod to me, Stan signaled our exit. At the door, he said to his father, "One of us has to attend John's funeral, Dad. I'll stick around to handle the phone if you'll go on to the service."

The old man pulled himself erect in his chair. He tugged at his shirt cuffs, flicked lint from his lapels, and straightened his tie. His complexion faded from grape to pink with amazing rapidity, and, as if his face were sculpted in wax, his expression melted down from ferocious to bland. In an instant, he was the very picture of a dignified funeral director.

"Thank you, son." He smiled graciously at me.

Stan Pittman quietly closed the door of his father's office, wearing the look of a lion tamer who has managed to escape with only flesh wounds.

He led me down a hallway that was lined with nineteenth-century American country antiques of the sort one finds all over Port Frederick. They are a source of local pride because they are homegrown, all of them having been constructed in the previous century at a local cabinetmaker's shop. Above the furniture, Stan's ancestors glared down at me from oil paintings, framed in rococo, on the walls. Most of them wore stiff white collars and grim expressions, with the exception of

23

one blond, mustachioed fellow who twinkled at me across the centuries.

As we glided past closed doors, Stan gave me a quick Cook's tour, pointing as he talked. "This is the management wing, Jenny. The public wing is through that door behind us, and the morgue is down that corridor to your right, and the crematorium is outside. This office belongs to Aaron Friedman, the personnel manager for all our companies . . . and this is Beryl Kamiski's office, she's our prearrangement sales manager . . . and this office is shared by Russell Bissell and our other salespeople . . . and my office is down here."

There was a single secretary/receptionist's desk midway down the hall, equidistant from Stan's office and his dad's, and a small reception area and a smaller lobby beyond that. The secretary's desk was at the moment unoccupied, though a plastic nameplate said the desk belonged to one Sylvia Davis. Neatly stacked piles of paperwork surrounded her electronic typewriter, and her telephone bore three rows of red, throbbing buttons. As we passed her desk, Stan punched down one of the buttons and lifted the receiver.

"Harbor Lights Funeral Home," he said pleasantly, and then after a few seconds, less pleasantly, "Yes, I know who's buried in Grant's Tomb!"

From the look on his face as he slammed the phone down, I suspected that Sylvia Davis had better return from lunch pretty soon if she valued her job.

We stepped into Stan's office—a smaller, plainer version of his father's—and he closed the door. I took a seat across from his desk. In his bookshelf there were framed photographs of a pretty woman with three small children and an inconspicuous sign: "Thou Shalt Not Be Unctuous."

Stan took the raincoat I had brought with me and hung it over a hook on the back of his door. Then he walked over to the chair behind his desk and slumped into it. "I wanted to be a writer," he said in wistful tones as he sat down. "That's all I ever really wanted to be, you know? I just wanted to sit in a small, quiet room at the top of a quaint Victorian mansion

24

and write Pulitzer Prize-winning short stories on parchment with a quill pen. Would you like some more coffee, Jenny?"

I accepted gratefully the hot refill he poured from a coffee-pot on his desk and sipped it while he took more calls from worried descendants of people who were buried in the Harbor Lights Memorial Park. Maybe, I thought, the caffeine would compensate for all the hours of sleep I had sacrificed on the altar of worry about this impossible task I had set for myself. One hundred and thirty-three missing bodies, indeed. Did I think I would find them under a few telltale humps in some-body's basement?

"But, sir," Stan said to one of his callers, "we buried your mother only last month, and it was an open-casket funeral. You saw her yourself." He paused to listen. "Well, every-body else said she looked just like herself." And to another: "He was cremated, ma'am. It would be difficult to identify the remains." And finally: "No, Mr. Riss, please don't call my father. I'll talk to you, although I don't know what I can tell you to help you with your story."

Stan answered the other flashing red lights by unplugging his phone from the wall. Then he leaned his elbows on his desk, placed his palms against his forehead, and grimaced. "Lord, I felt bad enough this morning, even before these calls started. We had our annual Founder's Day party last night, Jenny, and we're all a little the worse for wear. At least, I am. It's probably why Dad's such a bear today." He sighed, then picked up his coffee and drank it in straight gulps, then poured himself more.

"Do we," I inquired, after a tactful pause to allow him time to pull himself together, "do we have any reason to suppose those bodies were ever buried there at all?"

"Yes," he said with what sounded to me like regret. "Our diggers found evidence of cribbings."

"Cribbings?"

"Wooden planks. Nobody has been buried there since be-fore the turn of the century, which was also before the day of the backhoe. In those days, gravediggers had to drive planks in parallel to the sides of the grave to keep the dirt from giving

25

way and burying the gravediggers. You see, there wouldn't be any reason for cribbings if there hadn't ever been any graves.''

It seemed to me there was a slight flaw in his logic, but I let it go. ''Next question, Stan . . . if you don't own Union Hill, who does?''

''Well, actually, we used to own it, Jenny, but we weren't using it, so my father gave it to the historical society in, I don't know, the early 1950s, 'round about then.''

''That was nice of him.''

''Yeah, it was a nice tax deduction. And it was nice to get out from under the upkeep and the property taxes, that's how nice it was. Of course, now it's a not-for-profit organization.'' He was tapping his long, narrow fingers against a file folder on his desk and seemed hardly to be listening to his own answers to my questions. When he looked up at me again, he had a determined gleam in his pale brown eyes.

''You ever seen a grave dug up, Jenny?''

''Can't say as I have, Stan.''

''Probably not high on your list of fun things to do in your spare time.'' He smiled briefly. ''But as long as you're looking for bodies anyway, let's go find one. We can talk about Union Hill while I get this business over with. Kill two birds with one stone, so to speak.''

I thought perhaps *kill* was a verb better left unsaid in a funeral home.

''Whose body are we looking for?''

''Anybody's. Just to prove we've still got our bodies buried in our yard. I'd like to have positive, visible proof for that reporter when he shows up this afternoon.'' I glanced out the window at the drizzly day and felt dubious about the entire proposition. Stan was saying, as if to himself, ''I've already got the approval of the health department, and God knows we've got the approval of the next of kin.'' He helped me into my coat. ''You know, I've heard of runs on banks to get money out, but a run on a memorial park to get the bodies out? Give me a break.''

As we headed outdoors, Stan said, ''What I want to do is

prove the business in Union Hill Cemetery is an isolated case that has nothing to do with us.''

''You're sure that's true?'' I asked him.

He looked at me. ''Don't even suggest it, Jenny.'' With the unfailing courtesy of a born funeral director, he held open the front door for me. ''Whatever happened in Union Hill happened a long time ago, and it doesn't have anything to do with us.''

''If you say so.'' I stepped outside and pulled up my collar against the cold mist. ''But what will your father say?''

''The same thing he always says.'' Stan puffed out his thin cheeks in a passable imitation of his dad. '' 'You dumb bunny!' ''

I laughed sympathetically.

Stan steered me toward the entrance to the memorial park, a wide, green expanse of cemetery, which surrounded the funeral home on three sides. On its far northwest edge, the park abutted Union Hill Cemetery, from which it was separated by a century and a chain-link fence. ''We'll start at this end, Jenny. I don't think these late, great customers will mind if we disturb their slumber.''

''Slumber?''

Stan, who was looking at his feet as we walked, smiled at his shoes. ''That's funeralese for *dead*, Jenny. We do not die, you know. We rest, we sleep, we slumber.''

I thought about that.

''Listen, if these guys are merely resting, I'd like your personal assurance we won't wake them up. You know how cross Count Dracula could be when awakened early from his naps.''

Stan smiled at his shoes.

3

From inside a maintenance shed where they had been hovering to escape the weather, Stan retrieved three gravediggers to do the job. Under a rapidly lowering sky, we watched them remove squares of sod from atop a grave and then tear into the earth with a backhoe.

"We don't call them gravediggers anymore," Stan corrected me when I did that very thing. "They're maintenance men. Or groundskeepers. Like at a ball park."

"Or a ritzy home?" I suggested.

He smiled.

I raised my eyes from the macabre operation that was proceeding before me and looked across the park toward Union Hill Cemetery. I saw that a graveside service was at that moment being conducted near the fence that separated the two burial grounds. There was a green canopy to shelter the family, and even from that distance I could see that Spitt Pittman seemed to be patting a lot of hands.

Still farther on, across the fence, Union Hill looked like a playground for prairie dogs, or a bomb site; the "graves" had not been refilled since they were dug up. Their tombstones leaned forlornly over nothingness, like an existentialist's ultimate metaphor: Sartre would have loved it. If God was indeed dead, our twentieth-century churches marked, like those tombstones, empty graves. Or maybe God wasn't dead but only missing, like those Civil War corpses. Maybe angels had rolled away the stones from those 133 graves, and their occupants had walked, like Jesus, into immortality. Where, I wondered, do 133 dead people go when they're not at home?

Standing there in the near-rain, by a deepening grave, I shivered at the meanderings of my own imagination. If I weren't careful, I would be seeing ghosts.

Stan was staring at the far fence, too.

"In your wildest dreams," I mused aloud, "did you ever think there was nobody actually buried there?"

"Yes," he said. "I did."

"What?" I stared at him. "You *knew?*"

"Well, I never dug up a grave to check it out, but yeah, I've always suspected it."

I was dumbfounded and must have looked it.

"You ever walk around in an old graveyard, Jenny? You know how the ground is uneven? Because of the sinking of the graves?"

"Yes," I said shortly.

He flushed. "Well, you ever take a stroll in Union Hill?"

"Sure." I felt my eyes widen. "The ground is even, Stan! Flat as an ironing board!"

"Yep. It's decaying coffins and bodies that cause the ground to sink. That's one of the reasons that modern cemeteries require vaults. I mean, we don't want to drive our trucks over the ground and have them fall in a hole. But if there aren't any bodies or coffins, there's no sink. Believe me, nobody's ever had to refill the graves in Union Hill."

"You didn't tell anybody!"

He shrugged, but the flush remained on his cheeks. "Look at the fuss now that everybody knows. Weren't you happier when you thought your dearly beloved were safe and snug underground? Wasn't Miss Grant happier? What does anybody gain from this knowledge?"

"You think I ought to butt out."

29

He glanced at me. "Why not let sleeping dogs . . . bodies . . . lie, Jenny?"

I gestured impatiently toward the fence. "But those particular bodies aren't sleeping, Stan."

"Neither," he said firmly, "are they walking."

"Stan! We can't just fill in the dirt and prop up the tombstones and pretend our relatives are buried there! Do you think people are going to bring out their picnics and flowers on Memorial Day and sit there over empty graves? You think this town is going to rest until we find those bodies and bury them where they belong?"

"They're dead. What do they care where they're buried?"

"You surprise me," I said. "In the extremis."

His smile flickered. "Extremis. Very good. You're picking up our lingo like a born funeral director. Next thing you'll be saying 'remains' instead of 'bodies' and 'caskets' instead of 'coffins.'"

I let him change the subject. "What's the difference?"

"Only semantics, I suppose." He frowned. "They were generally called coffins until the nineteenth century. Then we pinned a label on them that connotes something fine and valuable. I mean, what would you put in caskets, Jenny? You'd put jewels, treasures, things of great worth, right? You wouldn't dump something you valued in a plain pine box, now would you? A coffin can be a plain pine box in which to dump a body, but a casket . . . now a casket is something fine and beautiful in which to secure the remains!"

"Fine, beautiful, and expensive."

He grinned. "Now you've got it."

"Stan," I said, "are you sure you're in the right business?"

"Yes," he said. I waited for him to expand on this seeming contradiction between his ironic view of his profession and his choice of that profession as a life's work, but he didn't. My old high school classmate was, it seemed, a more complicated man than I had previously assumed. I turned my attention back to the gravediggers.

Two of them descended into the grave with their shovels to

finish the job. The first one in was a white kid, maybe nineteen. His dark blond hair stood up in greasy, sculpted points on his head, like the spikes on a mace. He wore work boots and gray-and-white striped coveralls over a bulky gray sweater. A large gold earring—a skull and crossbones—dangled on a gold chain from his right earlobe. The other two gravediggers were black men, considerably older than the kid, maybe in their fifties, with creased and tired faces that said maybe gravedigging wasn't the worst job they had ever had.

As if he were suddenly aware of my gaze, the white kid stuck his shovel in the dirt and looked up at me from inside the grave. He stared at me out of dark, blank eyes. After a long, unsmiling moment, he lowered his gaze and let it travel slowly, insolently down my body. Then with a flicker of a private smile, he hoisted his shovel again.

I shivered. "How much longer?" I asked Stan.

"Not much."

A strong, moisture-laden gust of wind came off the ocean. I shivered again. The folks at the graveside service, even nearer to the ocean, must be freezing, I thought. I hoped their minister and our gravediggers hurried. I felt unaccountably chilled by something colder and more penetrating than the weather. I wished I were back at the office or, better yet, at home beside the fireplace.

"Who are they burying over there?" I asked, to take my mind off my misgivings.

Stan looked in the direction my finger was pointing.

"One of ours," he said. "John Rudolph. He was one of our funeral directors. That's his wife over there in the brown coat, and his kids." Stan, too, pointed, and said morosely, "I should be there. If it weren't for this disinterment mess, I would be, along with everybody else from our shop."

That explained the empty desks and the closed doors. Not to mention the unusual number of perfectly correct black suits, male and female, that I observed in attendance at the graveside. Maybe Sylvia Davis, the receptionist, had a good excuse, after all, for her absence from her desk. Or maybe she'd had too good a time at the Founder's Day party the night before.

"What did he die of, Stan?" It seemed somehow callous to watch a burial without becoming acquainted with the deceased, however slightly and posthumously.

"Terminal horniness," Stan blurted out. He blushed. "God, I shouldn't have said that. A heart attack, Jenny, that's what it was. Only thirty-eight years old. Built like a bantam rooster; you'd have thought he was one of those tough little birds who would live forever. Thirty-eight years old! You know, if I weren't already surrounded by plenty of evidence of mortality, that'd do it for me."

I hardly heard him. I was squinting into the rain at a most remarkable sight. I nudged Stan and pointed again.

He, too, stared at the unlikely vision coming toward us across the muddy lawn in the rain. "My God, I've never seen my father run," Stan said in awestruck tones. Then, half-jokingly, "What do you suppose the old man thinks I've done now?"

From inside the grave there came a disembodied bellow: "We've hit the vault!"

"Open 'er up!" Stan yelled back.

But we weren't nearly so interested in that operation anymore as we were in the arrival of Spitt Pittman. He came puffing up to us like a short, fat locomotive.

"Stanley!" It was all he managed to sputter before he bent over and placed his hands on his knees. Stan and I had to bend over, too, to catch his words. We must have looked, I thought, like penitents, or three drunks losing our lunch. Between gasps, Spitt issued commands: "Get over there, boy, and get that damn woman to calm down! Tell her it's in bad taste, tell her it's locked, tell her it's against the law, for Christ's sake!"

"Who?" Stan asked, reasonably enough, I thought. "What?"

"Muriel Rudolph, you dumb bunny!" Plainly, Spitt Pittman was furious and his son was the nearest handy target. The open grave behind us had become quiet as a, well, tomb.

32

The third gravedigger stepped back a few feet from the edge of the grave as if he hoped he could disappear between raindrops. "She wants the damn coffin opened! Says she's got to make sure he's in there! Says with all those bodies missing, maybe somebody has stolen John!"

Stan groaned. "Incredible."

"You're telling me?" His father managed to stand up, so Stan and I rose again, too. "What does the damn fool woman think, that we want to keep him around because we're so sorry to lose him? Hell, he was a pain in the butt when he was alive, so who'd want him when he's dead?"

"Now, Dad."

"Go," his father commanded.

Stan went, followed in single file by Spitt and, for lack of anywhere else to hang out in the memorial park, me. We approached the green canopy like referees approaching the foul line, and the occupants stared back like fans expecting to get the short end of the call. I heard, behind us, the sound of a forklift being started as the gravediggers prepared to lift off the cement lid of the vault.

I paused, with Spitt, on the far side of the coffin, opposite the mourners. Together we watched Stan go to the widow.

Muriel Rudolph was tiny, with lank, brown hair and sallow skin. She looked as if she were constructed of bird bones, and a wren's at that. She was plain as a wren, too, and haggard as any other widow, making it difficult for me to guess her age. Even from across the grave, I could see the blue pools under her eyes and the deep lines of weariness that no makeup could disguise. I watched her oldest child, a teenage girl, turn her two little brothers away from the grave and shuffle them off through the rain to one of the waiting limousines.

"Stan." The widow's voice was small and piping, a bird's chirp, ending in a sob. She stopped, bit her lower lip, risked one more word. "Please."

"Sure," Stan replied easily, quickly. A collective sigh escaped from the canopy like a soft wind. "No problem. You know we didn't prepare him for an open-casket service, Muriel, so maybe we'd better step on around to the other side of the box and just the two of us take a quick look. Okay?"

She sagged onto the arm he offered, nodding her head again and again as if she were beyond words. The top of her head came barely to the middle of his chest, so that she looked from the rear like a little girl all dressed up for a walk with daddy. At my side, Spitt sucked air like a flat tire. I supposed he didn't dare object, but God only knew what he would say to his son later.

With a show of sweet and gentle protectiveness, Stan ushered the widow to our side of the grave. He led her onto a relatively dry patch of earth a couple of feet from where the coffin was suspended for lowering into the hole. He squeezed her arm reassuringly, then walked alone to the edge of the grave. With quick, efficient movements, Stan unsealed the coffin. He wrapped his fingers around the brass handles and lifted the lid to reveal a plush interior upholstered in champagne velvet. From what little I could see, it looked warm and cozy on this miserable day. The body of the late John Rudolph, humped under a white sheet, waited a good deal more comfortably in there than the rest of us did outside. I did not, however, go so far as to envy him.

Stan turned back to face the widow.

"Muriel? Now?"

She nodded. He guided her forward, then he slowly drew back the sheeting that covered her husband.

Muriel Rudolph screamed.

"It's John," Stan said in a loud, stunned voice, ". . . and Sylvia."

4

Spitt Pittman clutched my arm. "Sweet Jesus," he breathed. Shrill cries and startled oaths flew up around us as pandemonium broke out among the crowd of mourners. There were a few in the crowd who screamed and ran away to their cars, as if they were afraid of being sucked, like matter into a black hole, into that crowded coffin themselves. But most of the mourners surged forward, to see for themselves. Spitt released the death grip he had on my elbow. He trudged toward the open coffin like a man who hopes that if he gives it enough time, the thing he doesn't want to see will disappear. I followed on unsteady legs.

I stared into the coffin.

Face down, the dead secretary embraced the dead funeral director, like a widow who has thrown herself into her husband's coffin in a fit of passionate grief. They fit snugly together in the deep coffin, as if they had fallen asleep after making love on a couch. Their faces were covered by a fan of her long blond hair, so that I couldn't tell if she had been pretty. But judging by the cut of her hair and by the plump firmness of her thighs, which showed beneath the skirt that was hiked up to her hips, I figured her to be younger than I, maybe twenty-five or so. Her suit looked new, the kind of unbecoming thing a young woman not yet old enough to fill her closet with clothes for deaths as well as for parties runs out at the last minute to buy for a funeral. If she had lived, she would have hated the suit, I thought irrelevantly; after a few years, she would have put it out in a paper bag for the Goodwill truck to pick up. Her white ruffled blouse and her backless high-heeled shoes were expensive looking but wrong; the sort of thing a young career woman buys before she acquires taste. I decided, however, that her taste was not nearly as wretched as mine was for conducting a fashion seminar over a corpse.

"Police," I said to Stan. "You have to call them."

"Police." The crowd took up the foreboding word like a chant, and it whispered all around us like a hissing breeze, "Police, police, police."

"She's right," said a baritone voice at our shoulders.

I turned to find that it belonged to a slender, olive-skinned man who looked about thirty-five. He wasn't wearing glasses, but he looked as if he ought to—thick, sturdy ones, with black frames. There was something about him, standing quietly there in the rain in his black suit, that made me think of a slim, young tree, in the late autumn when its leaves have fallen and its branches are plain and bare. He was saying in his pleasant, neutral voice, "And we'll have to tell her husband, Stan."

The crowd took up those words, too, like a second chorus to their chant: "Her husband . . . husband . . . tell her husband."

"I'll call him, if you like," the dark young man said.

"Oh, God," Stan replied, which the man seemed to take as assent, because he started to move away. But Stan suddenly began to babble introductions. "Jenny, I'd like you to meet Aaron Friedman, our personnel director. Aaron, Jenny Cain. She's an old friend of mine, and . . ."

"Police?" The widow had remained so quiet and frozen beside that awful grave that I had nearly forgotten her. Now her tiny hands were plucking at Stan, her colorless little mouth was trembling. "Police?"

Aaron Friedman placed a slim hand briefly on her shoulder.

Then he nodded courteously to me and walked off to perform his unpleasant duty. The whites of his eyes had been clear, the brown irises alert, and he struck me altogether as a man who would never have cause to regret the excesses of an office party. I watched him pause on the other side of the coffin beside a well-dressed couple: the man, tall and blond, in a dark blue suit and white shirt; the woman, elegant in a black suit with a white blouse. The two of them listened to Friedman, looked toward us, and then began to walk our way.

At the sound of the widow's voice, Stan seemed to come awake to the dreadful reality of her situation. "We have to get you out of here," he murmured in a distressed tone. He looked out over the staring, milling crowd. "Dad?"

The crowd took up the call: "Spitt . . . . Where's Mr. Pittman? Where's his father? . . . Spitt?"

But his father was busy yelling contradictory orders at employees: "Get that coffin up! Don't touch those bodies! Who closed this damn thing? Don't tell me, I don't want to know! Get back, get back! Come here, dummy!"

Stan raised his voice. "Dad? Don't you think you ought to take Muriel back inside, Dad?"

Spitt paused in mid-tirade.

"You poor, poor child," he said then, coming toward Muriel Rudolph with outstretched hands.

"Poor child," murmured the crowd. "Poor, poor Muriel."

Spitt jerked her hands out of his son's grasp. "What are you doing, letting this poor woman stand out here in the rain, you dumb bunny? Don't you know somebody ought to take her back inside?" Spitt wrapped an arm around her like a fond uncle. Without so much as a backward glance, he steered her toward the limousines, leaving his son to cope with the extra body in the coffin.

"What can we do to help, Stan?"

It was the tall blond man with the woman in black.

I stared again, only this time at a living, breathing wonder: Michelangelo would have carved a statue of this man and called it *David*. I found my glance caught in the amused contemplation of his companion, the elegantly dressed woman in the black suit. It was silk. Close up, it was also apparent that she was about ten years older than he, maybe in her early fifties. She was a big, handsome woman, but she had tamed the generosity of nature with fine tailoring. She had the knowing, understanding eyes of a good listener or a barmaid. Up close, I could also see that beneath the perfect makeup her skin sagged a bit, as if this barmaid had sampled a few too many of her own wares at the party the night before. I resisted a sudden urge to put my head on her shoulder and tell her all my troubles. I also resisted the urge to put my head on *his* shoulder.

"Help?" Stan parroted. He flapped his arms at his sides like long black wings, completing the image of a big, awkward bird. "God, I don't know, Russ. They didn't exactly cover this situation in mortuary science."

"Well, it's awful," the woman said in a strong, sympathetic voice, and I suspected the men suddenly felt as confirmed in their dismay as I did. If this woman said it was awful, then it must be. "I do not understand how this could have happened to that poor girl. I simply cannot imagine it. But you know we're here, Stanley, if you need us."

"Thanks, Beryl." He was grateful as a puppy. Somebody must have punched his courtesy button again, because he started making introductions. "Beryl Kamiski, I'd like you to meet Jenny Cain. Beryl's the manager of our prearrangement company, Jenny. And Russ, here, he's one of our top salesmen."

"Russell Bissell," the man said, and he held out a tanned, well-manicured hand to me. I thought he was living dangerously to offer any part of himself to a woman, because she might not give it back. I shook the hand, which was warm and muscular, then released it with regret. Close beside one of his broad shoulders, the corners of Beryl Kamiski's wide, red mouth turned up again.

Stan pushed his hair off his forehead with one hand. "See if you can get everybody to go home, will you, Beryl? And Russ, I'd appreciate it if you'd go back to the funeral home and sit on my father, see if you can keep him from having a coronary, okay?''

As one, they nodded. I received a parting smile, like a benediction, from Russell Bissell. My knees weakened, as if they wanted to bob in a curtsy. Beryl Kamiski tucked her hand firmly into the crook of his elbow and they walked away. It was impossible to tell who was leading whom, but such was the magnetic pull of his looks and her personality that I felt the urge to tag along after them. Compared to them, Aaron Friedman had been only a dim and narrow shadow.

''I'll bet the prearrangement business is pretty darned good,'' I murmured to Stan, but he was transfixed by the coffin again and didn't reply other than to whisper, ''Sylvia?'' and to shake his head.

''Sylvia?'' exclaimed a rougher, deeper voice.

The three gravediggers ringed us in a grimy trio, pushing us, with the intensity of their curiosity, closer to the edge of the grave. The mud from their previous endeavor clung to them, and was it just my imagination or did there also cling to them the hint of an odor one might not wish to identify? I began to breathe through my nose.

The two black men stared into the coffin with wide eyes and slack mouths, as if they'd never seen a dead body before. The young punk stared, too, but his pale face wore that closed and private smile I had seen on him before.

''Jesus,'' one of the black men spoke, reverently, like one who witnesses a miracle. ''How'd she get in there?''

''Didn't you guys close the coffin, Freddy?'' Stan asked in a high-pitched, querulous voice.

''Not me.'' The one named Freddy was defensive.

''Never seen her before,'' the other black man volunteered.

The white kid snorted, a derisive sound.

''But you guys moved the coffin, didn't you?'' Stan sounded more hesitant than definite. ''I mean, you had to move it from the morgue to the visitation room, and from there to the chapel, and then into the limo, right, Freddy?''

But it was the punk who answered him.

"So what? The lid was down, we didn't notice nothin' wrong, we didn't do nothin'. Sir."

"All right, Jack." Stan made appeasing movements with his hands. "Nobody's blaming you for anything."

"If she worked here," I interrupted, "why hasn't anybody missed her?"

"Everybody missed her," Stan said with a hangdog look. I was beginning to feel annoyed with him. "She didn't come to work this morning, and she didn't call in, and it wasn't like her to be so irresponsible. But she was young, and I thought maybe she'd never been to a funeral before, and . . ." He paused, as if aware of the absurdity of a funeral-home employee who was afraid of funerals.

The punk was grinning in open contempt.

"Didn't anybody call her husband when she didn't come to work?" I persisted.

There was an infinitesimal pause, during which I sensed, more than saw, a shifting of eyes, an exchange of quick glances among the people around the grave. Stan scuffed his good black shoes against the coffin and stuffed his hands into the pockets of his black trench coat.

"Uh, she was separated from her husband," he said. "She lived by herself."

"More or less," the punk said, and sniggered.

I stared at him. His response was to raise his upper lip in a lewd grin. I hadn't felt such an urge to slap the bejesus out of a man since college.

Stan, ironically, edged closer to me.

"Police," I said firmly.

Again, there was a sudden stillness around us, as if we stood in a shell. I had a fleeting impression of breaths held, bodies tensed. Then Stan cleared his throat. The world around the grave relaxed once more into movement, though it had a staccato, stop-and-go feeling, like an old movie. The mourners seemed torn between a desire to stay and satisfy their curiosity and a desire to escape from that awful graveside.

"Would you call them, Jenny?" Stan asked. And then he added, without inflection, "You know them better than I do."

I couldn't argue with that.

The punk shot me a quick, curious look, then just as quickly looked away. To Stan, he said, "Don't you want to know about the grave we just opened?"

Stan blinked.

"Everything's okay," the punk told him, then paused a beat. "Except for the headless dog . . ."

Stan looked as if he had been struck. "The . . ."

The punk burst out laughing.

I pulled Stan away before he could humiliate himself any further. We skipped the limos and slogged back across the memorial park in the rain. I kept my arm hooked through his to steady him and to keep us moving purposefully forward.

"Jenny, I'm sorry about all this."

"It's hardly your fault, Stan."

"No, listen, about your missing bodies . . ."

"I'd just as soon you didn't call them mine."

"Come back tomorrow, and I'll show you the archives from the old cemetery. We store them as a favor to Miss Grant. And if you catch my dad when he's not playing king, you'll find he knows a lot about the old days. It's part of our family heritage, you see, and that's important to him."

"I'll do that."

I tugged him along toward the inviting warmth of the funeral home and the telephone. He came with heavy steps, dredging his shoes through the mud like a small boy being hauled home by his mother.

"Do you think she was murdered, Jenny?"

"Well," I said gently, "the alternative is that she killed herself, then crawled into the coffin, pulled the sheet over her head, and closed the lid. I suspect that's unlikely, don't you, Stan?"

He hung his head and shook it, as at a dismal fate.

Once inside the funeral home, I divested him of his coat. I pushed him down into his own chair, poured him a cup of coffee, and called the Port Frederick police department.

"Thanks, Jenny," said Detective Geoffrey Bushfield. "I'll

41

send Ailey out with a crew immediately. You're all right, aren't you?"

"Sure, just a little shaky. I'll admit it's an awful shock to find an extra body in a coffin."

"I know a sure cure for shock," the policeman told me.

"What's that?"

"Bed rest," he said, and hung up.

I hid my smile from Stan.

"They're coming," I told him.

But I left before they arrived. Partly because I didn't want them to waste their time or mine in questioning me about a murder that was none of my business. Mostly because if I knew Detective Geof Bushfield, he'd want to question me privately. Alone. At home.

5

Late that night, I reluctantly rolled over in bed to answer the telephone.

"Jenny, this is Lew Riss." The reporter's voice sounded as if its owner abused it with three packs a day. I knew him, slightly, as the police reporter for the *Port Frederick Times*. "Let me talk to Bushfield, will you?"

"I would if I could, Lew," I lied. I put my hand over the receiver and glanced at the naked police detective in bed with me. It was officially his house and his bed, though we had shared both for nearly two years, and I kept promising to marry him and make them mine, as well. I mouthed the name "Lewis Riss" at him. Geof raised his eyebrows, rolled his eyes, lifted his hands as if to ward off a blow, and generally gave a good impression of a cop who didn't want to talk to a reporter. I said, "He's on his way to Philadelphia for some forensic seminars, Lew." That much was true. "And he's already gone. I took Geof to the plane myself not an hour ago." The detective nudged me in the ribs, a reminder that crooks and liars hang themselves by talking too much.

"Gone?" Lew's voice rose to a squawk. "How could he do this to me? What'd he say before he left town?"

I considered. I could tell him the police said that Sylvia Davis

43

had been strangled with her own long blond hair. I could tell him they thought she had been killed in the morgue at the funeral home, because that's where they had found a few of those hairs, pulled out by the roots. I could tell him they didn't trust their own estimation of the time of death, because her body could have been stored in the refrigeration unit in the morgue. Based on when she was last reported seen by other people, they did know she had died sometime in the early-morning hours before the Rudolph funeral; they just didn't yet know which hour.

"He said good-bye."

"Come on, Jenny!"

"It's not his case, Lewis."

"All right." Grudgingly. "But you were there, right?"

"Right."

"Well?"

"What do you want from me?"

"Good-looking women shouldn't ask leading questions like that, Cain. What I want from you is what it was like to be there when they found her body, for Christ's sake. What do you think I want? What about it? You gonna be my source, or what?"

I sighed. "I've never been a source before. God, what a thrill. Be still my heart."

"Jenny." Lew Riss was only a few months out of Asbury Park. His New Jersey accent came in handy when he wanted to sound threatening.

"Well," I began, as a prelude to no.

"Great. Meet me at The Buoy tomorrow night, sixish. We'll have a couple of drinks, map out our strategy on how I'm gonna get this story."

"Strategy? Wait a minute, Riss . . ."

But he had hung up. I decided I would meet him to suggest another destination for him.

"Go to hell," I said to the receiver, practicing.

Geof put down the police journal he had been reading. "Say what?"

"Not you . . . the jerk who just hung up on me. I think you ought to have him arrested."

He grinned. It was a nice sight—that wide grin, those brown

44

eyes, the wide, bare shoulders, the broad chest, and all that tousled brown hair against the white pillow. Two ex-wives had found him equally attractive, though they found his police work less so. I tried to concentrate on what he was saying: "It may be criminal to hang up on a beautiful woman, but to the best of my knowledge, it's not a crime. Besides, with me gone, he'll have to deal with Ailey. From your point of view, Jenny, anything more than that would be cruel and unusual punishment. Right?"

I lay back down beside him and pictured in my mind the coming confrontations between the egos of Lewis Riss and Detective Ailey Mason, Geof's young partner on the force.

"Yes." I smiled at the ceiling. "That will do."

"Jenny?"

I rolled onto my side to answer his inquiry and saw that he had suddenly turned serious on me.

"He's on his own," Geof said. He gazed at my face as if I were an idea he was considering. "Ailey, I mean. This is important, to see if he has what it takes to rise to any role of responsibility in the department. Particularly in dealing with homicides."

"What are you telling me?"

"He won't be reporting to me while I'm in Philadelphia." He nodded as if to say he noted my surprise, understood my doubts. "I know. I'm not convinced it's the smartest move I've ever made, but at some point I've got to let him sink or swim. I'd kind of been waiting for the next homicide, and when you called from the funeral home I thought, hell, this is it, perfect timing."

He paused, but didn't seem to be finished, so I said: "And?"

"And I don't want any news." He flopped over on his back, crossed his arms behind his head, turned his face to me.

"From me."

"From anybody. What I don't know won't worry me, and if I'm not worried, I won't stick my nose into his case. Then when it's over, we'll know that he managed it entirely on his own."

"Or he didn't."

The grin appeared, fractionally. "I am overwhelmed by

your confidence in my good judgment. I know you don't like him, Jenny, but that doesn't make him a bad cop."

"You forget that I am a fine judge of character. Why else would I choose to live with a former juvenile delinquent like you?"

"Jenny?"

This time, that single word held a different inquiry, one that carried a familiar, compelling invitation. I inched closer to him on our king-sized bed. We lay still for a moment, regarding each other without touching. Finally, I reached over to stroke his naked chest, from the curve of his left shoulder down into the hollow of his shoulder bone, over the bone, across the smooth width of his chest, and up the swell of the muscles on his other shoulder.

"What a lovely man you are. It's not just the way you look, it's your intelligence, your sensitivity, your sense of humor, your integrity, your . . ."

"I'll miss you, too, Jenny."

We smiled at each other then.

"Prove it," I suggested.

The detective presented evidence sufficient to convince a grand jury.

The next morning, when he did leave for Philadelphia, I felt bereft with an intensity that surprised me. I felt oddly vulnerable to the elements as well, as if I'd forgotten to wear a warm jacket on a cold day.

In the kitchen, I raised my coffee cup to absent lovers: *"E pluribus unum."*

After a quick breakfast of scrambled eggs and bagel with cream cheese, I called my secretary to let her know I might not get to the office that day. "I'm going to visit the cemetery this morning," I told Faye, "and I'm going to try to see Stan Pittman this afternoon."

"You're not going back there, are you?" she said in horrified tones. "Jenny, they found a dead body there yesterday, didn't you read this morning's paper?"

"I promise you, I'll stay out of coffins."

46

"But Jenny, it's miserable outside." Faye was taking her best motherly tone with me this morning. Usually that meant she was having trouble at home in getting her teenagers to listen to her. When that happened she tended to use me—or Marv, or Derek—as surrogate kids to discipline. Since Faye was long on heart and strong on common sense, we usually fell nicely into line for her. But on this morning, I was the stubborn five-year-old who wants, by God, to play in the rain. Faye was admonishing me: "It's cold and wet, and you'll catch your death of a pneumonia, Jenny. You don't want to go walking around in a cemetery in this weather."

"Yes, I do, Faye. I want to get a sense of the place. I want to know who was buried there, and when, and . . ."

"You couldn't just ask your old teacher?"

"She always told us to look things up for ourselves," I said. "Bye, Faye. I'll check in with you later."

I heard the sound of a "tsk" as I hung up.

I could have asked Miss Grant, yes. But I wanted to see for myself the names of the missing, the dates of their births and deaths, and the sentiments—loving or otherwise—with which they were ushered out of this world. Then perhaps I would know in which world I should dig, as it were, for their remains . . . the present or the past.

I climbed the stairs to the bedroom again to dress for the odd occasion: thermal underwear, blue jeans, red turtleneck sweater, green plaid wool jacket. I clamped my hair back with barrettes and threw on a waterproof, hooded black cape, and then I pulled black rubber boots over my thick socks and tennis shoes. I might not raise any ghosts this morning, but I suspected I could exorcise any fashion designer within a hundred miles. The thought gave me a perverse pleasure.

It occurred to me as I walked to my car that I was glad to be facing my mystery instead of Ailey's this morning—too few bodies, all of them long dead, are infinitely preferable to too many bodies, one of them all too recently and prematurely deceased.

6

The morning could have passed for twilight.

I stepped out of my car near the gate to Union Hill, pulled up the hood of my cape, and trudged off in the rain and mud to look at the tombstones.

"Damn."

I trudged back to the car to turn off the headlights. Then I returned to examine the first gravestone I came to. "Joshua Marsh," it said, "b. 1792, d. 1863." There had been an inscription once, too, but the years had worn it down to a shallow shadow in the stone, unreadable. "How you doin', Josh?" I inquired, taking my cue from Miss Grant's folksy approach to ghosts. "And where the heck are you doin' it?"

I moved on down the ragged row.

Edgar Allan Poe couldn't have picked a better day for tip-toeing through the tombstones. Fog. Mist. Tilted grave markers. Mounds of earth beside empty graves. In the distance, a dog barked, although howling would have better suited the atmosphere. I told myself it was only a rainy day on a dismal piece of real estate.

The earliest gravestone I found was dated 1848; the latest, 1886. That span of thirty-eight years seemed to account for every grave in Union Hill Cemetery. I recalled the dates 1861 and 1865 as marking the beginning and the end of the Civil War, so that meant the burials began about thirteen years before the first battle of Bull Run and they ended only twenty-one years after Lee's surrender at Appomattox. Beyond those historical benchmarks, I was getting an education in epitaphs. One grim little ditty in particular seemed to have been popular with the good folks of Port Frederick back in those days:

> "As I am now so you shall be,
> Prepare for Death and follow me."

I recognized some of the names I came across, including some Cains, the Grants, and a few Pittmans. Many of the stones were only modest slabs of slate a couple of feet tall, cut in a box shape with a half-moon rising from the top, with simply a name and birth and death dates below. The only truly grand monument was an Italianate bust recessed into a block of white marble. It was engraved: "Erasmus Pittman, b. 1810, d. 1886" and "Seraphim Pittman, b. 1816, d. 1879." And there was a motto: "Saving Grace."

It was the last stone I found, and it marked the end of my tour. I swept rainwater off the flat top of a gravestone next to the Pittmans', after first begging the pardon of one Sarah Clark, whose grave it was. Or at least was supposed to be. Her final "resting place" was deep and empty, like all the others. I tucked my cape under my rear and sat down on top of her gravestone to rest and to think.

This cemetery hadn't been anywhere near the center of town in those days. So why were these people buried way out here? Who buried them? Why did the burials cover this particular, relatively short span of time? Might grave robbers be to blame? But who ever heard of grave robbers taking all the bodies? Did that ever happen? When were the bodies removed, and why, and how, and by whom?

The Harbor Point foghorn blasted, and I felt suddenly warmed by the sound, just as mariners must have felt a century before when they sailed into Port Frederick. I suppose that to landlubbers it must seem a lonely sound, but to someone who has been raised by the sea, a foghorn isn't a lonely cry at all but a signal that somebody is near, that we aren't alone, after all, in the formless fog.

I squinted, looking for my car in the distance, and barely discerned its outlines. The world seemed far away, a century or more away. I looked in the direction of the funeral home, but it was only a twinkling of lights, cozy as a Christmas tree. The graves were only empty holes in the ground to me now; even the fog had turned warm and friendly after my exercise. I had seldom felt so utterly alone, and yet securely so, as if the fog had made me invisible—the ultimate security.

I didn't know anyone was behind me until he spoke.

"What are you doin' here?"

"My God." I whipped around to locate the source of the sound, and the sight that greeted me sucked the cozy warmth from the morning. It was the punk gravedigger. He was squatting on his haunches an arm's length away. The mist beaded on the greasy spikes of his hair like water on knives; I watched it slide onto his scalp, then onto the upturned collar of his brown leather jacket. The jacket was studded, and zipped to his throat. He was also wearing brown leather trousers that were so tight they looked as if they'd cut him off at the crotch, and hiking boots. He had in his right hand a long, silvery metal object that came to a point as sharp as a needle. He made a circle of the thumb and middle finger of his left hand and then he ran the metal object through the circle, slowly, repeatedly, his eyes on me. He had frightened me, and I was angry. "What are *you* doing here?"

"I like it here. What's your excuse?"

"I don't need one."

"Like hell."

I kept my eyes on his dark, blank ones.

He stood up and began slowly to circle me. Suddenly he made a fencer's jab at me with the silver spear. I caught my breath, jerked back. He laughed, a mocking sound that exploded my fear into anger. I stood up. "Stop it."

This time his answer was to press the needle point of the spear against the fabric of my cape, in the area of my heart.

50

I sat back down on the gravestone. The fear returned, crawling down my spine like a poisonous spider.

"You know what this is?" he said. I stared at him. "It's a trocar."

He waited, expecting a reaction from me.

"An embalming needle." He smirked. "You stick it in the body here . . ." He moved the needle down from my heart and jabbed it lightly into my cape, below my left breast. ". . . and you suck out the juice, and then you pump in the embalming fluid." He moved the thing back up to my heart.

"What's your name?"

"Cain."

"You're a good-lookin' lady, Cain."

I had been staring into his enlarged pupils for what seemed an eternity, and I still hadn't seen a glint of anything alive in those black depths.

Suddenly, he slapped the wand violently against his left palm. My hands flew up from my lap like startled birds. When he laughed this time, it was a low, knowing sound that sent the spider down my spine again.

"My name's Jack. They call me Jackal." His mouth hung open, he ran his tongue along the edge of his upper teeth. "I don't give a fuck about dead bodies. I only like 'em while they're still warm and breathin'. Are you still breathin', Cain?"

He began to circle me again, and to draw the tip of the embalming needle around my body as if he were drawing a line on it: cut here.

"Where you think the bodies are, Cain?" He was behind me now, whispering in my ear. "I hear there are cults that use dead bodies, you know what I mean? Satanic cults, like. Fee, fie, foe, fum, I suck the blood of an Englishman. They dig up the body, see, and they have this Black Mass, and they cut up the corpse, and they eat it. You think they cook it first, Cain?"

"I doubt it," I said in the coldest voice I could manage. "Roasted embalmed bodies taste like death warmed over."

There was a horrible beat of silence before he laughed. But

51

the laughter was worse than the silence; it echoed wildly, horribly, on and on into the fog, and stopped only a second before I broke. It would have been stupid to attack him; he wasn't much taller than I, but he had the extra weight and the advantage of a young man's muscles.

"That was good, Cain."

Abruptly, he pulled the hood of my cape down, jerking my neck back, exposing my head. With unbelievable speed, he raised the trocar in both of his hands like a club, and I knew I was dead. In the split second I had to react, I thought he was going to bring it crashing down on me. A scream caught in my paralyzed throat.

He dipped the wand delicately onto my hair. Onto my left shoulder. Onto my right shoulder.

"I choose you, Cain." It was a guttural whisper, nothing I recognized as human. "In the name of all that is unholy, I choose you." When I heard him next, it sounded as if he spoke from some distance away. "They're not all gone, Cain. Anybody tell you that? Some of them are still in the ground waiting for you."

After a few moments, I turned around, but the fog did not disclose him. I wanted to run screaming away from there, but instead, I picked my way carefully back through the obstacle course of heaped earth, tombstones, and deep holes. When I reached my car, I did not pause to think but started the ignition immediately and drove at all deliberate speed back to Geof's house.

"Where is a cop when you really need him?" I said aloud in the car, to see if my voice still worked. It did, but shakily. I bit my lip to silence the sound of my own fear.

If Geof had only been in town, I would have fled to the police station. As it was, I had nothing to report to Ailey Mason except that a teenager in a weird hairdo had freaked me out in a cemetery. And I knew what Ailey would say: "What were you doing wandering around by yourself in that cemetery?" "What difference does that make, Ailey?" "All right, did he attack you?" "Well, no." "Did he harm you physically in any way?" "No. . . ." "Did he threaten you?"

"Not exactly." "Then what do you expect us to do?" "You mean I just have to wait to see if he hurts me?" "He's just a punk, don't worry about it."

Thank you so much, Ailey.

I managed to get my car into the garage without hitting anything, and then to get into the house without tripping or dropping my keys.

I made myself walk slowly up the stairs to the fourth floor. In the bathroom, I removed my wet clothes, draped them over the counters to dry, turned on the water in the shower, stepped in, and pulled the curtain shut.

I stood directly under the water and closed my eyes.

Was he only getting his kicks? Was he trying to scare me away? If he was going to harm me, wouldn't he have done it then, when there was no one around to hear him and there was the fog to cover him?

My knees started to give out, and I sank down to the floor of the shower and sat there, naked, in the pouring water for a long time. It took a lot of hot water to wash the fear out of me. When it had all drained away, the residue left in me was a clear, sharp fury.

I turned off the water and stood up.

If the police could not help, at least I would have a sharp word with the Jackal's employer that afternoon.

I looked at the bar of soap still in my left hand.

My threat sounded so anticlimactic, even silly.

As if in response to it, the Jackal's sneering, leering face appeared in front of me in my imagination.

I threw the soap at it, hard enough to break the bar in two when it struck the faucets and dropped to the bottom of the shower stall.

"Damn you!" I said to his shattered visage.

7

I skipped lunch.

About one-thirty that afternoon, when I thought I could talk without twitching, I drove back to the Harbor Lights Funeral Home, only this time I drove up to the well-lighted front door of the management wing. The fog had lifted, so the day was presenting a more hopeful face, if still a gray one.

In the foyer I saw an empty bulletin board above an American country antique side table. There was a box of pushpins on the table, and a stack of photographs. I walked on toward the offices, only to stare in surprise at the smiling, middle-aged woman who greeted me from her post at the secretary/receptionist's desk.

"Hi, Jenny."

"Francie!" It was Francine Daniel, an old friend of my mother's. That's the thing about living in your hometown: you are always running into people who changed your diapers. It is why I get cravings for anonymity the way other people crave chocolate; they binge on Godiva, I fly to New York. I was, nevertheless, glad to see her. I heard unpleasant echoes of the morning as I asked her, "What are you doing here?"

"I'm what they call a 'temporary,' Jenny."

So was the last occupant of that desk, I thought morbidly.

"How's your mother?" she inquired, the sweetness of her nature showing in the concern in her eyes. In her buttoned-down shirt, red string tie, and wool skirt, Francie looked like somebody's aunt. But however kindly her question was meant, it was not one to lift the clouds from my mood.

"Oh, about the same," I said, and examined the painting on the wall behind Francie's head. My mother, a victim both of a chemical imbalance and imbalanced fate, had been a resident of a psychiatric hospital for several years. She had been more or less comatose for a long time now, always seeming near death, never quite getting there. "Would you tell Stan I'd like to see him, Francie?"

While we waited for him to respond to her page, I quizzed Francie about the police investigation from the funeral home's point of view.

"Well, of course, I wasn't here yesterday." She leaned forward, lowered her voice. "But I gather everybody was in a tizzy. Nobody likes to be questioned by the police, Jenny." She laid a finger against her cheek. "No matter how polite or handsome the detective may be. And some of them, if I may say so, are less polite than others, my dear."

"I detect the subtle tracks of Ailey Mason. I'm afraid you'll see more of him before this business is finished. Geof's out of town, Francie, so Ailey's got the case."

"Heaven help us," she said.

"From your lips to God's ears," said Stan Pittman as he walked up to her desk. His smile of greeting looked tired and forced. "We could use a little divine intervention around here." He picked up a staple remover from the top of her desk and began to snap it, like talking jaws:

"When did you last see the deceased, Mr. Pittman? At the office party? What did she say? Where did she go after the party? Where had she been before the office party? What sort of mood was she in when you saw her at the party? What did she wear to the party? How much did she drink at the party? Did she always drink so much? What was the nature of her relationship with the other deceased? Did she have any enemies? Did he? Do you know of anyone who would have a

55

reason to want to kill her? What did you do the rest of that night, Mr. Pittman? Do you have any witnesses to confirm that?''

Stan heaved an enormous sigh and tossed the staple remover back down. ''Poor Sylvia. Gosh, she'd have hated this. She always tried to make our jobs easier, and she'd have hated to think that her death was interfering with business.'' He grimaced, as if his words left a bad taste in his mouth. ''Well, come on, Jenny. I'll show you the archives for Union Hill Cemetery.''

He waved an arm at me in a halfhearted fashion.

''There's something else I want to ask you, too,'' I said. Stan looked back over his shoulder, raised an inquisitive eyebrow.

''Privately,'' I said, as I followed him.

As we walked down the corridor, past the first of the oil paintings, I hazarded a guess as to its identity.

''Your father?''

Again, Stan nodded.

It was a work of genius in its way, managing to transform Spitt Pittman into a man from whom you would not only buy the used car but the undercoating, as well.

I stopped to examine it, thus pulling Stan to a halt.

At that moment, the father himself materialized at my shoulder, over which he stared with apparent fondness at his own portrait.

''An excellent likeness,'' Spitt pronounced.

''Amazing,'' I countered, and moved quickly on down the line. ''Who's this one, Spitt?''

''That is my grandfather, Americus Pittman.'' He said it graciously, basso profundo, as if he were introducing us. ''And this,'' he said, moving on to the next painting, ''is his brother, Justice, who was my great-uncle. And his other brother, Honor, my other great-uncle. And here's their father, Erasmus Pittman, who was my great-grandfather and Stanley's great-great-grandfather.''

''Americus, Justice, and Honor?'' I asked delicately.

"Great-grandfather," Spitt said, "had a fine sense of patriotism."

Or a hell of a sense of humor, I thought. Old Erasmus was the twinkly one, the blond with the huge mustache. His three sons were darker, clean shaven, and dour looking, and who wouldn't be with a father who stuck them with those names?

We traveled on down the line of unsmiling male faces.

"This one is Amos Spencer," Spitt informed me, "who married one of my great-aunts and who owned the livery stable in town. And here's his cousin, Reynold Spencer. He was an upholsterer, married another one of my aunts, Libby, I think. Here's his son, old what's-his-name. And here's my great-great-grandfather on my grandmother's side, who had the forge in town, made horseshoes and nails and what have you, and here you have two of his sons. . . ."

Spitt was rolling now.

I interrupted the flow: "Why do you have paintings of all these fellows who married into the family?"

"Oh well, their businesses merged with ours, don't you see? We needed the horses from the livery to pull the wagon to the graveyard. And the forge supplied our hardware, and the upholstery shop supplied the lining for the caskers. Why, do you realize that very same livery stable became our present-day limousine service? And our cabinetmaking shop and upholstery shop merged into the coffin-manufacturing plant we still run to this very day? We had to close the forge, of course, when it was no longer economical to make our own hardware."

Spitt strutted on down the hall, applying names to frames. Finally, he indicated a small blank spot opposite the men's room. "And here's where Stanley will go someday. And then his son. . . ."

"You have daughters, too, don't you?" I inquired pointedly of Stan.

"Yes." He was rocking from one foot to the other and fidgeting with the change in his pants pocket. "Every now and then we allow women into the family, a necessary evil."

But Spitt was off on an introduction of the next ancestor in line. As I followed, I was struck by the strange similarity that each portrait had to the others. They looked as if they had been painted by successive generations of artists from the same family, all of whom had inherited identical artistic styles. A suspicion dawned.

"Spitt," I said. "There's no way you could have oil portraits of all these guys going clear back to . . . what?"

"The seventeenth century." He grinned at me like a boy who has been caught with his pet snake in his pocket, and then he smirked at his son. Stan had flushed red. "This girl's too damn smart, Stanley." Then Spitt said to me in a congratulatory tone, as if I had correctly answered the question that won the trip to Hawaii, "Jennifer Cain, you're the first person to guess our little secret. Of course we couldn't have paintings of them, not unless we were descended from John Adams or King George or some other blueblood. And to tell you the honest truth," Spitt lowered his voice, as if a reporter might hear, "these first fellows, they were just carpenters or cabinetmakers. That's how most morticians got started. I mean to say, they only made coffins as a sideline, you see."

"So how did you get the pictures?" I persisted. "If they go back to the seventeenth century, you surely didn't work from photographs!"

He chuckled. "Oh, but we did work from photographs. That painting there, Jenny . . ." He pointed. "That's from a photo in a history book. I think the real guy was a vice-president or something. And that one there . . . he's somebody's idea of John Alden, remember him and Priscilla? And we took that one over there from a bunch of old photos at a library, and . . ."

I was laughing, I couldn't help it.

"For God's sake, Dad," said Stan.

"Well, what the hell?" The old man winked at me. "Our own flesh and blood couldn't have looked much worse. Besides, it's not everyone who gets to pick his relatives."

We had reached Spitt's office, and he abruptly abandoned us to enter the room and close the door. I looked at Stan. His complexion had slid from crimson to white.

"I used to hope my mother would poison him," he said in mournful tones. "But I don't think she's ever going to do it."

I laughed, and finally he managed a smile, too. Then we resumed our trek down the hallway under all those somber eyes. Only this time I had the feeling that twinkly old Erasmus was laughing, too, behind his mustache.

8

Stan led me into a small, pretty room that was decorated in chintz and furnished with country antiques. There were chintz draperies, two armchairs, a loveseat, a coffee table, two large cardboard boxes, and a wall of tastefully displayed urns.

"For cremation," Stan said with a casual glance over his shoulder. He tapped one of the cardboard boxes with the toe of his highly polished left shoe. "This is it, Jenny, these are the archives. I wanted to give Miss Grant one of our old file cabinets, but my dad said, 'You think file cabinets grow on trees?'"

I smiled. "The old wooden ones did."

"I should have told the old buzzard that." He gently kicked the cardboard box. "Well, if you have any questions, you'd probably better ask Miss Grant, she's the expert on this stuff."

"I have a question, but not about that, Stan."

He stuck his hands in his pants pockets. "Shoot."

The pretty little room had given me a feeling of warmth and safety—except for the urns, of course, which only increased the feeling of warmth, but not of security—and the exchange with Stan's dad had lifted my mood, as well. But now the cold, wet fear of the morning came sliding back over me. "I'm sorry to tell you this, but one of your gravediggers—

that young one, Jack—played some sort of a weird, unpleasant game with me today. What do you know about him anyway?''

"Jack?" Stan looked over at the urns as if they had called his name. "He's okay, I mean, he's a damn good worker, I wouldn't want to . . ."

"I'm not asking you to do anything yet." I was puzzled by his reaction, and annoyed. "But what do you know about him?"

"Nothing." He was still looking at the urns. "I mean, I'm sorry if he, if whatever he did, if . . ." Stan glanced at me, flushed, began to back toward the door. "I've got to get back to work, I'm sorry, Jenny, I . . ."

Suddenly I was alone with the urns and the archives.

He hadn't even asked what happened to me.

But I couldn't see going over his head to talk to his father.

There was a phone beside me. I picked it up and asked the switchboard to put me through to Francie Daniel. Did I have the gall to ask her to risk getting fired on her first day on the job?

When she answered, I said, "Francie, this is Jenny. Please humor me and answer the following questions with a simple yes or no, and don't say anything else. First, will you do a favor for me?"

"Yes," she said immediately.

"Can you get to the personnel files?"

"Yes, they're part of the job."

"Please, just yes or no," I said quickly. "I would appreciate it if you would locate the file for one of the gravediggers, I don't know his last name, but his first name is Jack. Will you?"

"Yes."

"You don't have to whisper, Francie." God only knew what somebody overhearing her might think. "When you find the file, would you please bring it into the cremation-urn display room and give it to me? And please don't let anybody see what you're doing, all right?"

"Yes," she said, sounding conspiratorial. "10-4."

I sighed, and hung up.

In a very few minutes, Francie appeared in the doorway. She looked over her shoulder before sidling into the room like a spy. "Here's what you want, Jenny. Can you get it back to me tonight? The personnel manager in this joint strikes me as a man who always knows where all his files are all the time."

"I promise." I took the folder from her. "Did you have any trouble locating the file?"

She shook her head. "It's not as if they employ thousands of people, although heaven knows they own half the town, between this place and the other funeral homes and the casket factory and the florist's and the prearrangement company, and the limousine service, and the . . ." Francie lowered her voice to a near-whisper again. "You know, they say it pays to live a good life. Seems to me a good death pays a darn sight better. What's this for, Jenny, the police investigation?"

Because I live with a cop, people sometimes have an inexplicable tendency to invest me with police powers. I smiled at her, as though to say, what do you think? She put a finger to her lips. Then, her secret mission accomplished, Francie waved a silent good-bye to me, and fled. I assuaged my conscience by telling it that if I discovered anything incriminating about the Jackal, I would, indeed, turn the evidence over to the police.

I looked down at the folder in my lap and saw that the tab on its side said, "John L. Smith, Gen. Main."

John Smith—a name so ordinary as to go part way toward explaining his eccentricities, but certainly not all the way. It isn't everybody named John Smith who ends up with a skull and crossbones in one ear, just to be different. I slid my thumb inside the folder.

"Jennifer Cain." Suddenly, I heard the voice of my sixth grade teacher, speaking inside my head in her most no-nonsense tone. "Young lady, you have a previous assignment to complete. You will kindly finish your history lesson first."

It was not entirely with regret that I dropped the Jackal's file onto the carpet beneath the coffee table. "Yes, Miss Grant," I murmured. I got up and dragged over the heavy boxes of research. Obediently, willingly, I abandoned the threatening twentieth century for the comparative safety of the nineteenth century.

I quickly learned that life back then had its own unique hazards: men were kicked in the head by mules, women died of "tedious labor," infants succumbed to something called "summer complaint," while folks of sixty-five were said to have died of old age. Oh, there were plenty of "heart troubles," "kidney troubles," "female troubles," and even "brain troubles" to account for the passing in those days of the population of Port Frederick. But there were also cholera, typhoid, and other killers whose deadly powers have since diminished. There were cancers, which somehow surprised me, as if I had thought it was only a modern disease. And a few soldiers and civilians from the town suffered Civil War deaths, of course. But nobody in the middle of the nineteenth century died in an automobile accident. Nobody expired in an airplane crash. And not one person was listed as having been electrocuted when his hair dryer fell into his hot tub.

I learned all that from the "Funeral Record of Union Hill Cemetery," which Miss Grant had compiled, according to her written introduction, from tombstones, death notices, conversations with survivors, her own memories, and the city clerk's office. The modest appearance and size of her book—it was merely sheets of typing paper bound in a plastic cover—belied the scope of her effort. From the looks of it, she had researched every grave on Union Hill, and painstakingly included in her record the dates of birth and death, the places of birth and death, the cause of death, name(s) of spouse(s), children, and even the names of the parents of every citizen who was buried there, if the information was available.

I leafed through the pages, feeling unexpected pangs of sympathy for people I had never known but whose names I recognized. There was Ashley Leland—surely an ancestor of one of my trustees, Roy Leland—dead at the age of thirty-seven in the winter of 1853, of "lagrippe." Under "Remarks," Miss Grant had included a quote from the newspaper death notice: "A Baptist for thirty years."

63

And here was a death notice for a Pittman: "In this city, the twenty-first instant, Mrs. Sarah Clark, wife of Mr. Benjamin Clark, the proprietor of the local sawmill, in the twenty-fifth year of her age, in childbirth, infant not surviving. She was a dutiful wife, an affectionate daughter to Mr. Erasmus Pittman and his wife of this town, and a devout Methodist. May she rest in peace."

Feeling strangely nervous, I looked for evidence of the passing of my own relations and found three on my mother's side of the family. I touched their names, was sentimentally glad to see they had all lived into relatively old age and had died under circumstances that didn't seem to indicate any more than the usual amount of suffering to be expected from any disease that terminates in death. They had been Swedish Lutherans all, no doubt revolving in their graves every time I slept late on Sundays.

"Oh." I recalled. "No."

They couldn't roll over in their graves, although now there would be plenty of room for it, because their graves were empty. I returned to my studies with renewed vigor.

Here was a spate of Ottilinis, the name of another of my trustees, but wasn't the middle of the nineteenth century a bit early for the Italian migration? I shrugged away the temptation to meander down fascinating tangential paths and pursued my search for I didn't know what. Or whom. Or when. Or how, or why, or what.

Finally, I put aside the funeral record and turned to the other materials that Miss Grant had placed inside the cardboard file cabinets.

For one thing, she had put together a scrapbook of advertising for products relating to the undertaking business: "Lilac Soap is highly recommended for removing blood stains and unpleasant odors from the hands." "Dr. Holmes' Innominata Embalming Fluid, $3 a gallon. Dr. Holmes' Great Root Beer, $1 a gallon." "Smith Burial Shoes, With Laces, All Patent Leather." I needed all my willpower to stop reading after the first few pages and to move on to the other items in the boxes.

There were old catalogs from casket manufacturing companies, dating back to the late 1800s; books written about English and American funeral customs; books on genealogy; books on cemetery development through the ages; books on the Civil War; and a fair amount of material relating to the various Pittman business enterprises, including old ledgers detailing "Receipts" and "Accounts" for all the years of Union Hill Cemetery's existence. There were old newspaper advertisements that urged potential customers to "come to the Sign of the Cradle & the Coffin, opposite the Tavern, for the Finest Carpentry and Cabinet Work. Upholstery Done. Horses to Let. Custom Coffins Made." This was evidently before coffins became caskets, I thought, recalling Stan's wry words about his own business.

There was even an old black-and-white photograph—a real one—of men working in the Pittman Undertaking Parlour, taken at the turn of the century. I looked among them for twinkly old Erasmus but didn't find his blond head or that huge mustache; he must have been dead by then.

On impulse, I thumbed back through Miss Grant's funeral records.

There he was, by God, old Erasmus. And it looked as if he was the last person to be buried in his own cemetery, dead in 1886 at the age of seventy-six of "kidney troubles." Hmm. Did the old boy drink? Could that have been the source of his good humor, and the cause of his death? There was quite a long death notice extolling the virtues—and enterprises—of this "former church sexton, successful businessman, and leading citizen of Port Frederick." He was survived by "his grieving widow, a sister, three sons, three daughters, and twelve dear grandchildren, having sadly lost his first wife and one daughter in the blossom of her age." Erasmus was also survived, I read, by one undertaking parlour, one cabinetry shop, one forge, one upholstery shop, one cemetery, one livery stable, and a print shop. I wondered when the print shop had come into the picture . . . did one of his granddaughters marry a printer?

"This is all very interesting," I said aloud, "but where are those damn bodies?"

Feeling frustrated and weary, I picked up a volume entitled *The History of American Funerals,* and I began to read the chapter dealing with the Civil War.

"The War meant a bonanza for the businesses related to the funeral industry," the book claimed. "Not only were there hundreds of bodies to transport by train at great expense from battlefields to home, but there were also rich opportunities for tremendous growth in the new 'profession' of embalming. New embalming fluids popped up everywhere, with their makers ecstatically extolling their virtues of turning 'flesh to stone instantly' in order to preserve corpses from the ravages of the grave. When Abraham Lincoln's body was embalmed, the trend was launched in earnest."

My eyelids were drooping over the dry, academic phrases. I skipped a few paragraphs.

"Although the word *undertaker* had long been in common usage," I read, "it was not until the War that the word *undertaking* was coined to describe an actual and separate profession, which was appropriate since this was certainly the period in which undertaking came into its own as a lucrative and expanding business."

I continued to read until a phone rang somewhere down the hall.

It jerked me back into the twentieth century, a trip I was not entirely sorry to make. I became aware of the sounds of employees who were heading home for the evening. Feeling stiff and sleepy, I carefully returned the books and other artifacts to the cardboard boxes. Then I walked back down the corridor to Stan's office, musing that I was now smarter, which is not the same as wiser.

9

I leaned against Stan's door jamb and waited for him to notice me. After a moment, he did. The clock on the credenza behind his desk said 5:15.

"Did you know," I said, "that Port Frederick was ahead of its time in having a rural cemetery like Union Hill?"

"You still here, Jenny?"

"At this rate, I may be here until you bury me."

He nodded knowingly, his face giving no hint of the awkwardness between us earlier. "It is a bunch of stuff, isn't it? Well, just leave it, and come on back anytime you want to, Jenny. You're not in our way. That's only our display room for cremation urns, and nobody wants to get cremated anyway."

"Why not?"

"Beats me." He shrugged. "It's practical as hell . . . dust to dust, ashes to ashes, couldn't be more literal than that. It's been popular in Europe for ages, and it's catching fire in other parts of this country, but . . ." He noticed my smile, and he slapped his hand against his cheek. "Oops. Terrible puns are an occupational hazard around here. Sorry."

"Well, I suppose cremation is awkward if you believe in a material resurrection." I raised my voice to a professorial tone.

"Why, do you know that the Christian belief in bodily resurrection contributed in part to the rapid growth of the art of embalming in the nineteenth century?" I descended from my imaginary lectern and smiled at him. "Anyway, you know this town, Stan . . . ever the optimists. I suppose we hope that God or technology will reassemble us one day."

"Or maybe it has something to do with the price of caskets as compared to the price of urns." Stan propped his chin in his hand. He smiled at the ceiling, as if in contemplation of his profit sheet, but then frowned. "God knows I try to sell cremation, especially if I see a customer is hard up, but it gives people the creeps for some reason. Makes you wonder what they think happens to a body in the grave, doesn't it?"

"In this town, it disappears," I said dryly. "I have to disappear, too. But I'll be back tomorrow."

Stan picked up a brochure from his desk and held it out to me. "Ah, but one never knows, Ms. Cain, if one will truly 'be back tomorrow'! Why take the risk of burdening one's family with difficult decisions at a time of grief? Make your decisions about your funeral now, today. I'm sorry to say we don't take MasterCard, but I will gladly accept your cash or a check. Would you prefer to make a down payment today, Ms. Cain, or would you like to pay the entire amount at one time? Perhaps you just happen to have the money stashed away in a sock, under your mattress, as some of our elderly customers do. Just give us the cash, and keep the sock for a rainy day. Why, if you will just sign here, we will arrange for your bank to deduct your payments automatically each month, at no extra trouble or expense to you. Remember, one never knows how soon the future may arrive!"

"Is that a threat?" I laughed, and crossed over to take the brochure from his outstretched hand. Its cover said, "Harbor Security: the practical and loving approach to funeral arrangements." There was a name, Russell Bissell, and two phone numbers at the bottom. I folded it in half and stuffed it in my suit coat pocket. Stan was right. One never knew how soon the future might arrive. In my mother's case, it was taking its time, ambling along the sidewalk, kicking stones, delaying the inevitable. I was the one who would be making the arrangements one day; God knew my charming, irresponsible father wouldn't do it; he had already abandoned her anyway, for a second marriage. And my beautiful, not-so-charming sister wouldn't wish to be bothered with the details. Maybe I should think about doing it now while the final, wrenching emotions were still out there in the distance somewhere.

Stan was looking at me oddly.

"Good night, Stan."

"See you tomorrow?"

I grinned at him. "Who knows?"

I headed for the foyer and the front door.

"Oh." I stopped abruptly, embarrassed. Ahead of me, a man and a woman stood in the center of the foyer, embracing. I thought I had stumbled onto a moment of private grief, until I remembered this was the management, not the public, wing. The couple raised their heads.

The woman with the tear-stained face was Beryl Kamiski, the elegant middle-aged woman who had been introduced to me as the manager of Harbor Security, the prearrangement company. The man with his arms wrapped loosely around her shoulders was her salesman, the blond and beautiful Russell Bissell. I had, after all, disturbed some private sadness.

I smiled in embarrassed recognition. "Excuse me."

"No, please." Beryl tried to return my smile, failed, put a trembling hand to her mouth. In her other hand, she was holding some photographs. "I'm so sorry."

Russell Bissell nodded to me. Then quickly, tactfully, he led Beryl out of the foyer, away from my view. On their way out, she let the pictures fall from her hand onto the antique side table under the bulletin board.

I waited until they were out of sight before I crossed over to take a look.

First I looked at the photographs that had been tacked up on the bulletin board. They were pictures of what appeared to be a Harbor Lights office party. I noticed an interesting variety of smiles: some drunken, some disapproving, but most just wearing that self-conscious, oh-God-I-wish-I-were-some-place-else look that sensible people wear at office parties. There was one of Stan, staring at something out of camera range, with his pretty wife beside him looking as annoyed as most spouses do at office parties. Beryl Kamiski was in a photo where she was chatting animatedly with Spitt and with a thin, dark young man I recognized from the graveside, the personnel director, Aaron Friedman. A short, pretty blond woman stood beside Friedman. I stared for some time, admiringly, at a photo of Russell Bissell. Not surprisingly, he stood at the center of a circle of women whose faces were raised adoringly to his.

Finally, I picked up the photographs that Beryl had dropped to the table. There were only three, and each of them showed a lovely, smiling young woman who looked enamored of life. And, possibly, of men. In all three pictures, she had her arms entwined with male arms—once with Bissell, once with Friedman and Stan. The last photo caught her in a tight little group, all of them giggling into the camera: Freddy, the other black gravedigger, and the Jackal. From the expressions of guilty, silly surprise on their faces, I guessed the joke was not one you would tell at a family picnic.

I knew I was looking at Sylvia Davis on the last night, in the last hours of her life. If the pictures were a good likeness of her that night, she had been truly beautiful and really drunk. I wished Geof were available to tell me the blood alcohol content in her body, so I'd know if my conjecture was right.

Behind me, the door to the funeral home opened, admitting a chill breeze and a police officer.

"Hello, Ailey."

"Jenny." Ailey Mason had a build that was born to police work—muscular, stocky, taut—but not to the trench coats he affected as if he were Port Frederick's Kojak. He crossed over and took the photographs from my hands. As he flipped through them, he said, "You do turn up, don't you?"

Since he was given to clichés, I said obligingly, "Like a bad penny. Ailey, was she as drunk as she looks?"

"Yeah." He began to take down the other photographs

70

from the bulletin board. It wasn't the diplomatic way Geof would have handled the removal of evidence, but then it wasn't Geof's case. His broad, impassive face cracked a slight smile. "They won't have to embalm the broad, she was already pickled."

I thought of the pretty face in the pictures and had to wait a moment before I was sure I could speak civilly to him again. Finally I said, "Ailey, do you think there could be any connection between her death and the death of John Rudolph? Why was she in the coffin with him? Why not in somebody else's coffin . . . why his? They had other funerals that day, didn't they?"

"Yes." As he took down the pictures, he laid the pushpins on the table, and some of them rolled off onto the floor. I bent down to pick them up and laid them back on the table.

"Well?"

"The other one was an open-casket funeral, any other questions?"

"Yes. Was there anything funny about his death, Ailey?"

"Not unless you think heart attacks are funny." He directed another of those small, tight smiles at the bulletin board. "Some people think they're a real scream."

"Good night, Ailey."

"See ya."

At the door, I turned around again.

"Ailey?"

He grunted.

"There's a really weird gravedigger who works here," I said to his back. "His name is John L. Smith, known as Jackal, and he's maybe nineteen. I don't want to tell you your business, but I think you ought to check him out, because . . ."

"That's a good idea," he said. "About you not telling me my business."

I stared at the back of his trench coat for a moment longer. The belt was twisted over itself between the two back loops. I opened the door, stepped outside, and closed the door quietly behind me.

10

At six in the evening, on weekdays, The Buoy Bar & Grill is as noisy, smoky, smelly, and crowded as the English pubs on which it was modeled many, many years ago. Like generations of Port Frederickans before me, I can't think of any place I would rather go to drink and socialize. Sometimes. This was not one of those times.

"Cain! Jenny! Over here!"

The shout could have come from any one of a number of people there whom I would have been delighted to join. It derived instead from Lewis Riss.

I climbed over several pairs of knees to sit beside him on the long wooden bench that faced a long wooden table against the far wall. My name was carved in that table someplace along the line—the only bit of graffiti in which I'd ever indulged—along with dozens, maybe even hundreds, of the names of other graduates of Port Frederick High School. We had considered it proof of something back then, maybe coming of age, certainly not literacy. Because of the crush, I squeezed in closer to him than I really wished to.

" 'Allo, me beauty," he growled.

"Lewis."

Lewis was medium height, thin, late twenties. His heavy

mop of curly black hair hung down over his eyebrows, which were also thick and black and curly; his five o'clock shadow looked as if it dated from five o'clock on a previous afternoon. He had on a bulky, dirty white cableknit sweater over a black turtleneck over faded blue jeans. Somewhere under there was a basically good-looking man, but he was hard to spot, and I had no desire to search. He clapped a hand over one eye and leered at me like a pirate. There were curly black hairs on the backs of his hands. "What'll it be, matey? Grog 'n flog?"

"Grog," I said to the waiting, grinning waitress. "Hold the flog."

"I heard a great joke," Lewis said. He sucked on his funny cigarette and blew the smoke into my face. The unmistakable smell of marijuana drifted down the long bench; it was interesting to observe who looked up in startled recognition. He said, "It goes, 'Guess who's buried in Grant's Tomb?' "

"Are you out of your mind, Lew?" I coughed, waved away the smoke. "This is not Cosmopolitan, U.S.A., you know."

"No shit." He grinned through the smoke.

"Well?"

"I thought you said Bushfield's out of town."

"He's not the only cop in town, dummy."

"He's the only one with his brains in the right end of his anatomy." Lew was easy to insult, difficult to offend. But he delicately snuffed out the joint on the tabletop and slid the stub into his wallet. "All right, that's enough fun for one lifetime, let's get serious. What do you know about the murder of Sylvia Davis?"

"Probably less than you do."

He curled his upper lip in a show of skepticism.

"Honest, Lewis."

"Sure." He shook his head. "Okay, how did it feel to be there when they found her in that coffin?"

"You don't really ask questions like that, do you? How did it feel? It felt just peachy-keen, Lewis. How do you think it felt! It felt awful, shocking, scary, sickening, that's how it felt."

He smirked, as if I had fallen into a trap.

The waitress arrived with my draft beer.

"I hear you been askin' around about those empty graves on Union Hill," Lewis said quietly, as she placed the glass mug on a round cardboard coaster. "What's it to you? I mean, it's news, so it's a natural for me. And it oughta be for the cops, but they act like crimes committed in another century are out of their jurisdiction, for Christ's sake. I mean, you ever hear of a police force that defines its jurisdictions by *time?*"

"You've never come across the statute of limitations?" I waited for Lewis to pay the waitress for my drink. When he didn't, I dug the money out of my purse. "This is not Boston, Lewis, as you ought to realize every time you pick up a paycheck for that great metropolitan newspaper you write for."

"That was tacky, Cain."

"Well? These are the provinces, kiddo. Small town, small police force. It's all they can do to catch this year's crop of crooks, much less try to solve something that happened around the time of the Civil War."

"How do you know it happened then?" he asked sharply.

I sighed. "I don't, Lew. I was just . . ."

"This is what comes of living with a cop." He put his left arm over the bench behind me and leaned toward me, a severe expression on his face. "You get co-opted by the system, you start defending the gestapo . . ."

"Gestapo?" I laughed, drew back from him. "Lewis, the worst case of police brutality we ever had in Poor Fred was a couple of years ago when a traffic cop pulled over this old lady for speeding, and she bit him on the hand, and he bit her back, which God knows she richly deserved. Well, he got fired, and she never even had to pay the ticket!"

"Damn, I miss all the good stories." Lewis cocked an eyebrow at me. "So answer the question of this bona fide, genuine reporter . . . why the big interest in Union Hill?"

"You wouldn't understand this," I said a shade acidly, "being new to these sticks as you are, but we have a sense of community around here, Lew. And you don't move out of that community just because you die. I have trustees who want

74

to know where their ancestors are, and I'd kind of like to find my great-great-great-grandparents, too. Is that so hard to grasp, Clark Kent?"

He took a swig from his beer mug, wiped his chin with his sleeve. "You know who else is from near Asbury Park?"

I could only think of one man, "The Boss," the king of rock and roll. "You mean Bruce Springsteen?"

"Who else? He's big on community, like you. But you and he, you got the bucks, you can afford to be happy hicks. Me, I got a living to earn. And one of these days it ain't gonna be here, and it ain't gonna be in Asbury Park, New Jersey. I am only sticking around these sticks till *The New York Times* calls me to my natural home. And if I'm ever gonna get out of here, it's gonna be on the backs of murders and missing bodies. You hear what I'm saying? So while you're gettin' in my way, at least be useful, will you? For starters, you can get me in to see Miss Lucille Grant . . . the last time I called her, she corrected my grammar and hung up on me."

"She was only doing you a favor, Lewis. *The New York Times* is big on grammar."

I swallowed some beer.

"Well, you gonna do it?"

I looked him up and down. "You have a certain something, Lewis, an indefinable . . . something . . . that is remarkably easy to resist. No. You've hung up on me and insulted me, all in less than twenty-four hours. Why should I help you?"

"Would it have made a difference if I'd spaced it out a little, maybe given it a day or two between the hang up and the insults?"

I couldn't help but laugh.

He pounced on his advantage. "You should do it because if you do, I'll tell you everything I learn about the Davis murder."

"Why should I want to know that?"

"Because you were there when they found her, and you're dying of curiosity, and your number-one source is out of town, and your number-two source is a horse's ass."

"You mean you?"

"I mean Ailey." He grinned. "And God knows you can't believe everything you read in the paper. I'll give you a quarter to call her."

I didn't give in just out of curiosity, but because I didn't trust Ailey to be able to handle the case alone. Lewis Riss might turn out to be a valuable source of information for me to hoard for Geof, in case he had to take over the case when he got back from Philadelphia.

I raised my glass to his, just short of touching it. "Okay."

But he pursued my glass with his until they clinked.

He smirked. "Ambulance chaser."

After a second beer, I began to think it was a pretty good idea to visit Miss Grant. I called her from a public phone booth near the entrance to the bar. She, without hesitation, warmly invited me to drop by with "my friend."

"I should warn you," I began.

"Yes, dear," she said calmly. "When Mr. Riss called here, he reminded me a little of Teddy Magus, whom I had in sixth grade so many years ago. I doubt he's changed much, Teddy Magus, that is, although, goodness, he must be fifty years old by now. I suspect he has a very patient wife. No, Jenny, dear, don't you worry about me. I know just how to handle your Mr. Lewis Riss."

My friends, I noticed, were developing an unfortunate tendency to assign to me belongings I didn't want, like "my" missing bodies and "my" obnoxious reporter. But I hung up from talking to her with a sense of anticipation that very nearly amounted to glee. I turned away from the phone in time to see Lewis reach out and pat a waitress on her rear.

"You do that again, Riss," she said angrily, "and I'll serve your balls on ice."

When I walked up to him, he shook his head in a lugubrious fashion. "I can't make out with the women in this town, Cain. Including you, God knows." He held up his hands in mock defense. "I know, I know, a reporter can get into a hell of a lot of trouble for tampering with police property." Lewis leered, as Captain Hook must have at Wendy. "What am I doing wrong, anyway?"

"Beats me, Lewis."

"Hell, I would if I thought it would work," he said, but I saw that he was distracted by something over my right shoulder. I turned, to see the gorgeous Harbor Lights prearrangement salesman, Russell Bissell, walking by me on his way into the bar. I smiled, nodded. He looked from me to Lewis and back again, then smiled with a slow, easy flash of perfect teeth. Aaron Friedman was behind him, looking like a shadow trailing the sun. The personnel director frowned as if he were trying to remember where he had seen me before, and had not yet placed me at John Rudolph's graveside. I smiled at him, then followed Lewis, who had walked around me, toward the door.

He lifted a navy pea coat with gleaming brass buttons from a hook, and grunted as he slipped it on. "Women." The coat was a little snug on him; his wrists stuck out. "You're all alike. You want the tall, cool, pretty boys." He patted the pockets of the coat and brought out a pack of cigarettes. I was amused to see they were low tar, low nicotine, menthol. "But I'll tell you." He lit a cigarette, made a face at the taste of it. "Cool waters run shallow, kid."

"That will come as a surprise to deep-sea divers."

I slipped into my own raincoat and buttoned it. Once out into the cold, damp night, I hunched my shoulders, stuck my hands in my pockets. "Wish I'd worn something as warm as that coat, tonight."

"This?" He looked down at the pea coat, fingered one of the buttons. "Oh, it's not mine. I didn't wear a coat."

I stopped on the sidewalk and stared at him.

"Well, don't look at me like I'm some kind of ax murderer, Jenny. I'll return it tomorrow, for God's sake. You don't want me to freeze do you? Come on, we'll take your car."

Halfway down the sidewalk, he turned back to yell at me.

"Come on, Cain!" He stamped his feet, sucked impatiently on his stolen cigarette so the end of it glowed, a point of fire in the mist. "You don't want to keep an old lady waiting, do you? That wouldn't be very nice."

Cigarette. Fire. Cremation. I stood frozen to the cement, not only in shock at his theft but also because of my own stupidity: I'd left the personnel file on John L. Smith under the coffee table in the cremation-urn display room at the funeral home. Damn. I pulled back the left sleeve of my coat, checked my watch. Only 7:00. Funeral homes stayed open late, didn't they, for visitations, or whatever? Maybe there would be time to retrieve the file after we left Miss Grant's apartment. I hoped so, for my sake, but mostly for Francie's.

"Cain! Shake it!"

I stopped for gas on the way. Lewis didn't offer to pay for any of it. He did, however, promise me that he wouldn't ask Miss Grant who was buried in Grant's Tomb.

11

Miss Grant set down her teacup and smiled benevolently upon Lewis. He was seated on the floor at her feet, his knees drawn up to his chest, his arms resting on his knees. I was cross-legged on the floor opposite him. Miss Grant had on a flowered pink bathrobe and floppy pink slippers.

"My grandmother attended burials there, Mr. Riss," she said. "That's how I know the graves were not always empty, as they are today. Will you have another cookie?"

She held out to him a huge tin of imported English biscuits that she said a former pupil had sent her. Lewis took one. She smiled encouragingly. He took another, and laid them both on the lacy napkin that was draped like a bandage over one knee of his dirty jeans. He put one of the cookies to his mouth and a crumb dropped to the carpet; Lewis bent quickly to retrieve it. I watched, hypnotized, and waited for him to start eating out of her hand . . .

My, weren't those interesting articles that Mr. Riss had written about the trash dump? And, my heavens, of course she excused him for not having shaved, why she knew how very hard reporters worked at their craft, such long hours they devoted to their stories. And how thoughtful it was of him to visit an old lady . . . Jennifer always seemed to have such attractive, intelligent, nice young friends . . .

I was distinctly disappointed. I had hoped for something along the lines of a hickory stick to get him in line, not this sickening sweetness and light. As she talked, I munched grumpily on my third Scotch shortbread cookie.

"Every Decoration Day," she was saying, "my mother took us to that cemetery and related to us the details of the lives and deaths of our ancestors who were buried there, just as her mother had told it all to her.

"Why, Mother knew everything there was to know about the funerals, even down to such details as what kind of wood Erasmus Pittman and his boys used to make the coffins. Usually, it was oak, elm, pine, cherry, walnut, but hardly ever mahogany, since that had to be imported. And they used shiny brass fittings, of course.

"But the coffins were simple and dignified, Mother said, and in those days they were still shaped like bodies . . . you know, narrow at the feet and head, wide at the shoulders." Miss Grant traced a grim shape in the air. "It wasn't until long after the Civil War that the newfangled rectangular shapes and the fancy metal coffins became popular in towns as small as this one was."

She smiled down at us, and I felt my disappointment melt away. I was a sixth grader again, listening in rapt attention as she made history come alive with tales from her own memories. Lewis reached for another cookie. I sipped my tea; it was Earl Grey.

"Every Decoration Day," Miss Grant continued, "Mother made us trim the grass around the family graves and wash the stones. Can you imagine it? We had to dig the dirt out of every letter, with brushes! And we tended the flowers that my grandmother had planted. They were perennials, of course, can you guess why?"

Lewis and I glanced at each other in a panic.

"To symbolize rebirth," Miss Grant explained kindly. "I came by my interest in cemeteries through her, and through my mother." Lines appeared between her eyebrows. "Oh, Mother would be so very distressed to know . . . ."

"Stan told me that nobody has been buried in that cemetery since the last century," I said quickly. "I didn't think to ask him why. Do you know why, Miss Grant?"

"They ran out of room," Lewis suggested.

"Oh no," Miss Grant murmured. "There is ground remaining that might have served for burials for at least a few more years. I've always assumed that they wished to retain the open beauty of the property, rather than to crowd it fence to fence with tombstones."

"Early environmentalists?" I opined.

"Well, I've been thinking," Lewis interrupted, surprising me with the admission. "Maybe grave robbers did it. You know, for loot or for medical research."

Miss Grant pursed her lips, shook her head gently. "It is true that grave robbing for the purpose of medical research continued well up into the Victorian era. Resurrection men they were called, those awful men who robbed fresh graves for bodies to sell to the anatomists. Why there was even an infamous pair of them who killed wayfarers and sold their bodies!"

Like a child, I felt a delicious shiver run through me.

"Dreadful!" she exclaimed, her eyes wide. "That was one of the reasons that people took to erecting wrought-iron fences around family plots, you know, although it was mostly for show, to let the rest of the world know how rich and important they were. That custom never caught on in a small, poor town like Port Frederick, thank goodness. Such a silly, expensive conceit."

"So maybe it was the resurrection men!" Lewis insisted.

"No," I interjected. "Sorry to be morbid, but there were plenty of bodies around for the taking during the war years, without anybody having to resort to grave robbing."

"They robbed for loot, then," he said.

Miss Grant and I exchanged smiles, and I said, "There has never been much loot in Poor Fred, Lewis. Besides, you'll never catch a New Englander burying something that he might be able to sell for a good price later."

Miss Grant laughed into her napkin, quickly hiding the laugh when she saw the frustration on Lew's face. I could have told him he wouldn't find any easy answers, any more than I had so far.

But he leaned forward, not giving up. "I've been checking in the history books, Miss Grant, and I read that people used to be buried in churchyards or in commons in the center of town. So why did they bury people way out there at Union Hill? It must have been a good five miles from the center of town in those days."

"Well, my dears." She took an instructive tone with us. "The condition of those old graveyards was quite scandalous by the end of the eighteenth century. Just imagine . . ." Again, her hands moved in vivid concert with her words, ". . . there were scores and scores of bodies, all buried on top of each other in tiny, tiny graveyards . . . without the faintest regard for sanitation . . . the town's dogs dug up the bones . . . there were dreadful sights, horrible smells! Why, it became a matter of public health and decency to remove the burials to the countryside . . .

"The story that came down to me was that the town fathers of Port Frederick wished to move the cemetery outside of town, but the sexton resisted the idea. Sextons, you recall, were church officers who were charged with, among other duties, the rights and responsibilities of burial of the dead. They rang the bells, laid out the bodies, dispensed permits, collected fees, even dug the graves. It was quite a lucrative sideline, as you may imagine.

"At any rate, the sexton didn't want them to move the graveyard off church property, because he would lose the income from the burials! But he finally had to admit it was a losing battle, so he offered to open the new graveyard on his own property, and to sell plots just as some of the big modern cemeteries had already begun to do in the larger cities, like Boston. He was really quite ahead of his time, a shrewd businessman in that regard."

82

"It was Erasmus Pittman," I volunteered, and added for the benefit of Lewis, "That was Spitt Pittman's great-grandfather. He was the town sexton, as well as the cabinetmaker, the undertaker, and just about everything else."

"Was he, dear?" Miss Grant looked surprised, and pleased. "Why, I'd forgotten he was sexton, but of course, it stands to reason. So many of the men who turned to undertaking were sextons, or carpenters, or liverymen. It was a natural progression . . ."

"Life," Lewis pronounced suddenly, "is a natural progression." He stretched out his legs, rolled over on his side, crooked an elbow, and propped his head on his fist, looking set to wax philosophical. "Birth to death, love to marriage, marriage to divorce."

"So cynical, Mr. Riss?" Her tone was regretful. "Although, I must admit that your 'progression' from marriage to divorce seems more 'natural' now than it did during the era about which we were talking. Theirs was a hard life, but not a very long one for most of them . . . a small comfort to the unhappy, I suppose. It does seem to me that one of the reasons we have so much divorce nowadays is simply that we live too long for some marriages to endure. A soup with too little meat on its bones will not improve with time, no matter how long it's left to simmer." An expression of sadness crossed the broad, plain features of her face. "I never used to hear of divorces among my 'children.' Now it seems I learn of new ones every day. Sometimes I think I've lived beyond my time. I feel it particularly when I outlive one of my children. Dear, silly Sylvia. First that separation from her sweet husband, and now . . . this."

Lewis and I exchanged glances, and he sat up again.

"You knew her?" he asked.

"Of course," she replied. "Sylvia was in one of the last classes I taught before I retired. A beautiful child, but my goodness, what an outrageous flirt!" Her mouth drew up into a smile of fond memory. "Why, from the principal on down to the smallest kindergartner, Sylvia Davis had them all under her spell."

"Pretty is as pretty does," Lewis said, with a smug grin for me.

"No, no." She rebuked him sharply. "Sylvia was quite a nice and intelligent child, as well. She was one of my brighter and more responsible students, except perhaps when it came to the boys." Miss Grant gazed in a severe manner at Lewis. "Really, Mr. Riss, I expected better of you as a reporter than to parrot clichés. Just look at our little Jenny! If pretty is as pretty does, then pretty is exceedingly well. Wouldn't you agree?"

His nod was grudging.

"Little" Jenny, all five feet seven of her, tried not to grin.

"Lewis." I looked at my watch. "We've taken up enough of Miss Grant's time."

She cut the ground out from under me, of course, by smiling at him and murmuring, "I have far too much time, my dears, and every minute of it that you fill is time well spent for me." She gestured toward her knees, still tightly bound with bandages. "I still can't get around well at all, you see, at least not without the crutches my doctor gave me. I only wish I could attend the services for Sylvia tomorrow, but . . ."

"I'll take you," I said, before Lewis could.

Her eyes, behind the horn-rimmed glasses, glinted mischievously. "I rather hoped you would, Jennifer. Oh, I am a wicked old woman, aren't I?"

"Awful," I said fondly. But it was Lewis who kissed her on her cheek. I don't know who was the more surprised, Miss Grant or I, but it was clear which of us was the more pleased.

"Good night, my dears," she called to us as we locked and closed her door behind us.

I followed Lewis down the stairs. "Apple polisher," I muttered. To which he stuck out his tongue and replied, "Nya, na, na, na, na."

12

I waited until my car was moving before telling Lewis that we weren't going right back to The Buoy. "I left something at Harbor Lights," I said, with what I hoped was a winning smile, "and I need to run out there and get it before they close tonight. You want to come along?"

I stepped harder on the gas.

"No, I don't want to come along." He was sarcastic. "I want to pick up my car and then go to the police station to see what's new on the Davis murder. But I have a feeling I'm being kidnapped. Do I have a choice in this, Cain?"

"There's always a choice, Lewis. You could throw open the door and fling yourself to the pavement." I took a corner too fast; Lewis grabbed the edge of the dashboard to steady himself.

"Women drivers," he muttered. He leaned forward and dug for something in his back jeans pocket. "They don't call it power steering for nothing." He pulled out his wallet and removed the stubby joint. In a conciliatory move, I pushed in the car lighter for him.

"You're so cute when you're in a snit," I said.

He leveled his best New Jersey-gangster glare at me.

"I used to know a man," I told him, "who made plenty of money, but he refused to buy a car for his wife."

"Damn right."

"She left him," I said. "A few months after the divorce, her husband was mysteriously killed by a hit-and-run driver. But he, the husband that is, hadn't changed his will yet, so she got all the money. With the settlement, she bought a Mercedes dealership. Now she drives a new demo to work every day."

"You made that up," he said, but I heard amusement in his voice. The lighter popped out. I removed one hand from the wheel and held the lighter out to him so he could light the joint. Lewis leaned back against the seat then, and propped his dirty running shoes on my dashboard. He sucked energetically, then released the smoke with an audible sigh. He nudged my elbow and offered the joint to me.

I shook my head.

He grunted. "You hang around with too many cops." But he leaned back again and seemed content to ride along. I wondered briefly what my trustees would say to the idea of funding a study to examine the salutary effects of marijuana on hyperactive adults, like Ritalin on kids.

After a few more peaceful moments, we pulled into the parking lot at Harbor Lights.

"Hey," Lewis said lazily. "There's a party goin' on."

The lot was surprisingly full for the late hour. The funeral home, all lit up, did indeed look less like a mortuary than it did like a large private residence where the family was throwing a big party. I half expected a butler to take our coats and a maid to serve Dubonnet. All it needed to complete the illusion of affluent domesticity was smoke rising from a chimney. On second thought, maybe smoke rising from a chimney wasn't the most tactful note on which to greet visitors to a funeral home. I found a place to park beside a small brown station wagon.

"You're not coming in?" I asked Lewis.

"Brilliant deduction," he said. "Maybe you can lead me to water, baby, but that don't mean I got to drink." He had

86

removed a Baggie full of joints from somewhere on his person and was now smoking a fresh, fat one. After breathing the same air with him in the closed car, I was beginning to swim upstream myself. I shook my head to clear it, but only succeeded in making myself dizzy. I focused at a point over his shoulder to steady my vision.

The point materialized into a face, small and pale.

It belonged to a little brown-haired woman wearing a brown coat who was sitting alone in the brown station wagon, in the driver's seat. As if she sensed my observation, she turned her face our way. She met my eyes, then quickly turned away again to resume her straight-ahead stare out the windshield toward the funeral home.

I shifted my glance away from her before Lewis could notice. If the widow of the late John Rudolph wished to maintain a lonely vigil in the parking lot of the funeral home where he had been employed, that was her business. She didn't need a nosy reporter to probe her grief with his questions. What, I wondered, would Lewis ask her, given the chance? "Tell me, Mrs. Rudolph, how does it feel to find your husband in a coffin with another woman?" There was something about Muriel Rudolph—so small, so plain, so serious—that made me wish to protect her.

I felt my elbow jarred again.

Lewis, his face wreathed in the most relaxed and generous of smiles, held out the joint to me. Again, I shook my head. I realized with a shock that I had been sitting, lumplike, for several minutes in that car. I had to get out of there and breathe fresh air before I fell asleep. But I couldn't leave him there to discover the presence of the widow in the next car.

I roused myself to speech.

"Come with me, Lewis," I said in seductive tones. "If you do, I'll get you into the morgue to see where she died."

He sat up with surprising briskness and snubbed out the joint. Again, the stub went into his wallet. "On second thought," Lewis said cheerfully, his voice sounding unnecessarily loud to me, "I'm pretty damn thirsty, after all."

He started to turn toward the door.

"Lewis, wait!"

He looked back, eyebrows up.

I pulled down the mirror on the back of my visor and pretended to examine my hair and makeup. I took my time about applying new lipstick, pursing my lips at the mirror, running my tongue over them slowly, and blotting them caressingly with a tissue.

"And pretty damn hungry," he murmured.

I reached for the door handle on my side of the car, and Lewis reached for me. I slipped out of his grasp and was standing outside the car, looking down at him, before he was able to complete the pass.

"They don't call them power brakes for nothing, either," I said.

Lewis, sprawled over the driver's seat, stared up at me. Then he sang softly, "Hey little girl, is your daddy home, did he go and leave you all alone? Oh, oh, oh, I'm on fire."

I recognized the Springsteen, and smiled.

After a moment, Lewis grinned back.

I held out a hand to him to help him slide out of my side of the car. Once out, he tried to keep hold of me, but I took his hand and slipped it into the pocket of the pea coat. He laughed. We walked companionably up to the funeral home then. Lewis didn't so much as glance at the brown station wagon.

We tried the door to the management wing first, but no luck. Locked. My only choice, short of breaking and entering, was to go with the flow of mourners into the public wing.

Once in, it was not a butler but a short, fat, extremely neat man in a blue suit who greeted us. There was a sprig of baby's breath in his lapel. His shoes were shiny; so were his eyes, as if with repressed tears.

"Did you folks come for the Davis visitation?" He whispered, as if our visit were a secret he would tactfully keep for us. Lewis and I glanced at each other with "oh" in our eyes. That explained the full parking lot: the employees of the Pittman companies were here to pay their respects to Sylvia.

I nodded, signifying nothing.

The short, fat, neat man seemed to think my nod signified assent, because he pointed gracefully. "Down the hall, second double door on your right." He was still whispering, still keeping our little secret. It did seem bizarre, when I thought about it, for people to get all dressed up to go visit a corpse. Lewis, of course, was not all dressed up, but the little man bravely included him in our conversation anyway. In fact, when he looked at Lewis his welcoming smile grew even sadder and kinder, if anything, as if he understood that grief took all forms, even to the extreme of underdressing. He whispered, "It's in the Chapel of the Resurrection."

"Has it ever worked?" Lewis asked.

I grabbed his elbow to pull him away. But not fast enough. The short, fat, neat man innocently inquired, "What is that, sir?"

"The chapel," Lewis called back over his shoulder as I dragged at him. "Has anybody ever come back to life in it? Make a great story for the *Inquirer* . . ."

The kind, wet eyes looked hurt.

I pushed Lewis into an empty visitation chamber and then into an antique American country chair. "Sit," I commanded. I took off my raincoat and dumped it on his lap. "Stay. And keep your mouth shut so nobody starts asking what we're doing here and why I've wandered off into the offices at this time of night. And don't you go asking any of the relatives what it feels like to buy a coffin for their cousin when she already had a free one!"

His reporter's instincts were suddenly and obviously aquiver. "Hey, Cain, what are you after here? Maybe I'd better come with you, make sure you find it . . ."

"You want to see the morgue, or not?"

"Christ." He drummed his fingers on his knees. "All right, all right, but hurry, will you? I got work to do. If you're not back in ten minutes, I'll find old man Pittman and offer him a jay in exchange for information as to your whereabouts."

At the door, I turned back to examine him critically.

"Actually, Lewis, in that pea coat, you look halfway respectable."

His initial offended expression gave way to an ominous grin. "I'll see what else I can find on the coatrack. Shake it, Cain."

I stepped into the hallway with the idea of blending into the crowd of mourners so that I might work my way inconspicuously toward the door marked Staff Only. It's not easy to be inconspicuous when you're a tall female of Swedish descent, but I thought it was worth a try. Francie had trusted me, and I had let her down. I thought it was important to retrieve that file before it was found by somebody who might wonder how the new secretary could be so careless with confidential material. It wouldn't do for her to get fired on my account.

I reached the edge of the crowd and lowered my face but not soon enough. Across the hall, Aaron Friedman saw me, started to smile, then looked puzzled. His expression said clearly, "What's she doing here?" He started to make his way toward me, but suddenly stopped. He and I both stared at another woman who was just then walking through the front door. Again that puzzled expression crossed Friedman's face, but this time it also carried hints of "Oh, God."

It was Muriel Rudolph, come to pay her respects to the dead woman in her husband's coffin.

13

The little greeter held out his hands to her.

She swept past him, so that he was left in an awkward position, tilting forward like half a sculpture of reaching lovers. The expression on his round face changed from sympathy to surprise to embarrassment. He regained his balance and then retreated to his post beside the door, curling into himself like a wounded possum.

Muriel Rudolph walked toward the rest of us as if she were leaning into a high wind. Her arms in their brown sleeves were clamped tightly to her sides, but at the ends of them her tiny hands fluttered in nervous, leave-me-alone movements, like wings. She was holding her entire body so tightly clenched that it appeared a mere tap of a finger might shatter her. As she drew nearer I saw that her lower jaw was trembling.

One by one, the gathered relatives and associates of Sylvia Davis became aware of the widow's presence. One by one they looked, stared, grew silent. I sensed Lewis at my back, scrabbling a pencil across paper.

Directly in the widow's path, Aaron Friedman, looking nearly as tense as she, stood his ground. She stopped in front of him as if he had pressed a palm to her forehead. I heard him say, "Muriel," in a low voice, but that is as far as he got.

"Where's the slut?" The stiff brown arms came up in fists as though she would hit him. Friedman didn't move back or try to touch her. "Where is she, Aaron? I know everybody's here to honor the slut . . ."

Stan Pittman stepped quickly out of the crowd and walked to Friedman's side. I saw Spitt step forward momentarily, too, but then hang back, nervously massaging his hands. Beryl Kamiski and Russell Bissell glided up behind the widow so that she was trapped in a circle of Harbor Lights people. Stan said quietly, gently, "Come on now, Muriel . . ."

"Don't come on Muriel, me!" She screamed it, defeating the privacy fence that Stan, Bissell, Friedman, and Kamiski had erected around her with their bodies. There was a nervous flurry in the crowd as if everybody had stepped back a pace. I felt my own gut contract. Muriel Rudolph's birdlike voice, gone shrill and shrieking, stabbed my ears and traveled in a shiver down to the base of my spine. "Come on and behave, Muriel," she screamed furiously. "Come on and be a nice little lady, Muriel, come on and shut up, Muriel! I'm supposed to take it, is that right, Stan? I'm supposed to stand by and take it while you honor the memory of that slut who ruined my life? Well, I won't! I won't!"

Beryl Kamiski touched the widow's back and was immediately and violently shrugged off.

"How do you think I felt seeing him in there with her . . . my last memory of my husband! How do you think my children feel, oh God." She began to sob, but when Stan tried to steady her, she jerked back from him as she had from Beryl, as if their touch offended her. "And now all you fine friends of John, all you fine and decent people . . ." Her sarcasm curdled the words. "You're all here to pay your respects to her. Respects! Dear God! Do you think John was the only one? You know better than that, don't you, Aaron? Don't you, Stan? Don't you, Russell? My God, you know perfectly well she'd sleep with anybody around here who was still breathing! Respect! You couldn't even manage that for my John. When he died you didn't even have the decency to postpone your party, and oh boy, didn't she have a good time once he was gone, boy, didn't she dance on his grave!" Her voice caught again, cracked. "Oh, I heard, don't think I didn't hear all about it. And now you do this for her. How could you, how could you?"

"Muriel." Stan tried again. "Please."

"No, no, no, no." She wagged a finger under his nose in a taunting gesture. "The world's going to listen to me now. I'm going to tell the world how you pull out all the stops for the world's finest funeral for little Sylvia, and how awfully you treated my John. His beautiful, dignified funeral! Ruined! Gone! It was wrong, Stan, it was all wrong!"

"I'm so sorry," he said in a bleak voice.

"Where is she?" Muriel Rudolph was swaying like a punching bag. "Where are you keeping the slut? Got the best casket for her, I'll bet, nothing too good for the slut. Show me where she is. I want to dance! I want to pay my respects, too!"

"Come on, honey." Beryl Kaminski wrapped herself around the widow like a soft, enveloping mattress. But Muriel Rudolph went stiff, resisting, even as Beryl began to murmur to her in firm, comforting, lulling words that ran together like warm raindrops into a full stream: "Nobody meant any disrespect to John, Muriel, honey. We all thought the world of him, you know we did. It's just one of those awful, unfortunate things that nobody ever wanted to happen. Now let's come on along, Muriel, honey. We'll see you home, all right?" But the soft rain of her words was not absorbed into the hard, cracked earth of the other woman's emotions. The widow tore herself out of the comforting arms with an anguished cry.

"No!" She broke away and ran to the front door.

It was courteously held open for her by a scruffy-looking young man whose face was partly hidden behind the turned-up collar of a navy blue pea coat.

She paused to stare at him.

"You're that reporter," we all heard her say.

Lewis shrank further into the coat, but nodded.

She began to laugh, a wild and awful sound that mixed with her crying so the two ran together indistinguishably. "You want an obituary? I'll give you an obituary this town won't soon forget!"

Stan broke from the semicircle of Harbor Lights employees and began to walk quickly toward her. But she and Lewis disappeared out the front door together. It slammed behind them. Stan stood for a moment looking at it as if it might speak, then his shoulders came down in an apparent sigh. He turned back to face the crowd. I had the sense of a hundred other breaths released, too.

"I don't believe it," Aaron Friedman exclaimed in a shocked voice. His dark, narrow face registered, for the first time, strong emotion. "That's my pea coat!"

I thought I would take advantage of the general chaos to slip behind the crowd and sneak past the door of the Chapel of the Resurrection. But when I glanced in, my attention was momentarily caught by what I saw there.

At the far end of the large room there was an oddly feminine-looking coffin of pinkish bronze. It was closed. An arrangement of pink roses hung like a blanket over the lid.

A gray-haired man, midfifties, stood vigil at the head of the coffin, his hands clasped tightly behind his back. He had the crewcut of a man who will, at heart, always be a Marine, even if he was never in the service. His complexion was mottled red and white, as if somebody had applied suction cups to it, and he was staring stonily, blindly straight ahead. Her father, I thought. There were older women in the room, any one of whom might have been her mother, and there were young men who might have been her husband, but I couldn't pick them out so easily. His grief alone was visible and compelling, so that for a moment, I felt myself freeze in contemplation of him. It was like another person in that room, his grief: tangible, full-dimensioned, breathing, standing watch with him over the murdered daughter's coffin. There was no

94

way he could have escaped hearing the widow's accusations; they would have shot down the hall toward him like bullets, penetrating, wounding. The shock of them sat visibly on his rigid shoulders, clung to the hard, tightened line of his lips, stared out of his eyes.

I watched as one after another, single mourners in the room worked up enough courage to approach him. He ignored them and whatever words of solace or denial they offered. He stood in an invisible isolation booth that was constructed of his painfully transparent shock and grief.

I lowered my gaze from the sight of his pain.

When nobody seemed to be looking, I slipped through the staff entrance into the management wing.

When I reached the display room for cremation urns, I closed the door behind me. I didn't turn on the light inside, but simply groped my way across the small space to the coffee table.

I got down on my hands and knees and reached under the table. My fingers brushed the carpet. I swept in a wider arc, wider and wider, but my fingers only picked up a single small scrap of paper.

"Shit," I said elegantly to myself.

I'd have to switch on the lights.

I did that, only to prove the folder was, indeed, gone.

Francie would kill me and I would deserve it. Or had she come back to retrieve it herself, not trusting me to remember? Yes, surely that was it. I nodded to myself, feeling better.

Idly, I turned over the scrap of wastepaper in my hand.

A skull and crossbones was drawn on it.

"Oh *shit*," I said with more vehemence. I thought of that endearing World War II cartoon figure with the clinging fingers and the big nose: "Kilroy Was Here." This message was plain, too, but nowhere near as innocent. The tab on the edge of the Jackal's personnel folder had said, "Gen. Main." General maintenance usually included janitorial work, like cleaning offices after working hours. I had a sudden, overwhelming desire to go home.

To that end, I stuffed the drawing in my coat pocket, turned out the light, and slipped back down the dark corridor. It seemed, indeed, exceedingly black to me now. I opened the door a crack and peeked out.

Most of the crowd had fled, leaving vast, empty spaces in which I would certainly be seen if I walked through them. A few feet away from me, Beryl and Russell were picking up Styrofoam coffee cups and moving chairs back against the walls. Even nearer to me, Spitt Pittman picked up one of the used cups and held it to a light. I heard him say, "Hell, if we washed these, why couldn't we use 'em again?" Down toward the front door, a few remaining mourners were struggling into their raincoats. I saw the gray-haired man—his head bent, his hands pushed into the pockets of his black raincoat— wait for the little greeter to open the door for him. Then he walked out into the rain, which I could see falling in the illumination from the porch light. Worst of all, an agitated trio stood near the front door: Stan Pittman, Aaron Friedman, and Lewis Riss.

"You'd better be able to prove that's your coat, buster," Friedman said, "because I think you stole it from me at The Buoy tonight."

"Your coat?" Lewis plucked at one of the shiny brass buttons. His face was round with wounded astonishment. "Don't tell me I've done it again. I do this all the time. It's so embarrassing. I've got a coat just like this, and I'm always mistaking somebody else's for mine." I watched him look at Friedman with an eager, disingenuous expression in his eyes. "Boy, isn't this lucky I ran into you? I'll bet you walked off with my coat, too. Have you got it here? We can trade . . ."

"No." The anger in Friedman's voice and face was rapidly fading to confusion. "I didn't see another pea coat . . ."

"Oh well." Lewis waved a hand. "Don't apologize. I'll just drop back by The Buoy tonight and get it." He pulled his arms out of the sleeves and held the coat out to its owner with the air of a generous master offering a good dog a bone. "Here you go. You know, you've got a hole in the right front pocket. You ought to get that sewn up before you lose something out of it."

"Oh." The personnel director took back his coat and hugged it to his slender chest. "Thank you."

"Don't mention it."

Stan, who had been shifting his weight from one foot to the other during that exchange, finally interrupted it. "What did Muriel say to you out there?"

Near me, Spitt Pittman stood suddenly and absolutely still, a used coffee cup in his hand. I had the sense, in fact, of suspended movement from one end of the corridor to the other.

"Not a damned thing," Lewis replied. Spitt tossed the coffee cup into a wastebasket. There was a soft shuffle of people moving about again on the carpeting. "But I'm supposed to see her tomorrow afternoon. You want to predict what she'll say, Mr. Pittman? Or maybe you'd like a chance at rebuttal tomorrow, after I see her?"

"She's hysterical," Stan said, going all stiff and formal. "She's grief stricken. It would be an act of kindness to leave her alone. But if you insist on talking to her, I hope you'll let me present to you the other side of any facts that might be in dispute."

"Kinder to whom?" Lewis asked. "Her? Or the reputation of your funeral home?"

I heard a violent whisper near me. "Dumb bunny."

"To her, of course," Stan said.

"Well," Lewis said cheerfully, "good night, Mr. Pittman, Mr. Pea Coat . . ."

"Friedman. Listen, I hate for you to go out in the cold . . ."

"No, no." Lewis ignored the little greeter and opened the front door for himself. He turned back briefly to smile and to say with a sad, brave air, "I'm not nearly as susceptible to double pneumonia as I used to be."

The door slammed behind him.

Aaron Friedman slipped on his pea coat. He patted the right

front pocket, then the other pockets. "Damn. I could have sworn I had cigarettes in this coat."

I watched the rest of them pick up the last of the litter, finally put on their coats, say good-night to each other, turn out the remaining lights, and leave. Only then did I step back into the darkened public wing.

14

Moonlight filtered through the heavy draperies to illuminate my path to the front door, toward which I walked rapidly. But again, despite my general sense of unease and my desire to get the hell out of there, I stopped at the door of the Chapel of the Resurrection. Again, I was caught by the sight of the bronze coffin.

I stood there, staring, hoping the janitorial staff had all gone home and that Lewis was waiting impatiently for me.

The coffin looked lonely without the gray-haired man to keep it company. Sadness rose in my throat as I thought of that pretty young woman, so horribly strangled with her own long hair. I touched my own hair, which just brushed the tops of my shoulders. How hideous to feel someone come up behind you . . . reach over your shoulders to grasp the ends of your hair . . . cross them in front of your throat . . . pull them behind your neck, jerking you back, down, under . . . choking you with your own body. . . .

I grasped the hand that was creeping over my shoulder. "Don't you do that, Lewis," I said.

"Nuts," he replied. "How'd you know it was me?"

I turned to face him. He was wearing my raincoat. "There

99

is an air of vegetation about you. And I saw you come back in to use the phone, and then hide behind the drapes."

He arched his thick eyebrows and leered at me. "Show me ze vay to ze morgue, my pretty."

"Was that supposed to be Bela Lugosi? It sounded more like Maurice Chevalier. Lewis, it's late. Let's go home. To our respective homes, that is."

"You promised." He drew something shiny and metallic out of my coat pocket and dangled it in front of my face. "And I have the keys to your car."

I slowly pushed open the door to the morgue.

"Get a move on, will you?" Lewis whispered down my neck. "You think I like hanging around mortuaries in the dead of night?"

"Don't say *dead*," I whispered back.

He chuckled. It tickled the hairs on the back of my neck. I walked on in. Lewis followed close behind me, closed the door, and locked it. Immediately, we were engulfed in total blackness.

"No windows," I said. My voice sounded weird, eerie, like somebody talking in a shower.

"The folks in here don't need windows, Cain." His voice echoed strangely, too, sort of floating and disembodied. I reached back to grab his arm, just to make sure he was really there.

"Jesus." I felt him jump. "Don't do that!"

I smiled to myself in the dark, although I realized this was not turning out to be the best idea I'd ever had. Maybe I could get the car keys away from him.

"Got a match?" I whispered.

"Yeah, but what do they pickle these guys in? And why are we whispering? These guys keep secrets. I mean, do you think formaldehyde or whatever it is, is explosive?"

"Light the match," I said in a more normal voice. "If we explode, just think of all the time they'll save on our autopsies. No need to open us up and . . ."

"For God's sake, shut up." I heard him draw a match across a matchbook. The room became surprisingly bright as

100

the flame reflected off the white tile walls. No wonder we had sounded as if we were standing in a bathroom. Lewis was peering at me over the sharp point of fire. "You should see your hair in this light, Cain. It's like a halo."

He leaned toward me. I stepped back out of the circle of brightest light, but he kept coming, and this time it was he who grabbed my arm. In his low, hoarse, smoker's voice, Lewis began to croon another Springsteen song, "Can't start a fire without a spark . . . this gun's for hire, even if we're just dancin' in the dark . . ."

I shook my arm free. "Morgues don't turn me on, Lewis."

He snorted, then grinned. "Cain, this is stupid. If there aren't any windows, who's to see the light?"

"Right," I said, feeling stupid. "Right."

I found the light switch on the wall and flipped it. Fluorescent lights flickered, and then the room was brilliantly, blindingly bright. Besides all the white tile, there were a couple of drains in the floor, a lot of shiny chrome, a few plastic buckets, a lot of rubber tubing, a couple of deep washbasins, and two dead bodies on gurneys.

"This doesn't bother me," Lewis said in a loud voice. "Does this bother you?"

"Heck no," I said and moved over to stand close to him.

"You wanna move off my foot, then?"

I giggled nervously but quickly stifled it, feeling obscurely guilty, as though I might offend the bodies on the gurneys. I pointed to a long, silver object with a needle point. "That's a trocar, Lewis. They use it to remove the bodily fluids and then to inject embalming solution into the body."

"Thank you," he said. "Thank you so much for telling me that. I can't tell you how much happier I will be in my life now that I know what's waiting for me at the end of it. For Christ's sake, you wanna cut the ten-cent tour? Tell me what you know about what happened in here."

"I don't know much." I left his side and began to walk the floor. Near one of the drains, I bent over to study the tile floor more carefully.

"What's the matter? You sick?" Lewis asked anxiously.

"No. Look at this."

He joined me. I pointed to a number of scratches in the tile floor. "Geof told me they found evidence to make them think that she struggled while she was being choked. I'll bet you this is where it happened, because these are the sort of scratches a woman's heels would make on the floor." To test my theory, I walked a few steps away and scraped my own high heel against the tile. It left a mark like the others. I looked up at Lewis. "That's all I know."

"That's it?" He looked pained.

I nodded. "What do you know?"

"Rudolph's casket was in here that night."

I felt as if that fact ought to hold some meaning for me, but I couldn't think what it might be. I stared down at the scratches in the floor, hoping they might tell me something profound about the moment of life becoming death. Lewis began to circumnavigate the room, examining everything, picking up arcane tools, putting them back down again, peering into cupboards, opening drawers. Finally, he looked over at me. "Why in God's name did she come back here that night?"

I shrugged and said the first thing that popped out of my mouth: "To say good-bye to him."

Lewis's head jerked up and he stared at me. I felt a chill of recognition creep across my shoulder blades.

"Do you think so?" Lewis whispered.

I realized that was exactly what I thought. They were lovers, and she was drunk, and because he was a married man she wouldn't be able to cry for him in public, so she came back to say good-bye to him, privately.

"I don't know," I said.

"It's weird." Lewis seemed to discard the idea. "I'll bet she had some kind of weird fetish. Maybe she liked to do it with dead men. I mean, why would anybody want to work in a funeral home anyway unless they were kind of, you know, weird?"

"Why would anybody want to report on car wrecks and

rapes," I retorted, "unless they were kind of, you know, weird?"

He made a face at me and resumed his search.

"Lewis," I said, "I think she liked her men alive."

"Yeah." His tone seemed regretful. He picked up a large bottle of yellow liquid, squinted at it, made a face, put the bottle back down again. "It sounded that way from what Mrs. Rudolph said out there tonight. Man, that was a scene, wasn't it?"

"Are you really going to see her tomorrow?"

He was standing over one of the dead bodies, staring down at it. "Sure."

As I watched him, I considered which of my principles I should compromise: my belief in the sanctity of individual privacy, or my belief in the duty of a citizen to assist the police in the investigation of a crime. Finally, I decided.

"I'd like to go with you," I said.

He looked up. "Why?"

"Why not?"

He shrugged. "Suit yourself. It's three o'clock, twenty-five thirty-two Brooklyn Terrace. Let's get out of here; it's colder than Santa's butt."

I followed him to the door, where he turned off the fluorescent lights and then preceded me back into the hallway. "Oh." I tripped over him as I came out the door, because he had bent over to pick up something off the floor. "Lewis!"

"Where'd this thing come from?" he muttered, and straightened up again. In his hands, there was a manila file folder.

I grabbed it. "It's mine. I must have dropped it. Sorry."

"Some spy," he said irritably. "What is it, anyway?"

I held it against my chest so he couldn't read the tab on the edge. "It's the file I came back to get tonight."

"Did you have it when we went in there? I don't remember you having it when . . ."

"Oh, for God's sake." I hissed, and started to walk quickly toward the exit. "Move it, Lewis! And give me back my coat!"

15

This time I could hardly wait to drop Lewis off at his car so that I could go home to read the personnel file on Jack Smith. I took it and a glass of red wine with me to bed, and I spread out the pages in front of me.

Well, I had been right on the mark about one thing: he was nineteen. There in Geof's bedroom, with the bedside lamps shedding cozy light upon the pages, I looked at that number—only nineteen—and felt silly to be afraid of someone so young, still only a kid, really. And he hadn't actually hurt me, had he? But then I thought about all the "kids" whom Geof arrested for robbing liquor stores and beating up old men and raping neighbors. I thought of the grieving, gray-haired man, and of Sylvia Davis lying on the floor of that morgue, and of my own terror that morning, and I proceeded to examine closely every word of the stolen file.

He had filled in his employment application in a tight, secretive script. If what he had written there could be trusted to be accurate, the Jackal was born in Atlantic City, New Jersey, where he left high school at fourteen, though he claimed to have earned a GED. I leafed through the papers in the file, but I didn't find a copy of a graduation equivalent degree. No college or trade schools. Part-time jobs, all short-lived, a fact he hadn't tried to disguise on the application. He had been a waiter, a delivery boy, a janitor. Under "Reason for leaving," in each case he had written an ambiguous "No future in it."

I took a couple of drinks of wine, rolled my shoulders forward and back to release some of the tension in them, and thought about what I'd read so far.

Well, there was certainly "no future" in a job from which a person was fired. Had he been fired from all of those jobs, or had he quit? I flipped through the papers again, looking for references that might tell the tale, but there weren't any. Maybe they didn't think a gravedigger was worth the trouble of getting references. Or maybe there weren't many people who wanted the job, so they took anybody they could get, no questions asked. Did they tell him he had a future in funerals? I wondered if anybody had bothered to verify his claim that he had never been arrested for anything.

According to the application, he was unmarried, at least when he applied for the job, which was a year and four months previously. No children, at least none that he claimed on official documents. He had listed an address, on Ash, which was a few blocks away from where Miss Grant lived. He had gone to work at Harbor Lights for minimum wage, and had received cost-of-living and merit raises since then. Well, Stan claimed he was a good worker. I looked for his quarterly performance reviews.

As I read them, the picture of an ordinary file of an average employee fell apart.

"Mr. Smith's performance in the first three months of his employment has been unsatisfactory," I read. "He is chronically late for work, frequently absent, and his general attitude can be described, at best, as uncooperative. This evaluation has been discussed with Mr. Smith, who indicates an unwillingness to alter his work habits. Recommendation: Dismissal." At the bottom of the form there were two signatures: "A. Friedman," and "F. You." But that wasn't all. There was another notation scrawled in red across those signatures: "Place on probation for three months."

I sat up straighter in bed and drained the wine.

Whose handwriting was that?

They hadn't fired him, despite Friedman's strong recommendation and obvious cause. And when I read the subsequent reviews, I discovered the firm kept him on the job despite performance reviews that grew progressively more scathing. But each time, Friedman was countermanded by that red scrawl: "Probation."

This was getting more and more curious.

I picked up the most recent performance review, dated only this last month. It was terse compared to the others and written in a hand different from Friedman's neat, legible writing. "Performance improved," it said. "Recommend cost-of-living and merit raise."

I compared that handwriting with the red scrawl. They seemed to match. At the bottom of the last performance review there were again two signatures. This time, they were: "Stanley Pittman, Jr." and "Jack L. Smith."

"Oh, Stanley," I said to the mirror in the bedroom. "What's the little bastard got on you?" And what was the Jackal getting out of it for himself? Not a huge salary, that was obvious, or even promotions. And at his level of salary, the raises he got were too small to be worth the trouble of blackmailing somebody for them. Was he that desperate to hold a job? It didn't make sense. Stan would have to be paying him out of his own pocket, or out of the business. Had Sylvia found out about it? But if that was a motive for killing her, why hadn't he destroyed this evidence? Why had he, in fact, thrown it right back in my lap? God, I wanted to talk it over with Geof.

Would Ailey listen?

And did it really have anything to do with Sylvia's death? Or, if I reported it, would I only be pushing an old friend into an embarrassing situation? Maybe it didn't indicate anything more than bad judgment on Stan's part, although that didn't seem likely, considering his strange reaction that day to my simple question about the gravedigger.

"I don't know what to do," I told the mirror.

I closed the file, turned out the lights, and lay down. Maybe

106

I should try to talk to Aaron Friedman before I approached Ailey. That might be the thing to do. I closed my eyes.

I fell asleep to the sound of a certain former teacher droning on in my head, something about prior commitments and responsibilities.

When I woke up the next morning, I recalled which prior commitment she meant, and called her.

"What time is the service?" I asked.

"One o'clock, dear, according to the paper. You will want to allow a little extra time, Jennifer, since I move rather slowly on my crutches."

"Yes, ma'am," I said.

I called the funeral home then, to tell Francie I would be right over with her file, and to make an appointment with Aaron Friedman for that morning.

"He called in sick, Jenny," Francie told me. "Flu."

That probably meant he wouldn't attend the funeral, either. And there wasn't any excuse on earth that was good enough to get me into the home of a sick man I hardly knew to inquire about a gravedigger whose personnel file I wasn't supposed to have. Well, maybe he would return to the office tomorrow. And maybe Ailey was bright enough to look through the personnel files himself and draw his own conclusions.

I got dressed, had a bite of breakfast, and drove to the funeral home to drop off the file so it would be there if the police wanted it.

Then I drove to my office to see if it still existed.

Faye greeted me with a smile and a message: "Mr. Leland and Mr. Ottilini want to talk to you right away, Jenny." They were two of my bosses, the trustees of the Foundation.

I got us all together on a conference call.

"Found 'em yet?" Roy Leland demanded. He was the big, blunt chairman emeritus of United Grocers. I gathered he was referring to the missing bodies, several of which belonged to his wife's family.

"No, Roy." I knew better than to offer excuses.

The third party on the phone chuckled. It was Edwin Ottilini, a prominent and elderly local attorney. He said in his dry, wry voice, "It has been only a few days, Roy. We might give Jennifer a day or two more to locate the bodies."

"Jenny, you've got to find them," Roy insisted. "Doesn't look good for the town, you know what I mean, Edwin? Makes us look careless, losing our ancestors like this. We'll have a hell of a time convincing new industry to settle here if we can't keep our ghosts under ground where they belong. People don't like empty graves. Makes 'em nervous." A snort echoed through the lines. "Hell, it makes me nervous."

"Miss Cain will find them." Mr. Ottilini spoke with a calm assurance that flattered, but did not convince me. "Won't you, Miss Cain?"

"Sure," I said with more optimism than I felt.

I hung up only to find my assistant, Derek, grinning at me. "Listen," he said. "I heard about this great medium. She's a gypsy, see, and she'll raise the dead for only a small fee, oh, a hundred bucks a head. Let's see, at 133 heads, assuming nobody was decapitated, that comes to . . . thirteen thousand . . ."

"Oh, shut up," I replied.

I worked hard on foundation business until it was time for lunch. After a sandwich with Marv and Derek at The Buoy, I drove over to Miss Grant's to take her to the funeral.

108

16

All the way over, I fretted about how I would get the large and wounded woman down two flights of stairs to my car, but as it turned out I needn't have worried. She swung herself down to the bottom as if she had been born on crutches and then gazed back up at me with a modestly triumphant smile.

"I've been practicing. I have to get the mail each day, you know, and the newspapers."

"You couldn't ask your neighbors?"

"One mustn't impose, my dear."

I shook my head in mock disgust, then followed her out the front door of the apartment building. I had to hustle to keep up with her gaily swinging pace.

"Oh, it's grand to be outdoors again!" she said. "Oh, look up! Do observe those wispy cirrus clouds, Jennifer, like writing in the sky . . ."

"God's handwriting," I said, "with a message of hope for us to decipher if only we possessed the courage and the faith to read it."

Miss Grant stopped abruptly and swung around on her crutches. "You remembered," she said, with a pleased and surprised smile. "Did I really say it so very often?"

"Just enough," I replied.

She swung on down the front walk, then waited patiently beside my car for me to catch up with her. She wore a long-sleeved, full-skirted dress with a pattern of large lavender lilacs and pale green ferns and several inches of soft floppy ruffles down the front. She also wore black orthopedic shoes and a large black hat of lacquered straw, and she carried a large black purse, which was crooked up over one shoulder so her hands were free to ply the crutches.

I opened the car door for her. "You look pretty, Miss Grant."

"Impossible." But she turned a little pink nonetheless. With some lifting and pushing and grunting and shoving, we worked her into the front seat of my relatively small car and her crutches into the back seat. I got in, too, and started the car.

"Do you attend church, my dear?"

As I pulled away from the curb, I smiled and shook my head in the negative.

"You'd like my minister," Miss Grant said. "The only thing he takes for granted is his own faith, so his sermons challenge the intellect while they comfort the soul. He's a little older than you, and divorced." I glanced at her and she quickly glanced away, nearly managing to look innocent. "We must look for the potential of good, even in the awful wreckage of evil, you know."

"I have a special friend," I said. "He's a cop."

"Well, I'm sure your young man will like my minister, too." Her tone was pleasant but firm, the same one with which she used to assure us that we would learn to appreciate long division if we would only apply ourselves. "He performs simply lovely wedding ceremonies."

"Miss Grant, about the missing bodies . . ."

"We won't talk about that today," she informed me. "At funerals, paradoxical as it may seem, it is best to focus one's attention on life rather than on death. Did you fasten your seat belt, Jenny?"

I chose a route to the funeral home that took us past 1210 Ash, Apt. 4, as listed in Jack L. Smith's personnel file. It, too, was a brick fourplex but shabbier than Miss Grant's. If there was money changing hands, Smith wasn't spending it on fancy clothes or living quarters. Or course, I hadn't seen the interior of that apartment . . .

As funerals go, it was ordinary except for the presence of police officers and reporters in the rear. Both Ailey Mason and Lewis Riss were taking notes. The preacher tried to comfort the mourners by pinning the murder on God, who, we were given to believe, works in mysterious ways his wonders to achieve. Miss Grant made small, disapproving noises in her throat throughout. "Theologically unsound," she murmured once, and I half expected her to scribble "Needs more work" on a copy of the memorial program and pass it up to the front.

As we filed out of the chapel afterward, I watched the gray-haired man follow an elderly woman into a funeral-home limousine. Two younger people sat on the jump seats; a blond girl who looked like the pictures I had seen of Sylvia Davis, and a sad-faced young man with an abundance of muscles and blond hair. Younger sister and husband, I supposed.

"Her husband must miss her terribly," Miss Grant whispered, uncannily echoing my own train of thought, if not the exact car on the train.

"I thought they were separated," I whispered back.

"That would have been Sylvia's idea." She shook her head slowly. "Not Darryl's. He has never been one to so easily let go of anyone he loved, and I suspect he'll never really be separated from her, in his heart. Even as a child, Darryl Davis clung to his belongings and to his friends as if he would lose a part of himself if he lost any one of them. I wasn't at all surprised when he grew up and went into the military—he was just that sort of serious little fellow who would take things like God and country and marriage vows to heart. Why, I remember how he recited the Pledge of Allegiance every morning in my classroom as if he were taking an oath on the Bible. He had to leave the service when he was wounded, you know, and it must have been wrenching for him to go. I doubt that he has fully recovered even from that separation. No, Darryl would not be so easily parted from someone he loved.''

"Maybe he didn't love her.''

Again, that slow shake of the head. "No, he wouldn't have married her unless he loved her, and I suspect that once loved by Darryl, always loved by Darryl. I'm surprised he didn't marry his first sweetheart, that's the kind of loyal little fellow he was. She must have left him, because he would never have left her.''

"Who?'' I asked. "The first sweetheart, or Sylvia?''

"Both, dear.''

Darryl Davis sounded grimly possessive to me, but I didn't say so. Instead, I commented: "I do believe you've taught just about everybody in this town at one time or another, Miss Grant.''

She turned to smile at me, and her eyes were wise with eighty years of living. "But I have been a student, too, of all of you. We'll attend the graveside service, dear.''

"We commit unto your care, Oh Lord, our friend and daughter, wife and sister, Sylvia. May the Lord bless us and keep us, may the Lord shine His face upon us and . . .''

While the other mourners had their heads down and their eyes closed, I took the opportunity to stare at them. Stan Pittman and his father stood together near the coffin, their hands identically clasped in front of themselves, their feet identically spread about six inches apart, their heads deeply bowed. Russell Bissell and Beryl Kamiski stood behind them. Beryl, who was dressed in a navy blue dress that had the unmistakable look of high design, had a tissue clutched in one hand, a purse in the other, and her head was deeply bowed. I glanced down the gorgeous but sedate dress, past slim ankles to her shoes. They were a $250 number if they cost a penny; or maybe she was simply one of those shoppers who can smell a sale the way certain pigs sniff out truffles. I looked at the man next to her. At that moment, Bissell raised his golden head. I watched as he looked in the direction of the relatives, who were gathered under a green canopy. Then he seemed to look at the backs of the Pittmans' heads, and finally in my direction. When he saw me looking back at him, he looked surprised, then smiled a slow, sad, funeral smile. I nodded, then glanced away, only to meet the eyes of Lewis Riss. He grinned. I looked past him, on around the crowd until I came to Ailey Mason. He didn't grin at me, but jerked his head in a "come here" motion. I frowned back with a "wait a minute, for heaven's sake" expression of my own.

There was a lot of silent communicating going on around that grave, but it was the silent thoughts I wished I could hear. Were we all remembering that first, failed attempt to bury Sylvia? Was there anyone among us who was at that moment reliving the experience of placing her in that first coffin with the man who was allegedly her lover?

". . . now and forever more . . ."

I felt a large rough hand slip into my own. I squeezed gently, and hung on. Beyond the grave, the three gravediggers were leaning against a walnut tree. The two black men had their eyes on the minister, the white kid was staring at me. When I looked at him, he nodded as if confirming something. Feeling suddenly nervous, I finally bowed my head.

". . . Amen."

"Jenny, dear." I looked up to find Miss Grant gazing at me with a pained, puzzled expression on her face. "I'm afraid I have a touch of arthritis in that hand."

"Oh, I'm sorry!" I quickly released her hand, which I hadn't realized I was gripping so tightly.

"Is anything wrong, my dear?"

"No, no." I smiled at her. "Will you excuse me for a few minutes, Miss Grant?"

She said she would wait for me under the canopy, where she wanted to go to offer condolences to the family. Miss Grant swung away on her crutches, and I walked over toward the detective.

Ailey Mason stood on the hummock of a fresh grave, apart from the rest of the crowd. In his Kojak trench coat and slouch hat he couldn't have looked more conspicuous. I suspected the positioning, at least, was a purposeful move to agitate his suspects. Whether he had also considered its effect on the innocent survivors, I didn't know.

"Heard from Geof?" he inquired by way of greeting.

"Only on my answering machine," I replied. "You?"

He shook his head. "How come you're here? Did you know her? Or maybe you're one of those nuts who just likes to go to funerals?"

I waited a moment before I replied. "No, I didn't know her. But my sixth grade teacher did. I brought her as a favor."

"Well, since you been hanging around the funeral home, you hear anything I want to know?"

"I guess you've heard she was allegedly having an affair with John Rudolph?"

"Yeah, him and the Boston Celtics." Ailey's laugh was a short bark, like a bad-tempered dog's. "That broad oughta had a king-sized bed to hold all the men she was fucking."

"Rumors."

"Yeah, like the rumor that the sun comes up in the east. You hear any other names attached to those rumors?"

I thought back to Muriel Rudolph's hysterical accusations in the funeral home the night before.

"No," I said. "Do you have any good suspects, Ailey, or any motives?"

He laughed as if it were a stupid question. "I got a jealous wife, for starters," he said, ticking it off on a finger and saying it slowly, as to a dimwit. "And a husband she was cheating on. And maybe some jealous lovers. And for motives, I got sex, sex, and more sex."

"Did you come up with any fingerprints you can use?" He took it personally, as criticism. "You been promoted to captain or something, and nobody told me? Maybe I should make my reports to you now, is that it?"

Again, I waited a moment. "It was just a question."

"No," he said shortly, which I took as my answer.

"What about that office party?" I asked.

"You want to be a goddamned detective," he said then, "I tell you what you do. You take some of that money you got, and you buy yourself a nice jeweler to make you a sterling silver sheriff's badge, how about that? And maybe buy yourself some fancy bath powder, use it to dust for prints, you know? And then you buy yourself a little toy gun, like they sell in the toy store, and . . ."

"A trench coat," I said, and walked off.

It seemed Ailey was getting nowhere on his first solo case and feeling mighty defensive about it.

Miss Grant reached out a hand to me when I approached the green canopy. "Jenny, I want you to meet Sylvia's husband, Darryl Davis." The sad-faced young man who had been in the limo with Sylvia's sister had his right arm around a woman, so I didn't offer my own right hand for him to shake.

"Hello," I said, but he didn't even look up at me.

It was the much older man standing next to him who spoke—the man with a Marine haircut who had stood guard by Sylvia's coffin in the funeral home, the one I'd taken for her father. His hands were clasped behind him like a drill sergeant. I tried to cover my surprise, but it wasn't necessary. He met my eyes for only a second before turning his face to receive other expressions of sympathy. But in that second, I felt as if I were held in a fierce grip of anguish.

"I'm so sorry," I murmured to the side of his face.

How he must hate us all, I thought as I guided Miss Grant back to my car, for being witnesses to his humiliation and to the destruction of his beloved wife's reputation.

It was nearly three o'clock.

I sped Miss Grant home so that I could be on time for Lewis's interview. I figured I would hear Muriel Rudolph take what little was left of Sylvia's reputation and smash it to smithereens.

17

Lew's car was parked on the street outside the row of con-
dominiums where the Rudolphs lived on Brooklyn Terrace. I
parked behind his car then walked past the identical town-
houses until I reached 2532.

Like its neighbors, it was a narrow two-story house on
which thin boards and rough plaster were stuck to the facade
to simulate Tudor. The grass in the front yard had given up
the fight to children's bikes and balls, but someone—Mrs.
Rudolph?—had trimmed the hedges and set out early annuals,
which bobbed cheerfully in the light, cold breeze. Hello, hello,
they said. Not a bad place to come home to after a hard day
at a funeral home, I thought, a place that spoke of innocence
and caring, not of jealousy and revenge. If what the widow
had claimed the night before was true, however, the philandering man of the house had not been innocent or so caring
of the welfare of this household. I wondered, with a touch of
dread, how she would act this afternoon . . . would she still
be stiff and furious or would she be embarrassed, regretting
her promise to the reporter to air her family's laundry in public? Sex, sex, and more sex, Ailey had said. But Muriel Rudolph didn't look like a woman who, under normal

circumstances, would discuss that subject with strangers. But these weren't normal circumstances.

The front door was ajar, so I knocked lightly.

Lewis appeared instantly. He grabbed my wrist and pulled me inside. "Get in here," he said. "Don't touch anything."

"No," I said, not to him, but to the implication behind his urgency and his words. There are only a few reasons in the world to tell someone not to touch anything—one is to protect fresh paint, one is a warning to small children in glass houses, the third is for the benefit of the police.

"Oh, Lewis," I said. "Oh, no."

He dragged me by my wrist into the house, toward the kitchen. We passed through a tidy living room and a tidy, small dining room. I saw the sort of matching suites of furniture that young married couples buy on installment plans at discount stores; evidently, the financial strain of raising three children had kept them from replacing that furniture through the years. But she had kept it repaired and clean, so it looked merely old, not shabby. I saw fat, green Boston ferns in macramé holders that were suspended from the ceilings, and I saw that she had cut some twigs off a flowering viburnum and stuck them in water in a glass pitcher that sat on an orange runner on the dining-room table. The little white flowers had started to shed, forming a soft halo of snow on the table. Their fragrance filled the room with the smell of spring. Again, I thought, not a bad place to come home to. Tight budget or not, somebody had cared about this house. My heart was yammering unpleasantly, and my breath was coming short and fast.

Lewis pulled me into the kitchen.

There was a small black-and-white television set on a TV tray, turned on but with the sound off. I watched a beautiful man kiss a beautiful woman. There was coffee warming in a pot on the counter, but it looked thick and black as syrup, as if it had sat for hours. On the formica top of the kitchen table, there was a transparent glass mug of coffee, half-drunk, with a scrim of milk floating on top. A ballpoint pen lay beside an open morning newspaper, and there was half a plain cake doughnut and a little pile of crumbs beside a white paper napkin. I was absorbing every detail, because I was avoiding the larger picture. It was in most respects an ordinary picture of an ordinary kitchen where, after the kids leave for school, a mom sits down to enjoy her morning coffee, with a doughnut, the TV, and the word games in the paper.

This mom was still dressed in her nightgown, robe, and slippers, and she lay on her back on her kitchen floor near the coffee maker. Beside the Mr. Coffee, there was an empty mug, a clean spoon, a half-pint of milk—its mouth gaping like a thirsty bird's—and an open sugar bowl. If she were still alive, she might have been saying, "How do you like your coffee? Milk? Sugar?" Maybe she would have asked Lewis and me if we would like a doughnut.

"Just like the other one." He called me back to the way things really were, his voice sounding low, flat. "Just like Sylvia."

Muriel Rudolph's tiny hands were wrapped around her own hair and it was wrapped around her throat. Her face was dark, contorted, and dreadful. I thought of the teenage daughter I had seen at the memorial park the day John Rudolph was buried and of how protective the girl was of her younger brothers. She would lose her youth now.

"She had children," I said to Lewis. "She had children, for God's sake." I was suddenly, irrationally furious at a world that allowed people to go around killing mothers, as if there ought to be a special, unbreakable law against it.

"I'd better call Ailey," he said. His complexion was a sickly white against the black stubble of his beard. He still wore the tennis shoes, jeans, turtleneck, and sweater of the night before. "You don't have to stick around, Jenny. She didn't even know you were coming. You didn't find her. If you cut out now, I'll forget you were here."

It was the only thoughtful thing I had ever heard him say, and it made sense. Ailey would only waste time on me, when he could be looking for real leads. I tried to think what Geof would advise, and then I nodded.

Lewis stepped to a wall phone to make the call. I noticed

that he took a napkin from the table to cover the receiver, to protect any fingerprints that might be there. While he spoke to the police, I stared at the kitchen table.

She had sat there, drinking her coffee, eating her doughnut. Did her doorbell ring? Did she go to the door, invite the visitor into her home, offer a cup of coffee, a doughnut?

I stepped up to the table to look at it more closely. The newspaper that lay on it was turned to Lewis's most recent story on the murder investigation. She had circled his byline with her pen. I studied the napkin and the crumbs beside it, and then I turned the napkin over, though I only touched it by a corner. There, on the down side, she had written the name Riss across the top, followed by a list of other names—Pittman, Bissell, Friedman, Smith, Rudolph, and a few I didn't recognize. She had also written the word *party* and the word *bitch*. An angry hand had retraced each letter of the last word several times until the letters ate into the thin paper of the napkin.

"Jenny, what are you doing?" I turned around to see that Lewis had hung up the phone. "Don't touch anything!"

"Look at this, Lew." He walked over to stand beside me, and I pointed at the napkin. "She was making notes to herself about what she was going to discuss with you. Look at these names."

"Guys that Sylvia was . . . ?"

"I guess Mrs. Rudolph thought so."

"How'd you find this?" He sounded annoyed, as if he had missed a trick.

"What do you do if you're having a bite to eat and you suddenly think of something you want to jot down? You dump the crumbs off your napkin, and you write on it. I saw the pen, and I saw the crumbs, and . . ." I shrugged.

"But she turned the napkin over." He said it slowly, as if he were thinking as he spoke. "Because . . . because she didn't want the person who was here to see her list! Because he was on it! Jesus, Cain. I think what we've got here is your basic dying woman's last words! And a nice little list of suspects. Too bad she didn't circle one of them for us, you know what I mean? Like 'this is the one who done it, guys, lock him up.' "

I glanced at him, then away.

"I know," he said quickly, angrily. "You think I don't know? She got killed because I was coming to see her. You think I'm stupid, Cain? You think I don't know that?"

"Keep your voice down."

"Screw you," he said bitterly. "This ain't the way I want to win a Pulitzer.'

"I know that." But I couldn't bring myself to offer a touch or words of comfort. Maybe she would have died anyway because the killer didn't want her to talk to anybody, ever, about Sylvia's love life. But maybe, in the absence of a curious reporter, she would have calmed down, kept quiet, stayed alive. We would never know, but I suspected it was a question that Lewis would ask himself all his life. Stan had asked Lewis to leave her alone, saying she was hysterical, saying it would be a kindness to leave her alone. God knows he had been right about that.

"I'm leaving," I said.

On my way out, I stopped to sneak a look at some papers that were spread out on a coffee table in the living room. It looked as if she had been going through the file that contained her husband's estate planning. Using a handkerchief, I moved the papers slightly so I could skim their contents.

There was: a simple will, everything straightforwardly left to her and the kids; a key on a string, labeled "safety deposit box"; a passbook-savings book with a balance of $10,972; a term life-insurance policy to pay off their home mortgage if he died; another policy to pay her a small amount if he died; titles for two cars; the deed to their property; mortgage loan papers from a bank. That was it—a simple estate left to a small family by a man of modest earnings. Unless there were investments that weren't reflected in this file, she would almost certainly have had to go to work to support herself and the children. But he had seen to it—or she had insisted that he see to it—that she would have the house free and clear, a little money, a couple of cars, some savings. Maybe he had cared, after all, in his fashion.

A siren sounded not far away.

I looked up to find that Lewis was standing in the kitchen doorway, shaking his head at me. "You ever think about going into journalism, Cain? Anything interesting in those papers?"

"No. It all looks normal to me."

The siren was getting closer.

I nudged the front door open with my elbow, and left. As I pulled my car away from the curb, Ailey Mason and two other cops were striding up to the front door of the Rudolph home. Ailey wore his trench coat, and the belt was still twisted in back. A body wagon came down the street at a sedate pace and double-parked beside the squad car.

As I drove, I couldn't get out of my mind the picture of Muriel Rudolph's teenage daughter and small sons. They would be at school now. Who would pick them up, who would tell them, and, in God's name, how? Who would love them now, who would care if they went to college, who would convince them that a world that took both of their parents from them was a world worth living in? I felt sick to my stomach with sadness for them, and helplessly angry.

It occurred to me that helpless was not a state of being for which I had much talent. Maybe now was a good time to go back to the funeral home on the pretext of continuing my search for the missing bodies. Maybe I would just happen to be there before Ailey Mason showed up to question the people whom Muriel Rudolph had listed on that napkin. After all, nobody knew I had been at the scene of the murder, and nobody knew I had knowledge of that list. Maybe I could use that private knowledge to the detriment of the person who orphaned those children.

"I'm sorry," I said silently to Miss Grant, "but your missing bodies will have to wait a little longer." It wasn't as if they were going anywhere. They had already gone.

18

It felt odd, surrealistic, to return to the Harbor Lights Funeral Home and to force a smile, to offer banal greetings, all the while holding to myself the awful secret of the murder of Muriel Rudolph. It felt as if the world should have stopped for at least a moment, that the clocks should reflect a pause in time, and have to be reset; that the people I saw in the streets and in the funeral home ought to look at each other with wide eyes and with slack mouths that released words of shock and horror; that everywhere, people should reach out to touch a solid object to reassure themselves of the reality of the moment, and their own existence in it.

"Hi, Jenny." Francie greeted me with a cheery smile and a steaming cup of coffee. I took the cup from her and then stared at the rising steam for a moment, collecting my thoughts and my emotions, and probably hoping for a message like the ones that Miss Grant claimed to read in cirrus clouds in the sky. If I stared long enough, would the steam form letters, and spell out the name of a murderer, the reason for life, the excuse for death? Was there any excuse for a death like the one that Muriel Rudolph had suffered? Francie asked me if there was anything wrong with the coffee or the cup. Was the coffee too strong? She would water it down. Was the cup chipped? She would fetch me another.

"It's fine." I took a sip, swallowed over the apple in my throat. I forced a smile. "Francie, do you know what time school starts around here?"

"School?" She blinked. "Which school?"

"Elementary. High."

She smiled. "You are talking to the mother of four and the grandmother of five. Of course I know what time school starts. Seven-thirty for high school, eight for elementary. Unless you're talking private?"

"I don't think so."

"You don't think so?" She arched an eyebrow. "Could there be something you'd like to tell an old friend of the family, Jenny?"

I forced a laugh at her unexpected implication, "No, Francie, I have an old friend I'd like to surprise some morning, but I want to be sure her kids have all gone off to school before I drop by."

Francie laid her chin in the palm of one hand. "Oh, how well I remember those delicious moments after the last child waved good-bye. I'd have a cup of coffee and watch a game show. 'Concentration,' I think, or maybe it was 'The Price Is Right.' For years, Jenny, those were the only cups of coffee I ever got to drink that stayed hot from beginning to end."

"Unless a salesman came to the door, right?"

"Oh well, there aren't many salesmen out and about at that hour of the morning," she informed me. "If anybody came to the door, it was usually one of my neighbors after her kids left for school." She grinned. "You'll never truly appreciate a cup of coffee, Jenny, until you have children and they leave for school in the morning."

"I believe it. Who's here today?"

She groaned. "Everybody."

"Except Friedman."

"No," she said surprisingly, "he dragged in just after the funeral, sneezing and sniffing and looking like death warmed

123

over. Honestly, a sense of duty is a fine thing, but not when it spreads germs, you know?''

"But everybody else was here right on the dot of . . ."

"Eight," she filled in for me.

". . . eight. Piling the work on you as if you were three secretaries instead of just one overworked temporary.''

"Oh well, salespeople are never on time," she said vaguely and waved a hand in the air. "Of course, Spitt throws a tantrum every time they walk in late. 'Your dawdling costs me dollars!' he says. And pity poor Stanley if he's a minute past eight, oh my."

I tried to look sympathetic. "Was he late today?''

"Stan? Oh, he hasn't come in at all. It's his day to call on the other businesses, plus he had that funeral, Sylvia's, you know. But you can bet that everybody else has been in and out all day: 'Type this, Mrs. Daniel.' 'File this, Mrs. Daniel.' 'Hold my calls for an hour, Mrs. Daniel.' " She sighed. "The reason they call this a temporary position, Jenny, is that nobody could stand it on a permanent basis.''

"You love it," I said.

She grinned. "I love it."

I sipped my coffee and tried to sound casual. "Who had you hold their calls for an hour, Francie?''

"Spitt," she replied promptly. "But his button was lit up the whole time, so I guess he was on the phone anyway. Before he had me hold his calls he asked me to get him the number of *The Wall Street Journal.*"

"The Wall Street Journal?"

She shrugged. "Don't ask me. Nobody tells me anything.''

"Was Spitt mad at the salespeople this morning, Francie?'' I wondered how long I could keep up the questions before she began to wonder about the odd angles of my curiosity. I could only hope she possessed the normal amount of vanity that makes most of us feel flattered if somebody shows an interest in our jobs.

She was chuckling. "Oh, they've got his number. Beryl and Russell show up at 7:59, make a big point of saying good morning to Spitt, and then they disappear. On sales calls, they say.'' She made a moue at me that said ''sure.''

I joined in with a cynical chuckle.

''And then they go out for coffee, right?''

''Or back home to sleep, more likely!''

''Is that what they did this morning, Francie?''

She nodded.

''And the other salespeople?''

''They're part-time, I hardly ever see them.''

''What about the gravediggers?''

There it was, she was beginning to look at me oddly. But she replied, ''Well, I don't know, but they have to punch in, so it would be easy to find out. Is there some reason you'd like me to find out, Jenny?''

''No, no, just curious.'' Even if the Jackal had punched in, the nature of his job probably would allow him to leave the premises anytime. But long enough to drive to the Rudolphs', kill Muriel, and get back to work without anybody noticing that he was gone?

Francie shifted her gaze to the pile of work on her desk, and I knew my source of information was about to dry up. I also knew that I probably only had a little while longer to prowl around before Ailey showed up.

''Francie,'' I said, ''would you ask Aaron Friedman if he would see me?''

''When?''

''Now.''

He stood up behind his desk to greet me. But then he bent over, grabbed wildly for a tissue from a box on his desk, and sneezed violently. It seemed to blow all the air out of him, because he sat back down abruptly.

''Excude me.'' He looked at me, with every appearance of true misery, out of watery brown eyes, and said, ''God a awful code. Wend oud without a code last nide, and caught dis code.'' He seemed suddenly to be aware that the vaudeville accents sat oddly with his otherwise dignified appearance, and he blew forcefully into another tissue. This time when he spoke, it was more normally. "I apologize, but I seem to have picked up an awful cold. I was at The Buoy last night, and a fellow stole my coat, and I went out in the cold, and got this . . ." He waved the used tissue, as if displaying proof. It occurred to me that as acts go, faking a cold is an easy one to manage. Just sneeze and cough a sufficient number of times and you'll convince anybody that you're truly contagious. Although, I had to admit, this cold seemed real enough.

He sneezed twice more before I got in a word. Finally, he sighed as if exhausted, and leaned back in his chair and gazed at me.

"I don't know if you remember me," I began. "I'm Jenny Cain. Stan introduced us at the graveside the day of John Rudolph's funeral."

"Sure," he said, in the same exhausted tone.

"I'm sorry to barge in like this," I said then, "but I have a problem I hope you can solve. You see, I'm the director of the Port Frederick Civic Foundation . . . you've heard of it?"

His nod of assent turned into a sneeze.

"Bless you," I said, with some hesitation. "Well, we have a client, a nonprofit group, that operates out of a small building here in town. They called me this morning to say their janitor quit yesterday, because he didn't get the pay raise he wanted. Maybe you know how it is with the social-service sector; there's never enough money to pay decent wages. At any rate, my clients have enough to do without cleaning the building, too. So I thought I'd ask around to see if any private companies—like this one—would lend them a janitor for a few days. Just till they get somebody to replace their old one."

I smiled sincerely, to encourage him to buy this unlikely story. The lower half of his face was hidden behind a tissue, but above it the intelligence in his eyes had come awake; he looked alert and aware, despite the bleary appearance of his eyes and the dark circles below them. I had a sudden, strong feeling that this man played one hell of a bridge game.

He lowered the Kleenex. "Who are your clients?"

Damn. I thought quickly. He looked like a Republican to

me. Was there any social-service agency that might awaken the sympathies of a Republican?

"Youth for Christ," I blurted, before I remembered he might be Jewish. I covered one of my hands with the other, crossed my hidden fingers, and plunged on without giving him time to reply. "Just one man would do a lot of good, and I noticed the other day that you have at least three maintenance men. Do you think you could spare that young one for a few days?"

"You don't want him." Friedman snapped off the words. Without knowing I was doing it, I seemed to have diverted him from my problematic "client." He began to rip the tissue apart with both hands. "Believe me, you don't want him. How about one of the older men, instead? We'll have to check it out with Stan, but I could probably get Freddy or Lennie to help you out for a while."

I feigned a surprised air. "What's wrong with the young one? He looks strong and capable to me, just the sort of fellow they need."

"No." He grabbed another tissue from the box, began to tear at it. "He's lazy, he's insubordinate, and he would be a terrible influence on young people."

"Why do you keep him around?"

The dark, angry eyes looked once, briefly, over my shoulder as if checking to see if anybody was listening. "If I had my way, I would fire the son of a bitch this afternoon," Aaron Friedman said with a passionate bitterness. I decided he might be a Democrat, after all.

"Why don't you?"

"Because . . ." He stopped, stared at me, then down at the mess of torn tissues on his desk. He began carefully and slowly to brush them into a neat pile. Then he swept them off his desk into his hand, leaned over, and dropped them into a wastebasket at the side of his desk. He looked back at me, gave me a smile that seemed forced, shrugged. "Because the boss will not let me. He says the kid has potential. Potential! He has the potential to mug his grandmother, that's what kind

127

of potential he has. No, I will let you have one of the other men, if they're willing to do it. All right?"

"Yes, thanks." I dug into my purse for a business card, and reached across his desk to hand it to him. "Would you call me as soon as you find out? If you can't reach me at the office, my number's in the phone book." I had a separate listing of my own, at Geof's place.

He nodded, took the card, put it down to grab a tissue, tried to reply, sneezed, sneezed again. I said, "Bless you," thanked the top of his head, and departed. I hadn't managed to slip in any questions about his relationship with Sylvia Davis or about the night she died. Maybe I would find the opportunity when he called me later . . . if he called me later.

Francie stopped me as I came out of Friedman's office.

"Jenny," she said in a near-whisper. "I checked the time cards. All the janitors were here on time this morning." She seemed to wait for me to explain my curiosity.

"Thanks," I said. "May I see Spitt?"

19

We went together to stand in the doorway of Spitt's office When we saw that he was in conference with Russell Bissel' and Beryl Kamiski, we started to turn away, but Spitt noticed and called out, with a commanding wave of both hands.

"Come on in here, girl!"

Francie and I looked at each other, and silently, mutually, decided he meant me. She turned back to her own desk, while I went on into Spitt's office to sit in the only empty chair. Russell Bissell, Beryl Kamiski, and I nodded at each other.

"Damage control," Spitt said next, and pounded his fist on the top of his desk. "It's too damn late to prevent the publication of that damn story, so what are we going to do about it now that it's out?"

His employees appeared to be hanging on his every word, so he answered himself.

"Complain to the damned newspaper, that's what, raise holy hell like I did with the *Journal* this morning. I told that congenital idiot of an editor exactly what was wrong with their story, you bet I did, and I demanded that she print our side of things. 'No two ways about it,' I told her." Spitt slammed one meaty fist into the other. " 'Fair's fair!' I told her. You got to be tough with these jokers or they'll kill your business with their goddamned do-gooder journalism.''

He sat back and nodded as if he agreed with himself.

I hadn't the faintest idea what this was all about.

"Good for you, Spitt," Beryl said. I looked over at her. She had on yet another elegant business suit—this one a muted red silk with a creamy blouse—and a fresh and expensive hairdo and the sort of perfect makeup that is only sold in salons where the saleswomen wear pink smocks and serve tiny cups of coffee. And yet, beneath it all, there was that barmaid I had originally seen in Beryl—the old-fashioned kind to whom tending bar is a profession, almost a mission in life. She would cross her arms on the bar, this one would, and lean forward on them until a bulging wave of bosom showed above the low, ruffled neck of her blouse, and she would offer friendly advice or a bit of a morale boost to her customers. She would have a lot of regulars, this barmaid, and she would know their favorite brands and their ex-wives' names, and each one of them would think she secretly loved him, and that she would have told him so long ago, except that she didn't want to hurt the feelings of her other regulars. And she would make a lot of money in tips, enough to pay for pretty clothes to wear in her real life, which existed outside the imaginations of her customers. I brought my own imagination under control long enough to hear her say, "Did they agree to print a retraction, Spitt?"

"They damned well better."

She didn't press him for a clearer answer, but gave way to Russell, who had leaned forward, his forearms pressing on the arms of his chair. He didn't look like a man who would frequent Beryl's bar; he looked more like a man who had spent his youth lifeguarding on a California beach and lifting weights and eating health food. If Aaron Friedman played bridge, this man played racquetball, and when he sweat, it only made his body glisten. In my imagination I put his blue suit back on him, and listened. "Well, it's lucky for us," he was saying, "that most of our customers aren't the type to read the *Journal,* you know?"

"Yes." Beryl nodded. "Russ is right, Spitt. Even if they don't print our side of it, I doubt we'll lose any business because of it. We've weathered worse criticism than this. One little article in one little newspaper shouldn't do any lasting damage."

I was intrigued to hear *The Wall Street Journal* called a "little newspaper." I cleared my throat and said, "If you don't mind my asking, what's up?"

Spitt turned his face toward me. "Just when we've had all this publicity about Sylvia, the fools start climbing all over prearrangement again!" He turned back to face his salespeople and spread his arms wide as if gathering their agreement.

"They don't write about all the thousands of people who are happy they've prearranged their funerals, oh, hell no. No, they've got to find the one or two bad apples in the business and tar and feather the rest of us with them." He turned back to me. "You're an unbiased observer. Which would you believe . . . some unfair criticism in some snotty New York paper . . . or the word of an old and respected company that has never lied to you in your own hometown?"

It had been an interestingly mixed metaphor, and a leading of the witness to which any prosecutor would strenuously object. I pretended to consider his question.

"Well," I said, "to tell you the truth, I have such faith in you that I'm kind of interested in looking into prearrangement myself."

The effect of my words was electric: three heads swiveled toward me, three mouths fixed themselves in warm smiles, three pairs of eyes focused brightly on my own. I hadn't felt so interesting since I starred in the senior play.

"Smart girl," Spitt said.

"Very wise," Beryl murmured. She placed her hand on the arm of Russell's chair.

"I'll be glad to tell you about it," he offered.

"Would you?" I turned a disingenuous smile on him. "That would be lovely, Russell. When would it be convenient for you? I'm afraid, the sooner the better." I cast my eyes down briefly. "It's for my mother, you see, and she's not well."

"How about now?" Beryl said. "Russell's free now, aren't you, Russ? And heaven knows, there's nothing more important than taking the time to make the proper arrangements for one's family, don't you agree, Miss Cain?"

I nodded.

"Of course you do," she said. "Russell, why don't you take Miss Cain into your office?"

"This is a fine young man," Spitt assured me, winking broadly. "Single, too, never even been married, but then I expect he's never found a girl as pretty as you before! Jenny, here, she's never been married, either, Russell. Quite a co-incidence, I'd say! Why, this boy's hard-working, ambitious, smart, and honest as the day is long. They don't come any better than Russell, here. He'll take good care of you and your dear family, my girl."

"Just like Stan," I said.

"What?" Spitt looked puzzled.

"Hard-working," I said. "Ambitious, smart, honest."

Russell and I stepped self-consciously out of Spitt's office just as Ailey Mason and two other cops stepped into the foyer. I touched Russell's arm, and he turned immediately, a slightly wary look on his face, as if he were afraid that I'd taken Spitt's matchmaking too immediately to heart.

"Russell," I said. "I'm sorry, but I've just remembered another appointment. Do you think we could postpone this until later today?"

"Sure." He looked over my shoulder, back into Spitt's office. Unexpectedly, he said, "Are you free for dinner?" Now I was afraid *he* had taken the hint too readily. But then he added, "We'll let the company treat us, and I'll tell you all about how to preplan and prefinance your mother's funeral."

I could have thought of subjects I'd rather cover at dinner, but this was no time to object. I said, "As a matter of fact, I am free. Where shall I meet you, and when?"

He named a seafood restaurant down at the harbor, 7:00. I smiled my assent, then left in a hurry, by the back door.

* * *

I stood on the back stoop in the cold sunshine and looked out over the memorial park. Just inside the gate, in a stand of evergreens, there was a small stone building that looked like a crypt but was really a maintenance shed. The gravedigger named Freddy was sitting on the grass at the side of the shed, his back against a fertilizer bag. His feet were flat on the ground, his knees pulled up, his hands hung limply over them. His head lay back on top of the bag, and from where I stood it looked as if his eyes were closed.

I looked out over the rest of the park.

About a hundred yards away, the other black gravedigger had hold of the base of a ladder whose top was lost in the branches of a tree. I watched until I saw a white arm reach down for a saw. The Jackal was trimming branches this afternoon. Having ascertained his whereabouts, I walked quickly toward the shed. Since Freddy was resting on the side away from the other gravediggers, they would have to come around the corner to see him, or me. And I didn't want to be seen.

"How you doin'?" said a deep voice as I approached.

"Okay." I stopped a couple of feet from him. "Yourself?"

His eyes opened wider. "I know you?"

"Yes, but don't worry about it. We all look alike."

He grinned then. "You be that woman friend of Mr. Pittman's, come to see us dig up the old lady the other day. Am I right?"

"Yes."

His look changed to one of suspicion. "You ain't come to get us to dig up anybody else, have you? I ain't fond of puttin' them in the ground twice. Once ought to be enough for anybody, it sure ought to be."

I sat down on the grass. "It wasn't enough for poor Sylvia, I guess. Did you know her, Freddy?"

"Sure. Everybody know'd her." His expression was impassive, giving nothing away. Unexpectedly, he added, "Friendly girl."

"I guess she was pretty upset by Mr. Rudolph's death."

He sniffed. "Not so you'd notice."

133

"What do you mean?"

He dragged a cigarette out of his shirt pocket, lit it, pointed it at me. "Let me put it to you this way. Your man dies, you be partyin'? You be drinkin' and carryin' on, like nothin' happen?"

"No, I wouldn't do that."

"That's right." He stuck the cigarette in his mouth.

"Maybe she was trying to forget," I suggested.

This time the sniff was more like a snort. "Well, if she be trying to forget, she done give herself some new things to remember."

I nodded as if I knew what he was talking about. "I guess she got pretty loaded at the party. It's a wonder she could drive home, drunk as she was."

He squinted at me through the smoke. "Drunk don't begin to tell it."

I tried again. "Well, if she was so drunk, you'd think somebody would have gone with her, to drive her home safely."

He shrugged. "It don't be that far."

"What?"

"Her house don't be."

"From where? The party?"

"The Seaman," he said impatiently.

"Oh." I tried to assimilate this information. The Seaman was a bar for pool players and hard drinkers, one where Geof had made plenty of arrests over the years, not a few of them for charges that were as serious as they got. "You mean she went to The Seaman after the party? With you guys?"

Suddenly he sat up straighter, and took the cigarette out of his mouth as if he needed to do that to concentrate. "What you got all this curiosity about, huh? You be some damn lady cop or something?"

I gave him a look that said, "You crazy?"

He settled back onto the fertilizer bag, but there was a wary stiffness to him now. I was rapidly losing the trail I had only begun to sniff out.

"Well," I said after a moment, "I hope you didn't tell the

cops about being with Sylvia after the party." When he didn't say anything, I added, "They would try to make something out of it, you know?"

"I ain't stupid."

We sat without speaking for a few moments. I had the feeling he was making up his mind about me. Finally, he stretched out his legs, folded his hands over his chest, and closed his eyes to half-mast. I've lost him, I thought.

"We was takin' care of her," he said in a low growl. "Leastwise, Lennie and me was. She don't be in no shape to drive, that for sure. Jack, he drive her to The Seaman. All we done is, we had us more drinks, feelin' pretty good, you know. But she commence to climbin' all over him, so they gets up and leaves. Lennie and me, we didn't think that be such a good idea, but what we gonna do about it? We didn't want to be messin' with young Jack, he got a mean streak. So me and Lennie, we leaves and goes on home. I don't be askin' no more questions about it, and I be recommending that course of action, you might say, to most anybody who might be happen to ask me. You get what I be tellin' you?"

"Yes," I said.

He nodded, and crossed his feet at the ankles.

"What do you mean, she was climbing all over him?"

His eyes flew open and he looked at me with disgust. "Your problem is you be a slow learner. And you know what happen to slow learners? They be learnin' hard things the hard way."

Freddy stared at me as if trying to impress some vital piece of knowledge onto my brain, then leaned back, closed his eyes again.

I waited a moment to see if anything more was forthcoming. When I saw it wasn't, I got to my feet, and said goodbye to him.

He didn't open his eyes. "Yeah."

Before walking out into the open, I looked around the corner of the stone shed: the Jackal and Lennie were still trimming trees some distance away. I walked quickly to the cover of the funeral home, and then around it to my car.

* * *

From the nearest pay phone on the road into town, I called the *Port Frederick Times*.

"Have you got your story written?" I asked Lewis when he came on the line. When he told me he had, I said, "Well, considering what you've been through today, I suspect you could use a stiff drink."

"Is that an invitation, or an observation?"

"An invitation."

There was a moment of silence. "This is you, isn't it, Cain?" And when I assured him it was, he asked, "When? Where?"

"Now. Do you know The Seaman?"

"I never would have picked you for a Seaman type, Cain. What's the matter, are you ashamed to be seen with me again at The Buoy?"

"Well," I said, "it is true that if you pinch a waitress at The Seaman you will be singing tenor in the boys' choir this Sunday."

"You're a hard woman, Cain," he said.

"Move it, Riss," I replied, and hung up.

20

He looked the worse for wear, even for Lewis. He still hadn't shaved or changed clothes. But the easy, impudent grin had disappeared, and his eyes were those of a man who was considerably older than he had been when he woke up that morning.

"Do you feel as bad as you look?" I asked him when I joined him on the sidewalk outside The Seaman. He looked so worn and exhausted I was prepared to call off this excursion, if necessary.

"Listen." His voice was as raw as a man with a sore throat. "Compared to the guys you're gonna see in here, I look like a goddamned preppie. Do me a favor, Cain. When we sit down, don't order a wine cooler."

"Or nachos?"

A corner of his mouth lifted.

"Really, Lewis, are you all right?"

"You saw the same dead body I did, lady, and you're still standin'. Come on, let's get a load on." He shoved open the screen door to the bar, and I followed him inside.

It was dark enough to blind us, and we stood in the doorway until our eyes adjusted. Even blindfolded, I would have known it was a bar, though: the smell was that warm, pungent, unmistakable one that permeates old taverns as if they mopped the floors and wiped off the tables with rags dipped in buckets of stale beer. With my other senses heightened by the loss of sight, I was also acutely aware of the near-total silence that greeted my entrance.

"I could have walked in with a two-headed cow and been less goddamned conspicuous," Lewis whispered. "You couldn't at least have changed into jeans, Cain? You had to wear that I-been-to-college-and-do-you-know-a-good-tax-shelter suit?"

I laughed softly. "Yes. I did have to."

A long, drawn-out wolf whistle floated in from the back of the room. It was followed by male laughter, and then there was a subdued rush of ordinary bar sounds, like water released from several dams all at once. I heard a clatter of ivory balls, a rumble of male voices, a surge of Marvin Gaye from a jukebox. I smiled grimly, inwardly, at the dramatic irony of his song: "Can I Get a Witness?" Still the bar stayed quieter than it had been when we were standing outside the screen door, and as my eyes adjusted I met several appraising, cool stares.

"Just tell 'em you're selling Mary Kay cosmetics," Lewis said out of the corner of his mouth. "And you just wondered if they could use a little fine pressed powder. You know they think you're slumming, don't you? They resent it."

"I know. I don't need an interpreter."

"Yeah? You're in a foreign country, Cain."

"Don't worry. I've got a passport."

I walked past him toward the bar and sat down on one of the high, metal, revolving stools. It had a torn, red plastic seat from which brown padding stuck out like knuckles. Lewis slouched after me, but instead of sitting down on the empty stool next to mine, he stood between them. He turned around and faced the room, leaning his upper back against the edge of the bar, crossing his legs at the ankles and his arms over his chest.

The bartender, a mountainous black man, called down to us: "Yeah? What'll it be?"

"Beer," I said.

"What you got on tap?" Lewis asked.

"Bud," the bartender called back. "Busch."

"You got Beck's?" Lewis asked.

"Are you kidding?" the bartender said.

"Busch," I told him, and Lewis nodded.

"Two Busch it is." The bartender poured the draws and brought them down to us, placing them on paper napkins that bore cartoons that featured women in bikinis and men in suits. On the flap of his shirt pocket, he had pinned a large brown button that said "Ted" in white letters. Ted leaned on the bar directly in front of us. The skin around his eyes was dark, as if he hadn't slept well in years, or had been punched in the face too often. He said, "So what do you know?"

"Nothin'," Lewis said.

I brought the beer to my mouth with both hands and drank. Then I lowered my head. I shook it in the negative. The bartender started to move away.

"You could call this a sentimental journey," I said, my voice thick. "My sister was here the night she . . . died. I just . . . I just want to be where she was, you know? She kind of liked this place . . ." I looked around me. "God knows why."

The barkeep had turned back when I started talking. Now he laughed once, explosively, like a car backfiring. Immediately, he looked embarrassed, as if he were afraid he had offended me in my hour of grief.

"You don't look much like her," he said coming back to lean on his bar again.

"You remember her?" I stared at him with what I hoped was pathetic interest in my widened eyes. "You remember Sylvia?"

He exchanged a glance with Lewis who was now facing me with an unreadable expression on his face. Ted said, "You and your sister, you ain't exactly the run-of-the-mill type of lady we get in here, you know what I mean, ma'am? Listen, you want another beer? On the house, memory of a nice lady. What's her name? Sarah? Susan?"

139

"Sylvia." My smile trembled. "No, thank you. If it's all right, I'd like to buy the house a drink. In memory of my sister, as you said. Do you think they'd mind?"

Again, an exchange of wry looks with Lewis.

"I'll try to persuade them," the bartender said.

"Oh," I said. "Thank you."

He set up a long row of tall glasses into which he dumped a couple of ice cubes apiece. Then he lumbered up onto a step stool and lifted down from an upper shelf a dusty half-gallon of Wild Turkey.

"Hey," Lewis said sharply. "How 'bout your bar brand?"

From his perch, Ted looked down at me. I was reminded, incongruously, of those old cartoons where an elephant climbs up on a chair to escape a mouse.

"No, no," I told him. "Make it good, please."

He filled the glasses with my dollar bills. Beside me, Lewis grunted, "My mother was right; it is just as easy to fall in love with a rich woman as a poor one." Then he raised his voice to Ted again. "Hey. My friend here, she'd kind of like to hear about her sister's last night, you know what I mean? Where'd she sit, who'd she drink with . . ."

"Shut up," I hissed, as Ted frowned at him, then at me.

I let my lower lip quiver, and I wiped at one eye with the tips of the fingers of one hand. "I know who she was drinking with . . . it was some guys she worked with . . . Freddy, Jack, and Lennie, I think. They were just trying to keep her from driving home drunk." I said it as if appealing to Ted to understand. "They knew she'd had too much to drink, and they were just trying to protect her, isn't that so?"

"Sure," he said kindly.

"Nuts," Lewis breathed at my side.

A waitress in black slacks and a pink V-neck sweater began to distribute the memorial drinks. "Who?" said a loud male voice at one of the tables. "Sylvia," she told him in a discreet stage whisper behind my back. "Well, shit," he said, "here's to your health, Sylvia." There were muffled whisperings, giggles. "Forget it, Sylvia," the same voice said, with a drunken sadness, "too late." There were more giggles.

"Sorry," Ted said. He yelled over my shoulder, "Shut up, assholes." And then again to me, "Sorry."

"It's the liquor," I told him, as if revealing a great and surprising truth. "That's what it was with Sylvia, too. They should have kept her from drinking any more, shouldn't they? If she hadn't had those last drinks, she wouldn't have started climbing all over Jack like she did . . ."

Ted grunted, and nodded. "Man, she was hot at him, I never seen her so pissed off before, excuse me, ma'am. Yelling at him. Man, she was beating on him like a crazy woman. I thought he'd have to beat the shit out of her before he got her out of here." He flushed. "Maybe I shouldn't have said that. Shit. Sorry."

"No," I assured him. "It's okay. She was my sister, I know what she was like sometimes. But I never knew her to get so mad at Jack. What was it about, do you think?"

Ted shrugged. "We get a lot of that, folks arguing at each other, I mean. I don't listen much anymore. Ain't my business. Selling drinks is my business. Fightin' ain't my business. Used to be my business, but it ain't no more."

"Well, I know what they was into about," the waitress said. She had come up during the last exchange. Her button drooped over her left breast and said, "Marie." Marie looked about twenty-two, with skin the color of oyster crackers and red hair that hung in long twists, like curling ribbon, and huge, eager eyes in a thin face.

"What?" I asked her.

"She goes, 'I thought you was my friend!' " The waitress's face was animated, as if she were reliving the emotions as well as the words. "She goes, 'I trusted you!' She just keeps yelling that, your sister does, over and over. And this Jack guy, the creepy one, he was just laughing at her to start out, you know, like she was drunk and he was laughing, but pretty soon he starts to get real mad like her, and then they was really into it, you know? He goes, 'You done it to yourself, fool,' or something like that, and she goes, 'I wouldn't of told you if I didn't trust you,' and he goes, 'So what' and the other two guys, the black dudes, they're saying, 'Hey,

141

take it easy, man,' you know. Stuff like that. And pretty soon she gets up and stomps out, you know, and Jack, the creepy one, he goes after her, and then the other two dudes, the black guys, they leave, and, you know, that's how it went down.'' Abruptly, she stopped, shrugged. She patted my shoulder in an awkward, kind sort of way and turned to answer the summons of another customer. The red curls bounced against her scalp as she walked.

''Well,'' I said.

''Nutso.'' Ted shook his head.

''I need another drink,'' Lewis said.

I gave him time to drink it, and then I nudged him out of there, leaving tips for Ted and the waitress. ''Thanks,'' Ted said, with a tip of his hand to his forehead. ''You take care now,'' the waitress called out, and waved. A few of the customers nodded to us. One or two said, ''All right.''

Outside, Lewis cornered me.

''Who's this Jack? Who's Lennie? Who's Freddy? And how come you didn't tell me before we went in there what you were up to?''

''I only wanted an escort,'' I said bluntly, ''not assistance. I have an appointment I have to keep now, Lewis. But I'll tell you all about it later.''

''When later?''

''Nine.'' I fumbled in my purse for paper and pen and scribbled down an address for him. ''Here.'' I shoved it at him as I walked away. ''Meet me there around nine. But stay in your car, Lewis. I'll find you.''

''What the hell, Cain? Why do I have the feeling I'm being used again? Hey!''

I raced to my own car to keep my dinner date with Russell Bissell.

21

The restaurant, down at Liberty Harbor, was a popular seafood place, the C'est la Vie. It was all fishnets and pink shells, and couldn't have been a greater contrast to the bar I had just left. Nor could the man I joined there have been a greater contrast to Lewis, or to the other customers of The Seaman. Russell Bissell sat in immaculate, glowing, blond masculinity in the center of the room at a table for two, drawing female glances as the tide draws sand. A couple of thin waiters with very short hair were eyeing him as well.

He got up to pull out a chair for me, then sat down again.

"Russell," I said at once, leaning toward him. "I just heard on the radio about Muriel Rudolph. I was so shocked. Do you know anything about it?"

He shook his head no but then contradicted himself. "The cops came out to the funeral home to interview all of us. I guess she made some sort of list, and we're all on it, if you can believe that." He made a face that said he couldn't. What I couldn't believe was that Ailey Mason would divulge a major clue to prime suspects. "They told us she was strangled, just like Sylvia. Gosh, it's awful, isn't it? But I don't know how they could think any of us did it, I mean, she was a real nice lady, and we all liked her real well."

"Did you know either of them very well, Russell?"

"Sylvia and Muriel, you mean? Huh uh." His startlingly blue eyes didn't waver from mine, but neither did he appear to be forcing himself to look at me. "I only knew Sylvia from work, and I guess the only times I met Muriel were at Christmas parties, that sort of thing. They were nice, though, I liked them both, and I feel real bad about all this."

The way he talked—short words, simple statements—made me see him again as that tall, blond teenager on the beach. Even now, in April and twenty years later, he had a gorgeous tan.

A waitress in a floor-length, clinging jersey dress appeared to take our order. She didn't once look at me, so I could only assume she heard me order iced tea and stone crabs in garlic butter. As she walked away from the table, her left arm brushed Russell's shoulder. He didn't appear to notice. I recalled how Beryl Kamiski clung to him at John Rudolph's funeral, and how I had touched his arm earlier that day in the funeral home. He'd probably gone through life being patted, stroked, caressed, and all the while his physical beauty had grown lustrous, like pewter, from loving and constant buffing. I wondered if Sylvia had longed to touch him, too. Had she succeeded in doing it, and at what cost?

"What was Sylvia like, Russell?"

He fiddled with the heavy silver knife at the side of his plate, appearing to think about the question. Finally, he said, "Like I said, she was nice. And a real hard worker. She was real friendly and nice."

"Yes." My tone was insinuating. "I heard she was a real friendly girl."

He looked up at me quickly, then away. "I don't know anything about that. I only knew her at work. And she was always real . . ."

"Nice." I was getting nowhere with this gorgeous, inarticulate, overgrown lifeguard, so I decided we might as well get on with the excuse for this dinner. "Well, these murders surely do remind us of our own mortality. I believe I told you, Russell, that my mother is very ill . . ."

144

He nodded but looked blank, so that for a moment I thought he wasn't going to take the cue. I prodded him a little harder by adding, "The doctors say she could live for years, but it's also possible that we might lose her at any time."

At that, he seemed to rouse himself.

"You're a loving daughter to consider prearrangement for your mother, Jenny." He smiled sympathetically, as if someone had pulled a cord in his back, setting him in motion. The words of more than one syllable alerted me to the fact that we had now moved into the canned portion of the evening. I wondered who'd taught it to him—Beryl? "I'd be grateful to be of assistance to you, if you will allow me to tell you all about it."

I allowed him, while we cracked and ate stone crabs. As he talked, I tried to look attentive. But, as the shells piled up until our table looked like a crustacean burial mound, I began to feel desperately tired and bored. I was wasting time and energy on this dinner. I'd seen a terrible and very real death that day, not this safe, sterile, prearranged business he was talking about. Not that it was fair to blame him for the powerful contrasts in my day, but dear God, I wished he'd shut up.

"There are literally dozens of decisions to be made at the time of death, Jenny," he told me. "Large decisions, such as how much to spend on the funeral, and small decisions, like what music to play. As you can imagine, it's difficult for a family to make all of those decisions, all at once, right when they're feeling the worst of their grief and shock."

He seemed to be waiting for a reply.

I swallowed some crab, pink and white like the restaurant decor. Did the owner plan her color scheme around her menu? Maybe that is why steak houses tended to be done in meaty reds and salad-bar restaurants were so often decorated in lettuce green and squash yellow. I tried to remember what Russell had just said to me, and, failing, offered a generic reply. "Yes, I can see that."

It seemed to satisfy him, because he continued: "Preplanning and prefinancing allow you to make all of those decisions now, while you have the luxury of time and the freedom from devastating emotional distress. Jenny, are you beginning to appreciate the value of preplanning?''

"Isn't the prefix redundant, Russell?"

He stared at me.

"I'm sorry. Never mind. What have you got there?"

He had pulled out a portfolio which could be mine if I chose to preplan through Harbor Lights. There was a brochure, a "Personal Record Book" for recording vital statistics, a "Notice of Moving from Service Area" to instruct the funeral home what to do with me if I moved out of town, a medic-alert card to carry in my wallet, a prearrangement agreement, a checklist of "Important Facts," a prefinancing contract, and a Check-o-Matic agreement. While he explained what it all meant and how it worked, I thought about what I knew so far of Sylvia's last night on this earth. What happened between the time she walked out of that bar and the next day when Stan opened that coffin?

"Jenny, you can finance your mother's funeral by paying for the whole thing at once by cash or check, or by making a down payment and taking several years to pay the balance, whichever method of payment is more convenient for you. We can even arrange for your bank to transfer funds from your account into the prearrangement trust account each month. Does that sound good to you, Jenny?"

"Sure."

"What more do you need to convince you, Jenny?"

"Well." I pretended to think it over. "I'll take these papers home and read them, and I'll want to run them past our lawyer. I'm sure you understand, Russell."

"Absolutely." He shuffled the contents of the portfolio back together and handed it to me. I took it with a greasy hand and slipped it down beside the table leg. With any luck, I would manage to forget it. "Jenny, I'd like to see you again to answer any questions you and your lawyer may have. Would next Monday be good, or would the week after be better?"

"What about tomorrow?" I'd expected a harder sales pitch, a request for a down payment, at least. His low-key effort made me scurry to devise an opportunity to see him again, much sooner than next week. "I'll talk to my lawyer tomorrow morning. Come to my house tomorrow evening, why don't you? I'll broil the lobster, you bring the wine."

The skin above his cheekbones reddened again. "I'd love to, Jenny, but I have plans. Thanks a lot, but could you come to my office instead?"

"Fine." I smiled, to cover the awkward moment. It struck me that despite my initial awe at his physical beauty, there wasn't enough chemistry between us to fill a test tube. Not that I wanted chemistry from anyone but Geof. Still, I had hoped for another less-public opportunity to probe Russell's defenses. Failing that, I made a final, awkward stab at delicate subjects. "It's good to keep pleasure and business separate, Russell. It's one reason I hate office parties, you know?"

"Boy, do I." He said it with feeling. I was reminded of the photograph of him surrounded by admiring females. Most men would love any function that brought them that kind of attention. I wondered if a person could get too much loving attention in his lifetime, too much petting and stroking so he grew satiated and tired of it. It probably happened to movie idols and rock stars. And to extraordinarily handsome men?

"I guess Sylvia had a good time at her last office party." I feigned a smirk, hated myself for doing it. "Seems strange to me though, considering a good 'friend' of hers had just died."

"So what if she was having a good time?" The pink patches returned to his cheeks but this time in evident anger. "What's wrong with that? She wanted to be with her friends, drink a little, try to forget for a while. But she was hurting, let me tell you."

"I thought you said you didn't know her very well."

"I didn't." He clamped his lips together, then seemed to remember that I was a customer he didn't want to offend. "I'm sorry . . . I didn't mean to . . . I shouldn't have . . . it's just that I feel so bad about . . . I could just tell she was hurting, that's all. She came in looking kind of sad, and then she got to drinking and laughing and carrying on, and all of a sudden she was real quiet again, and then she was gone."

147

He lowered his gaze to the table. "I didn't get to say good-bye to her."

"So that's the last time you saw her?"

He nodded, still looking at the table.

I looked at my watch. It was getting on toward nine.

"I have to go, Russell." I declined his offer of coffee and dessert and said, "Thank you for dinner, and for this." I touched the portfolio. There wasn't going to be any way to leave that restaurant, under his gaze, without taking it with me. He paid the bill, then walked me out to the parking lot. My last view of him was of his blond, sculptured head, framed in profile like a Classic Greek portrait, in the window of a baby-blue Mercedes sedan.

It was 9:05 when I located Lewis, down the street from 1210 Ash, and joined him in the front seat of his old, battered, orange VW Rabbit.

"You're a weird lady, Cain." He was slouched up against his door, smoking a joint. The air in the car was still fairly fresh, so I figured he hadn't been waiting long. The second thing he said was "Talk."

"Sylvia went to the Harbor Lights' office party to drink away her sorrow over the death of her lover, John Rudolph," I began. "And she had a good time, for a while. I know, because I saw evidence of it in some photographs that were taken of her at the party, and I have at least one witness. She may have been grieving, but she didn't show it.

"But something happened at that party to upset her. If the person I talked to can be trusted on this point, Sylvia suddenly became quiet, and then she just disappeared from the party. You and I know that she went to The Seaman, where she continued drinking with Jack, Freddy, and Lennie."

"Whoever the hell they are."

"Gravediggers."

"Holy shit. Your 'sister' was as weird as you are."

"Think of them as maintenance men," I advised him. "It doesn't sound so strange that way. Okay, so we know she fought with the one named Jack, that she accused him of betraying her, but he claimed it was all her own fault. We don't know what any of that means, but I think she found out about this 'betrayal' at the office party. That's what upset her. By the time she got to The Seaman, she was ready to let him have it. They fought, she got up and left, he followed her.''

"Then what?''

"I don't know," I admitted. "Did she and Jack go to the funeral home together? Did he kill her there?''

"You're asking me?''

"I'm asking you to help me find out, Lewis.''

"That's why we're parked in a dark car in this charming neighborhood, I suppose. In case Bushfield hasn't shown you the crime stats for Port Frederick lately, maybe you'd like to know this area is big on people who are directly descended from highway robbers and horse thieves. You do know the nicest places, Cain.''

"Let me tell you my plan," I said.

"That would be a welcome change.''

"This gravedigger, Jack Smith, lives on this block.'' I pointed out the window. "Over there. I want you to go up to his apartment and pretend to interview him, say you're interviewing friends of Sylvia's for a human-interest angle on the murder. And then when you get in there, ask him about that night, look around for evidence of whatever . . . such as the possibility that he has a lot more money to spend than a gravedigger probably earns. There's a strong possibility, Lewis, that he's blackmailing somebody at the funeral home.''

"Who?''

"I can't tell you.'' I leaned toward him in the dark. "Will you do it, Lewis?''

"It won't work.''

"Oh, come on.''

"Really, Cain, it won't. If he's guilty of anything, he's already suspicious. And even if he's not, it's gonna look damn suspicious anyway for me to haul my ass up there to get a story from some peon gravedigger at this time of night. I wouldn't buy it, you wouldn't buy it, why should he?''

"You're right." I sighed and leaned my head back against

the seat. Weariness poured over me. "It was a stupid idea. Anyway, I wouldn't want to put you into a dangerous situation."

"You wouldn't?"

"I guess we'll have to go to Ailey, but I hate to do it without any more to go on than guess and gumption. He'll probably throw me out of his office and tell me to mind my own business. Damn, I wish this were Geof's case."

"Don't give up yet, hotshot. There's another way to do it, much easier. Believable, even. I can get us in there in the next five minutes, no problem."

I opened my eyes to stare at him. "How?"

He stubbed out the joint in his ashtray.

"It just hit me. This guy, Jack Smith . . . he go by the name of Jackal?"

"Yes, but how . . ."

"He lives in the third building, upper right?"

"Yes, but . . ."

"Jenny," Lewis said with a patient air. "You know these funny cigarettes I smoke? Well, in an uptight town like this one, where do you think I get my stash? From another New Jersey boy, that's where. The Jackal's my man, Jenny. Come on, let's go."

22

"Us?" Adrenaline came rushing back into my body as if I'd taken a handful of uppers. "Why should I go, too?"

"Because you might notice something I don't, because you might see something I don't, because he's not as likely to do something stupid if there are two of us. Drug dealers ain't partial to drop-in visitors, Jenny." Lewis reached over me to open his glove compartment. He fished around inside of it until he came out with a miniature tape recorder, which he stuck down in his right front pants pocket. "Small but powerful, like some women I've known." He opened his door, got out of the car. When I continued to just sit there, he leaned back in to quote Springsteen at me: "No retreat, baby, no surrender."

"Baby, I was born to run," I threw back at him, having Springsteen albums of my own to quote from. Lewis was laughing as he slammed the car door. I put a hand on my door handle, but still I sat there. I didn't know what to do. On the one hand, I didn't want him to go alone; he was right about all his reasons for wanting my company. But I wasn't eager to encounter the Jackal again, and I couldn't predict how he would react to my presence.

"Cain, it's cold out here! Shake it!"

Thinking was getting me nowhere. I tried listening to my feelings, instead, and what I discovered there was that residue of fury, left over from the previous morning. Suddenly, I realized how badly I wanted to nail this guy, especially if he'd killed his "friend" and poor Muriel Rudolph. We would go carefully, Lewis and I would, to minimize the risk to ourselves, if indeed there was any risk at all. I told myself to stop selfishly worrying about my own skin and to start thinking about Sylvia, about Muriel, and about ridding our town of this drug-dealing, murderous, spike-haired menace. I got out of the car.

There were no flowers outside this building, only dead-looking shrubs with bare branches. An empty plastic holder from a six-pack of cans was snagged over one of the twigs; yellowed newspapers, still wrapped in their rubber bands, were piled up against the bottom of the outside wall like logs, along with a blue plastic sandal with a broken strap and a couple of old diapers. I wasn't crazy about the idea of children living in this place. In the lobby, three of the four bulbs in the overhead light fixture were burned out. There was a basketball in one corner. It looked incongruously innocent, a big, ripe, healthy-looking orange, growing out of season in poor soil, like the teenager who probably left it there. Maybe it was the Jackal's. No, the image was impossible.

"How can you stand to come here?" I said.

Lewis sniffed. "It does kinda smell like a back alley in Tangiers. I always expect some dude in a turban to pop out and offer to sell me his little brother."

"If I had to go to a place like this to get a drink, I'd stop drinking."

"If God meant you to preach, he'd give you a pulpit."

We started up the stairs.

"I'm beginning to wonder if he really is blackmailing anybody," I whispered. "This is hardly living in the lap of luxury. I mean, where's the money going?"

Lewis glanced back down at me. "You're the one with the MBA, Cain, you figure it out." He was whispering, too. We stopped on the landing and stood close together. "He's probably putting it back into his drug operation," Lewis said, "like the good little capitalist he is. It's just a little outside financing . . . no taxes, no interest, no penalty for early withdrawal. Hell, he's gone from selling a little pot to a full-service pharmacy, just since I've known him, and you don't get that big that fast on sellin' a few joints. I think you better wait here until he says it's okay for you to come up."

"All right." My voice sounded faint.

Lewis climbed on up to the second-floor landing and knocked a peculiar knock on the door to his right. I heard the sound of light footsteps on old floors, like somebody in his bare feet, and there was a pause, as if that person were peering through a peephole. When the door opened, it was the Jackal's voice I heard, although from where I was standing I couldn't see him.

"Hey, man." Smith sounded sleepy and annoyed. "You forget how to use the phone? What day is it anyhow, this ain't your day, is it?"

"I got a guest, kid." Lewis's New Jersey accent came on stronger, as if he could relax and speak his own language with another native. "She's got a hunger for a sugar cake, and I ain't got the eggs to bake it. You got enough on hand I could buy a few extra off you?"

"I don't like strangers, man."

"Come on, I know her, and you know me, so what's the problem? You got the stuff or not? I got the cash, and it ain't cryin' for me to spend it here."

There was a long moment of silence at the top of the stairs. How in God's name would he react when he saw who the visitor was?

"All right," the Jackal said, and then he laughed, a low, wicked, rumbling chuckle that flattened me back against the landing wall. "You're lucky, Riss. I got plenty of sugar on hand. And I got me a delivery of farm-fresh eggs just this very morning. I got brown ones, I got white ones, I got speckled ones, I got pretty little red and blue and pink ones. Your lady into eggs of any special color, man?"

"You can ask her," Lewis said. "She's here."

I heard the Jackal come out of his apartment, and then his head, with its blond, spiked hair, appeared over the bannister. He was wearing jeans, the earring, and a wide gold watch on his wrist. It looked like a Rolex. I probably expected tattoos, but there weren't any visible. He stared down at me, showing no surprise.

"Well," he said softly. Then he jerked his head at us. "What's the matter with you, you like standin' in halls?"

I climbed the stairs on shaky legs and followed Lewis into the Jackal's apartment. His interior designer had a taste for the macabre. The walls were covered in black lacquer, and the carpet was black. He had removed the lid from a silver casket, tossed in black pillows, and called it a couch. The lid, turned upside down, served as a coffee table. There was a monstrous television screen, and enough stereo equipment to alter the vibrational rate of the earth's rotation. How did the neighbors bear it? On the other hand, once having seen this apartment, who'd have the courage to complain? Around the room, he had scattered tools of the funeral trade, the way some people scatter knicknacks . . . hooks, knives, tubes, a couple of trocars, and bottles in which gray fleshy objects floated in greenish liquid. I felt my stomach contract, and I looked quickly away, at the Jackal. The pupils of his eyes were enlarged, shiny, black, and focused steadily on me. In a low, intimate tone, as if we were alone in the room, he said, "You like candles? I'll put out some candles." He dug beneath the pillows in the casket and came up with several thick black candles, which he placed in silver holders around the room and lit. "Shut the door," he instructed Lewis, who did it. "And turn off the lights."

It was like being plunged into a black night with a quarter-moon rising and fires burning in the forest, flickering against the wall of night. The Jackal switched on the stereo next. Male voices, accompanied by screeching guitars and pounding drums, screamed unintelligible things at us. When he turned the volume down, it made it worse, because then the voices seemed to be whispering obscenities from behind the trees in

154

the forest. If Sylvia had played around with this guy, she'd had a dangerous taste for the strange and the ugly.

We were standing in a triangle, facing each other. Jackal broke the geometry by leaning back against a wall, leaving his lower body in candlelight, his upper body and face in shadow. "So, what'll it be tonight, girls and boys?"

I saw Lewis reach into his right pants pocket and knew he was switching on the tape player. He then said, in a quiet, serious tone of voice, "I got to level with you, Jackal, I didn't come here to buy. You know me, I'm a reporter. I deal in news, the good and the bad. I'm afraid I've got some real bad news for you tonight."

The Jackal came out of the shadows. He looked like a wary animal, tense and ready to spring. His arms hung loose at his sides, he flexed the fingers of his hands. "What's going on here, Riss?"

"Listen to me, Jackal." There was, in Lewis's tone, a note of friendly urgency, nothing threatening, nothing tough. "The police know that you went drinking at The Seaman with Sylvia Davis the night she died. They know you had an argument and that you followed her out of there. Jackal, they think you were the last person to see her, they think maybe you killed her. You have to get out of Port Frederick, immediately."

There was silence for a moment as the Jackal just stared at him, then at me. And then the dark, blank eyes began to shift to the right, the left, as if he were frantically looking for a way out. He took a step toward us, backed off, then turned back into the shadows and I heard him strike the flat of his hands against the black wall. Suddenly, he was back in the light again, as if he'd pushed back from the wall. "Why are you tellin' me? I know you, Riss, you don't do no favors. What do you want?"

Lewis spread his hands wide, in a display of honesty. "I want your side of it, Jackal. I'm a reporter, man, and I want the whole story, not just what the cops say. I'm not gonna print it, I just want to know what happened. Like, why was she pissed at you?"

"How do I know you won't print it?"

155

"Are you kidding?" Lewis was all disbelief. "If I print it, the cops are going to ask me how I know all this, and they're not going to like it that I just happened to talk to you just before you just happened to leave town. Come on, man, I'm doin' you a big one, do this one for me."

The Jackal shrugged, as if the truth were the least of his worries. "She was screwin' around with Pittman, and I was making some bucks off him, only she didn't know that. Then when she finds out, she's ticked off at me, like it was my fault she was an idiot. We get out to her car, man, and she's crying and carrying on that she's gonna lose her job, and it's my fault, and, I mean, who gives a shit? But I wasn't the last person to see her, man, 'cause she said she was gonna go talk to somebody, see if he'd remind Pittman what a"—and here he sneered—"good little worker she was."

"Who?" Lewis asked quietly.

The Jackal smiled that private, knowing smile. "Friedman, man. You want to know what happened to little Sylvia, you ask Mr. Personnel Prick, little Mr. Aaron Asshole Friedman."

Lewis had grabbed me by an elbow and was pushing me toward the door. I had my hand on the knob when Smith said, "I got another favor for you, but you gotta tell me something first."

"What?" Lewis said.

"Why'd you bring her?"

"She's the one who told me about the cops," Lewis lied. The Jackal shifted his gaze to me, and the smile played at his lips again. "Come here," he said, and he moved over to the casket/couch, where he picked up the black pillows and threw them to the floor. Lewis dragged me over there, and we looked inside to find a cornucopia of drugs: pills in bottles, cocaine in wrappers, pot in plastic bags. "Take your pick," the Jackal said, "it's on the house . . . and thanks, man." But he was looking at me when he said it.

Lewis plunged with both hands into the casket, coming up with enough illicit substances to fill every pocket.

"Go on," the Jackal said softly to me. "You, too."

I started to shake my head, but Lewis nudged me with his knee. He grabbed my purse, opened it and stuffed it full, then gave it back to me. Again, he took my elbow and steered me to the door. We were down to the first landing when I looked back up. The Jackal was leaning over the bannister again, staring at me. Lewis looked up, too, and said to him, "You better get gone, man."

23

"How could you *do* that?" Full of righteous indignation, and pent-up fear, I threw my purse, hard, across the front seat of Lewis's car at him. It struck his chest, and he instinctively brought his arms up to protect himself as it fell to his lap.

"Hey!" he said.

But I was rolling now. "How could you warn him like that? How could you give him time to get out of here before the police catch up to him, before they even know they want him? How could you do that? Anything for a good story, is that it, Riss? And these drugs!"

He ignored me, and reached through the open space between the front seats of his car and fumbled around in back, coming up with an empty plastic shopping bag into which he began to dump the illicit contents of my purse and his pockets. The corners of his eyes and mouth lifted into a huge, wondering grin.

"God, will you look at this?" His voice squeaked, like an excited boy's. "I won't have to deal with reality for the next six months. Do you have any idea how much this stuff is worth, Cain? Jeez, remind me to do a few more favors for drug dealers, will you? And to think you almost didn't take any!" He stopped his sorting long enough to stare at me as if

I'd suddenly grown two heads. "I'll bet you don't mail in your entry in the *Reader's Digest* sweepstakes, either." When he saw me open my mouth, he said quickly, "Jenny, if he didn't kill her, it's not so important for the police to find him right away. Anyway, how long do you think a guy who looks like him can hide?"

"He might comb his hair," I said acidly.

Lewis looked doubtful for a moment, then perked up. "Calm down, Cain, I did okay for us, and for the cops." He scooped up a pile of drugs with both hands, let them trickle down through his fingers, and laughed wildly. "God, I guess I did okay. Sure you don't want any of this?"

"No. Do you believe him?"

"Probably, but let's take it to Ailey, see what he thinks."

"Ailey?" I put out a hand to stop him in the middle of his happy sorting. "*You* calm down, Lewis, and listen to me for a minute. We can't go to Mason yet, because we might put an innocent man in a bad situation, on the word of an extremely unreliable witness. I think we should give Friedman a chance to tell us what happened. And you'd better let me do it alone, because I don't think he's going to want to see you again."

"Why?" Lewis looked puzzled. "Do you think he's the type to hold a grudge? I'll swear, some people have no sense of humor."

Finally, we agreed that I would telephone Friedman and try to persuade him to allow me to see him that night. For safety's sake, Lewis would follow me in his car. Before I returned to my own car, I said to him, "Please, put that stuff in the trunk, Lewis. And for heaven's sake, don't eat any of it. I need you sane and sober."

He sighed. "Reality sucks, Cain."

"Please."

He sat still for a moment, his head down, and when he raised his face, I thought it would be to make another smartass remark. Instead, he said quietly, "I keep seeing her face, Jenny. And it's like she's looking at me, and saying it's my fault she's dead, like if I hadn't agreed to interview her, it wouldn't have happened. I've seen a lot of dead faces—car wrecks, homicides—and I don't like it, but I get used to it, it doesn't keep me awake. But I don't think she'll let me sleep, you know? I want to sleep tonight, I don't want to be lookin' at her face in my dreams. So don't bug me about the drugs, Jenny. We all got our escape routes. You travel yours, I'll travel mine, all right?''

I placed my hand, briefly, on the curly, springy black hair above his forehead but couldn't resist chiding him gently, "I don't think Bruce Springsteen would approve, Lewis.''

"What do you know?'' he said, but managed a slight grin. Then, more flippantly, "That was only an editorial comment anyway, not necessarily representing the views of the management. Go on, I'll follow you.'' He tied the ends of the plastic bag together, took the keys out of his ignition, and walked around to the back of his car. As I walked away, I heard the trunk lid slam.

I pulled in at the first convenience store I came to and used an outside pay phone. First, mostly to give myself time to cool down, I called Geof's house to pick up the messages on the answering machine. As I dialed, then waited for the machine to reply on the third ring, I watched Lewis get out of his car, go into the store, and pause by the magazine rack. Thank goodness, I thought, they usually keep the *Playboys* behind the counter in these stores, so he couldn't steal one.

"Hello,'' I heard the answering machine say to me. "This is Aaron Friedman. It's five-thirty. Your client can have one of our maintenance men for the rest of the week. Call me at home tonight if you want to, 352-8623.'' That's what I call perfect timing. I put in more change and called Friedman's number.

"Hello?'' said a light, female voice. Wife? Girlfriend?

"I'm calling Aaron Friedman.'' I tried to make it sound businesslike, neuter, unthreatening, as not all women like the idea of unfamiliar female voices asking to speak to their husband/lovers, especially so late at night. "May I speak to him?''

"Gee, I'm sorry," she said as if she meant it. I pictured a pretty, pleasant blonde who was probably even nice to telephone solicitors. "He just stepped out for cigarettes. May I take a message?"

I thought quickly. If Friedman wasn't there, maybe I could find out some valuable information from her. "Is this Mrs. Friedman?"

"Sort of." She had a nice laugh.

"Well, I represent Multi-Markets," I said in a bright voice. "We're employed by the Columbia Broadcasting System to survey viewers about their opinions of television shows. May I ask you—very quickly, because I don't want to take up any more of your valuable time than necessary—were you or Mr. Friedman at home watching TV on the night of April third? That would have been, um, this last Tuesday night."

"Well, part of the time we were."

"Do you happen to recall if you watched television between the hours of six and eight?"

"No, we were at a party, and we didn't get home until nearly nine-thirty. Not nearly soon enough if you ask me, God, do I hate other people's office parties." I smiled to myself, thinking how people are inclined to tell a lot more about themselves to strangers than they have to. I hoped this very human tendency would play into my hands in this case.

"What about between eight and ten?" I asked.

"No, no, we were just getting home." That sounded as if she lived with him. How could he have left home to go to the funeral home to kill Sylvia, without arousing the lover's suspicions?

"What about between ten and midnight?"

"Yes, I'm sure we watched the nightly news, and then we turned on the movie."

"Well, it's the movie we're interested in," I said. "The one that comes on at eleven-thirty. Did you watch the entire movie, ma'am?"

"No, we didn't."

"I see. Could you tell me if one of the following responses indicates why you did not watch the entire movie. A: It was on too late at night; B: It did not hold our interest; C: We were interrupted in our viewing by the phone or the doorbell; or D: We had seen it before.''

"C," she said.

Damn, I thought, I should have split that into two questions; now I still didn't know if Sylvia actually dropped by to see Friedman or if she only called him. "I'm sorry," I said, as if I hadn't heard her. "Did you say doorbell or did you say telephone?"

"Doorbell."

"Thank you, ma'am. I'll only keep you a moment longer. For how long would you say the interruption of your viewing continued?"

"How long?" She was beginning to sound less forthcoming and friendly, more suspicious. I would have hung up on me long before, but she was evidently the type who tries to please everyone, even strangers who ask impertinent questions. "Maybe a half hour, forty-five minutes."

"And did you both resume your viewing when the interruption was completed?"

"These are really strange questions," she said. "What . . ."

"It's very helpful for the networks to know these things," I said in a voice so smooth you could have slid on it. "And it's so reassuring for the programming people at the network to know that viewers are not turning them off because of the network programming, and that viewers will resume viewing the programming on the network if given the opportunity, if you see what I mean."

"I guess so," she said doubtfully. "Is that all?"

"I'm sorry." I gave a little laugh. "But this little list I have in front of me says I have to get an answer to that last question or I don't get credit for this call. Did either you or Mr. Friedman resume your viewing when the interruption was completed?"

"No." And then she added in a funny voice, "It didn't seem as interesting as real life anymore."

"Not as interesting as real life," I repeated, as if I were

162

writing down a criticism. "Would you care to expand on that . . ."

"Wait," she commanded.

I had the feeling she had put her hand over the receiver, and I heard a murmur of voices, as from a television. I nearly hung up then.

"What did you say the name of your company is?" She returned so suddenly my heart jumped.

"We're a survey company for . . ."

"No, what's the name, please?"

"The name?"

"Yes."

I couldn't for the life of me remember what I had said it was, and I was on the verge of hanging up without another word when a male voice came on an extension.

"You sound like Jennifer Cain." It was Friedman, sounding furious and something else . . . nervous? Scared? "What kind of trick is this?"

"I'll explain," I said.

"Yes, you will," he said, and rapped out his address.

The girlfriend, still on her extension, said in a wounded voice, "Now that I think about it, the movie wasn't even on CBS."

"I'll be—"

One of them hung up.

"—right—"

The other one hung up.

"—there, folks."

I hung up, walked over to Lewis's car, and leaned down to the driver's seat.

"She was there," I told him. "And I'm going there now."

He said he'd follow me. It was then I noticed the copy of *New York* magazine that lay open on his lap.

"I don't believe you!" I exclaimed. "Lewis, you have to take that magazine right back into that store this very minute!"

"Take it back?" He screwed up his face at me. "Are you kidding? I just paid two bucks for it, I'm not taking it back! What do you think this place is, a library? Honest to God,

Cain, sometimes I wonder about you." He reached down between the seats and brought up a white Styrofoam cup with a lid. "Here, I think you need this."

It was hot coffee.

"You bought this?"

He nodded.

"For me?"

He nodded.

"Thanks." I returned to my car, holding my head and the coffee cup high, trying to look dignified.

24

"This is my friend, Sonya Klein," Friedman said when I stepped into his house. His tone was as flat and inhospitable as a dry wind across a prairie. He was wearing clean, pressed jeans and an immaculate long-sleeved black knit shirt, so that he reminded me again of a slim tree with bare branches, as he had that day when I had first met him, beside John Rudolph's grave. But this time, he held himself so stiffly that I thought maybe he had run a steam iron over himself, as well as over the pants and the shirt.

"Hello," I said.

Instead of reaching for my hand to shake, she reached for one of his hands to hold and only nodded at me. Sonya was a short, pretty blonde, about ten pounds overweight, wearing a pink terry-cloth jumpsuit and pink bunny slippers. Like him, she looked about 35. Her smile kept flickering on and off like a light bulb with a bad connection. All in all, the atmosphere was thick with nerves and incongruity and caution.

I waited for them to make the next move. That seemed to confuse them, for they glanced back and forth as if each one hoped the other would take the lead. "Your turn," his dark eyes seemed to say to her. "But it's your house," her big blue eyes seemed to plead with him.

"Could I have some coffee?" I asked.

"Coffee?" He stared at me, then at her. Again, they communicated with their eyes: "Do we have any coffee?" "Should we give her coffee?" "Are you going to do it?" "No, you do it." I could almost hear the words; it was the sort of extradimensional communication that goes on between twins or lovers.

"Instant's fine," I said, looking at him.

Friedman jerked out of his paralysis and walked stiffly toward the kitchen. I turned to her then, and suggested: "Do you think we could sit down?"

"Parlor," she said, and led me there.

The house was a small two-story Victorian that had probably once been advertised as "a handyman's dream." Somebody had laid loving hands on it, however, and worked it into a modest showplace of hardwood floors, refinished antiques, and stained-glass windows.

"You've done beautiful work here," I said. When she didn't deny the compliment, I felt sure they had renovated the house together. I tried buttering her up. "I've always admired people with these sorts of talents."

"I'm an interior decorator," she said, and then blushed. She gave me a frightened look, as if she'd made some incriminating admission, and pressed her lips together. But it wasn't in her to be rude. She opened her plump lips to suggest that I sit on the love seat. "The cushions are stuffed with real goose down," she told me in a hesitant, chatty way, "so it's not as hard as some of this other stuff. Aaron and I got into antiques because we like the way they look, but I guess we didn't think about actually sitting on them. He says we can thank television for comfortable furniture. I mean, it's impossible to imagine a Victorian sitting in a reclining rocker, isn't it?"

"Especially a vibrating one," I said, and she bit her lower lip to keep from smiling. I added, quietly, carefully, "But I guess they didn't watch many Sunday-night movies." She flushed and pressed her lips together again. This time, she was going to wait for him to come back.

When he did, it was with a coffeepot and three cups.

Once he had poured for everybody, he settled close beside her on the settee and lit one of his filtertip, menthol cigarettes. Within seconds, the room smelled like burnt breath mints. I suspected they could communicate by the nudge-and-press method as well as by eye contact, and that put me at a disadvantage. If I'd been a cop I'd have separated them, even sending them to different rooms to question them, to break their vibrational field.

"What's going on here?" Friedman blurted, certainly not the first person to do so that evening.

I looked him in the eyes, then her, in an effort to seem honest and sincere. She was round and sunny; he was a thin, dark shadow. It was like looking at noon and midnight of the same day. I regarded the united intelligence opposite me and opted for the Lewis Riss method of criminal interrogation. "I think I ought to tell you the police know that Sylvia Davis was here the night she died."

"Oh," Sonya said, with a moan escaping from her lips, and she took one of his hands into her pink terry-cloth lap. They very carefully did not look at each other.

"That's crazy," he said.

"She got drunk at the office party," I said. "While she was there, Stan Pittman told her their affair would have to stop, because Jack Smith was blackmailing him. That really upset her, because she hadn't known about the blackmailing, and she was afraid she'd lose her job over it. She left the party to go drinking with the three gravediggers, and got into a fight with Smith, accusing him of betraying her. I gather that she had confided in him about her affair with Stan, and now she was furious to find out that he'd used that information to blackmail her boss and lover.

"She stormed out of the bar, Jack following. She told him she was coming over here to see you, Aaron, to see if you'd help her keep her job. She stayed about forty-five minutes, according to Sonya. I think it would be a good idea if you could prove those were not the last forty-five minutes of her life."

This time they looked at each other. The silent communication lasted a long time, and I would have given anything to have been privy to it.

"She was here," Friedman finally said. He looked as if the words hurt. "She told us about the blackmail, and she pleaded with me to help her." He frowned, gazed at the carpet. "She was crying so hard, and she was really drunk. It was like seeing a whole different side of somebody I thought I knew." He glanced up at me. "I really liked her. She was always nice to everybody, and she worked like a dog. She was a very responsible person, at least when it came to her business life. So sure, I was going to help her if I could . . ." His voice trailed off; he looked away again. "God, it was going to be so embarrassing, but I was going to talk to Stan about the situation the next day and tell him that if he was going to fire anybody it ought to be Jack."

"You wanted to fire him, anyway," I said.

"Yes, but Stan always said no. And now, of course, I know why." He paused to look at Sonya, then back at me. "Listen, there's one thing though . . ."

"What?"

"Sylvia wasn't having an affair with Stan."

"But you just said . . ."

He shook his head in tight left-and-right movements, the sign of a man who is going to be obstinate about something.

I sighed. "All right, skip that for now. What happened after you said you'd talk to Stan about his being blackmailed for . . . ," I let my voice grow sarcastic, ". . . not having an affair with her."

"She was grateful, and she started to cry again." Friedman looked at Sonya as if pleading with her to take over the story from there.

"Sylvia began to tell us how much she missed John Rudolph." Sonya's voice was sweet with sympathy. "She hadn't really loved him, she said, any more than she loved any of the others, but she'd spent a lot of time with him, and she missed him. I think . . ." Sonya looked into Friedman's eyes, then back at me. "I think . . . she was grieving for a lot of things that night, maybe even her marriage. The poor little

168

thing, she just kept saying, 'I'm so lonely . . . I just want somebody to hold me.' We tried to get her to stay here with us, to sleep it off, but she wouldn't. She was really kind of out of control. Aaron tried to get her keys out of her purse, but I guess she'd left them in the ignition, and we didn't think of that. So we couldn't force her to stay, and we let her go." The sympathetic voice trembled, then stopped.

"And neither of you left the house again that night?"

"No," she said, at the same time he said, "Of course not."

"And," I looked at Friedman, "you were home sick this morning when Muriel Rudolph was killed."

"Yes," he said, at the same time Sonya said, "I stayed home to nurse him."

"Where did Sylvia go when she left here?"

They looked at each other, shook their heads.

"You don't know. And you didn't tell any of this to the police," I guessed, "because you didn't want to hurt Stan or his family."

As one, they nodded.

"But if he wasn't really having an affair with her," I said insistently, "how could the truth hurt him?"

They looked at each other again, passed some sort of unspoken words, then simultaneously took up their coffee to drink. They didn't meet my eyes over their cups.

"Please," I said.

But they had gone dumb on me.

"I'll have to ask Stan," I told them.

They looked shocked, as if that possibility hadn't occurred to them, and then they looked resigned.

"I suppose so" was all Friedman would say.

"Please." Sonya glanced from me to Aaron and back again. "Please, tell him that Aaron tried to protect his family, please tell him that."

"All right." I was growing tired of these decent, careful people who had not volunteered this information to the police and who would not take me further down the road toward the truth. It was exasperation and weariness that made me take a last, mean shot at him.

"Did you sleep with her?"

He blinked, looked into his lover's eyes.

Again, as one, they shook their heads.

I gave it up and let them walk me back to the front door. They seemed relaxed now, as if all were forgiven, as if they were glad to have gotten it off their chests. And who was I to think they should confide in me?

"Good night," I said, none too graciously. And then to Friedman, "You sure got over your cold fast."

"I took an antihistamine and a decongestant this evening," he said promptly. "Cleared up the symptoms right away."

"Another modern medical miracle." I turned to go.

"Jenny?"

I looked back to see them standing together in the doorway, their arms entwined. She smiled sweetly at me.

"Multi-Markets," she said.

This time, Lewis was waiting for me in the front seat of my car, nearly giving me a heart attack when I came upon him there.

"Dead end," I said, when I could breathe again. I told him what little more I knew of the last night of Sylvia's life. "Of course, we have only their word that Sylvia left here alone that night, or that Friedman really was sick this morning."

"Why would he kill Mrs. Rudolph?" Lewis asked.

"Maybe he didn't want Sonya to know he'd had an affair with Sylvia?" I shrugged. "I don't know. We don't even know if he did have an affair with her. Would you kill two women to keep another woman from finding out you were unfaithful?"

"Only if I thought she'd kill me first if she found out," Lewis said, and grinned. "Does this Sonya look like the violent type?"

I thought about the pink jumpsuit and the fluffy pink bunny slippers and said, "What do I know? Maybe we ought to take this to Ailey now, and see what he thinks."

"But we still don't know who did it."

"Perfectionist! We know she went to The Seaman, we know

170

she fought with Jack, we know she came over here to Friedman's, and that he and his lady friend claim that when she left them she was still alive. I think we've found out a lot, and I'll bet you it's more than Ailey knows.''

"All right.'' Lewis nodded. "We'll tell him tomorrow.''

I touched his hand. "Do you think you'll be able to sleep tonight?''

"Sure. I've got more than one good night's sleep locked up in the trunk of my car.'' He shrugged wearily, but then made a valiant effort to leer at me. "I'd manage it a lot better if I had a little company.''

I shook my head, smiled. "Not if she fell asleep on you.''

"That might have its pleasures, too.'' He shrugged again, then opened the door. "Oh well, you're an upper and the drugs are a downer, and if I tried to take you both at the same time, I'd probably send my system into toxic shock.'' Lewis got out of my car, then leaned back in to say, "Thanks all the same, but not tonight, Jenny.''

"Did I offer?"

But he had already closed the door, and was walking to his car.

I watched him go. I desperately wanted to go home to bed myself, but I was momentarily unable to summon the energy to turn the key in the ignition. Instead, I leaned my head against the seat and stared at the roof. The overhead light was still on because Lewis hadn't gotten the door closed entirely when he left. I reached over and slammed and locked it. The light extinguished, leaving me alone in the dark.

It was beginning to feel eerie, this business of tracking the path a woman had taken on the night she died. I was following in her footsteps nearly to the hour she took them. When I left Friedman's, it was going on eleven; when she left there, it was nearly midnight.

I closed my eyes and tried to imagine what it was like to be Sylvia Davis that night. She was frightened of losing her job, hurt over the betrayal by her friend, and grieving over the death of her lover and the failure of her marriage. She was lonely, so lonely she ached for somebody to hold her, and she was drunk. I tried to imagine the emptiness she felt that night, and the guilt? She was a woman who loved the company of men, and she was losing the main ones in her life in rapid order . . . her husband to divorce, one lover to death, another to fear, her friend to greed. She was used to being loved, but who was there now to love her when she needed it most? The grief and the loneliness she would have felt if she were sober would have been doubled, tripled, quadrupled—must, indeed, have been multiplied exponentially—by the alcohol, until that grief inhabited every cell of her body. Like a demon, it would have taken possession of her brain, filling the hemispheres, squeezing out any other thoughts, certainly any rational ones. It would have filled the ventricles of her heart, pouring in like wet cement and hardening, until her very ribs hurt from the hideous pressure of grief in her chest. This was no intelligent, conscientious, "pleasant" Sylvia; this was the after-hours woman, the voluptuous child who was irretrievably possessed and driven by her own desires and emotions. By the time she left Sonya and Aaron, Sylvia Davis would have been a quivering, aching pool of self-pity.

"I'm so lonely." I said it aloud, trying to mean it, trying to feel the ache. "I just want somebody to hold me."

But not just anybody, not this woman. Aaron and Sonya would have patted and comforted her, if all she needed was a friendly hug. No, it wasn't the embrace of platonic friends—if indeed, Aaron was such—that she desired. For this particular woman, in those particular circumstances, only a certain kind of somebody would do, and that body would have to be male: sexually, attractively, desirably male. She might have known a thousand men who fit that description and fled to any one of them after she left Friedman's. Certainly, she didn't go home; she was too lonely to go home. But I suspected there were only a few of those thousand men who were high enough up on the ladder of desirability, and difficult enough to obtain, to satisfy her ego that night, to reassure her that she, a woman who was losing her men, could still attract whomever she wanted, whenever she wanted. And only a few of them would have been living, conveniently, alone. Well, there was an obvious possibility, and I was supposed to see him in his office tomorrow . . .

My attention was suddenly dragged down from the roof of my car to the side mirror. I watched as an arm retreated back through the open window of a car that was parked a few lengths behind me, as if somebody had tossed out a cigarette butt. It occurred to me that meditating alone on a dark street is not the safest form of recreation for man, woman, or beast. A sudden memory of Sylvia Davis lying facedown in her lover's coffin, and then of Muriel Rudolph's contorted face, and then of the Jackal proffering his drugs to me as if he were offering his trophies in some bizarre courtship ritual gave me the energy to start the car and to drive home. I chose a route down major streets where there was still considerable traffic for as late as it was.

There were moments that night when I envied Lewis his drugged sleep. Muriel Rudolph kept me awake for a long time, as did her dead husband and his lover, and a pair of dilated, shiny black eyes that were focused steadily on me.

25

I didn't wait for Russell Bissell to call me the next morning, but telephoned him first thing, from my office. I told him I'd already talked to my attorney, who had given her blessing to my desire to buy a prearrangement plan for my mother. I would like to sign the contract immediately, I said . . . could he see me now?

"Come on over anytime, Jenny." His voice had that warm, lazy, liquid tone that pours out of salespeople when they successfully close a sale. "Will you be making your down payment by cash or check?" He laughed pleasantly. "I always have to ask. You wouldn't believe how many little old ladies keep their life savings in hundred-dollar bills rolled up in coffeepots."

I forced a responding chuckle and said, "Check."

After Russell hung up, I thought about the visit that Sylvia Davis might have paid him the night she died. Beautiful, bachelor Russell must have seemed just what the doctor ordered for a lovely, lonely lady. But I wondered if she got the reception she expected.

With that on my mind, I placed a call to a local health club to speak to an old friend.

"Robbie?" I said when I was connected with Robert Morrison. "It's Jenny Cain."

"Wonderful!" he exclaimed, in the familiar warm voice that made everybody who knew him feel welcome in his life. "God, it's been too long, lovey. I don't suppose you've called to take advantage of our two-for-one membership sale, have you? I'll sell you a year's membership, and that gorgeous hunk of a guy you live with can get in free."

I laughed. "You'd let him in free, anyway, Robbie."

"You're right." His chuckle was warm and rich as plum pudding, a laugh that sounded as if it derived from a chubby body, not a tough, muscular one like Robbie's. "He wouldn't have any cop buddies he'd like to fix me up with, would he? I've always kind of liked authority figures." The merry laugh rolled out of him again, giving no hint of the agonies of identity he had endured in his early life, including his time on the football squad in high school. Now, Robbie was about as well adjusted, as unself-conscious as anybody I knew, and his loving personality won over almost everybody and made him extremely popular in the small, discreet gay community in Port Frederick.

I decided to be as straightforward as he was.

"Robbie, if I mention a name to you, will you tell me which way he swings?"

"Only if it's a public swing, lovey."

"I understand, and if it isn't, I know you won't tell anybody I asked. His name is Russell Bissell."

"The beauteous Bissell?" Robbie whistled lightly. "I can tell you that now and then he drops into my favorite bar, but that might not make him anything but curious. Or thirsty." Robbie laughed. "He does allow the rest of us to buy him drinks, sort of like the prince consorting with the commoners. Royalty doesn't carry cash, you know. But he's not a regular, and I've never seen him leave with anybody. Jenny, I wouldn't want to plant a seed here that won't grow flowers. Maybe he just likes to get away from all the women who'd like to catch him and eat him for breakfast."

"That," I said, "is entirely possible."

"On the other hand," Robbie said, thoughtfully, "I know some mighty ravenous men, too. About the only place he'd be safe is on a desert island, alone. And even then, I'd worry about the monkeys."

"Thanks." I laughed. "And I'll think about the membership, seriously. My head still feels as if it's under thirty, but my thighs are coming up on forty."

Next, I called Lewis at the newspaper to suggest that we meet at police headquarters in two hours. I told him that I thought I'd figured out where Sylvia went after she left Friedman's and that I was going over to the funeral home to see if I could confirm my suspicion that she attempted to get a little tender loving care from Russell Bissell.

"So if I don't show up, Lewis," I said, "tell Ailey to check all the newly buried coffins for an extra inhabitant, a tall female with long blond hair."

"You sure you want to do this alone?"

"Well, I don't see why not," I said, truthfully. "After all, it's broad daylight, and there will be plenty of other people around. What can happen?"

"That's what George Custer said before he rode into the Valley of the Little Bighorn," Lewis said in an ominous, knowing tone, "and look what happened to him."

"I'll keep that in mind," I said.

In truth, I was nervous, but not necessarily because I feared Russell. I didn't particularly want to run into Aaron Friedman, and I felt equally anxious about the possibility of seeing Stan, because if I saw him, I would feel compelled to ask him about his affair with Sylvia Davis, and the blackmailing. The truth was, I simply hadn't believed Aaron and Sonya when they denied Stan's affair with Sylvia. Ironically, the affair and the blackmailing had too much of the ring of truth when the Jackal told it. I thought of all the years I had known Stan and liked him, and of the photograph in his office of the pretty woman and the three children, and I felt disappointed and saddened. Well, Geof often said that criminal investigation was the peeling away of illusions, and sometimes the peeling was painful.

I had to visit two water fountains and a public rest room before I worked up the courage to walk back into the funeral home.

As it turned out, Francie ushered me right into Russell's office, then started to shut the door behind her. I reached out for the inside knob and tugged the door away from her grip. "Do you mind if we leave it open?" I smiled at Russell. "It's kind of stuffy in here."

He didn't object.

I moved a chair up close to his desk so that I could be seen from the outer office but not overheard. He was pulling papers out of a desk drawer, and when he looked up, he seemed startled to find me so close to him. He pushed his wheeled chair back slightly from his desk, opening more space between us.

"Russell," I cleared my throat to cover the shakiness in my voice, "before I sign anything, may I ask you another question?"

"Of course." His smile held all the confidence of a coach whose team leads the game by a field goal in the final seconds. "Ask me anything you want, Jenny."

The night before, he'd used that old sales gimmick, the "give a choice" close on me. I thought I would try it on him. "The night Sylvia died, did she visit you at your home before midnight or after midnight?"

The other team seemed to have made a miraculous interception, because the coach suddenly looked stunned and confused. In the face of his staring silence, I once again traced Sylvia's path, claiming the police knew all about it, ending with, ". . . and after she left Friedman's, she drove to your house, looking for a little love and comfort. Did you give it to her, Russell?"

"No." The magnificent blond head began to shake violently back and forth in denial. "It isn't true."

"Which isn't?"

"The last time I saw her was at the party."

"No, no," I said with a patient air. "I just told you the police know all about her visiting you. They have a witness, Russell, a neighbor who saw her go into your house."

177

The time-honored lie seemed to work, because he suddenly put his head in his hands. When he looked up at me, the handsome features had gone haggard and nearly ugly with fear. "Oh God, I killed her."

I stared at him. Had he just admitting to killing her, just like that? Yes, there it was, and it wouldn't seem to sink into my dense skull. It couldn't be this easy. If it were this easy, even Ailey would be a good cop. Could this be admissible in court? But wouldn't they say I'd trapped the witness? No, that was crazy, I wasn't a cop or a lawyer, just an ordinary citizen. But of course he would deny it, and they would never get him to admit it again. Oh Lord, who did I think I was, playing cop? All I had wanted was an admission that she was there, so I could take the news to Ailey. And now look what I had done! Not having the least idea what else to say, I repeated his words. "You killed her?"

"By sending her away." His blue eyes were on me now, but I had the feeling he was staring into the past, down some vast psychic distance. His voice had softened to just the other side of tears. "I'll always know I killed her, because I didn't let her stay with me that night."

Now there were tears in the blue eyes.

"But you didn't strangle her," I said, feeling an absurd relief that rested mainly on the hope that I hadn't screwed up the investigation entirely.

"It doesn't matter."

"Of course it matters!"

"No," he shook his head in obstinate misery. "Even if somebody hadn't killed her, she'd have died on the highway, drunk as she was. Probably had a wreck and killed somebody else, too, a family of five or something. And I'd be responsible, because I sent her away. I should have let her stay, or driven her home, or something, God, something."

"Why didn't you want her, Russell? And why didn't you tell the police she'd been there?"

He took a deep, shaky breath and stared down at the contracts on his desk. "Because they'd have asked me the same question you just asked . . . why did I send her away? I'm a

single man, Jenny, and I live alone, and women . . . like me
. . . and the police wouldn't believe me if I said this beautiful
woman came to my door and offered herself to me, and I made
her leave.''

"*Why* did you make her leave?''

"Like I said.'' His glance held mine for a second, then
flickered, and fell. "I didn't want her.''

"When did she leave, Russell?''

"About fifteen minutes after she got there. I told her she
couldn't stay, that I didn't want her, and she asked to use the
phone, and I let her, and then she left.''

"Did she say where she was going?''

He shook his head.

"Whom did she call, do you know?''

"I don't know, honest to God, I don't know. I just keep
remembering how she looked when she left my house. She
was crying and hugging herself and kind of stumbling, like a
little girl, like this sad, lost, little girl.''

He sucked in another deep, shaky breath.

"Who do little girls want to talk to when they're feeling
sad and lost?''

"Mom or dad.''

I hadn't realized I had spoken the question aloud, and I was
startled to hear his voice. "What did you say, Russell?''

"She couldn't have called her mom, because she lives out
of town, and I'm pretty sure it wasn't a long-distance call, at
least I don't think so. And she couldn't call her dad, because
he died when she was just a kid.'' He looked up at me with
blue eyes that were full of the tears of the self-pity of guilt.
"Sylvia didn't have a father.''

Oh yes, I thought immediately, grimly, she did.

Suddenly, I wanted very badly to talk to another woman.

"Is Beryl in the office today, Russell?''

He half rose out of his chair. "Why?''

"I want to talk to her, that's all.''

"You can't tell her about this.'' His tone was urgent, pleading, and I suddenly had a distasteful sense of power. "She's
my boss. I might get fired if they find out. You can't tell her.''

"Fired?" I found it hard to believe, but I had to accept that he knew better than I the limits of other people's tolerance. "No, of course I won't mention it."

He admitted then that she was in the office.

"Russell." At the door of his office, I looked back at him. "Go to the police, before they come to you. Tell them she was drunk and disgusting, tell them whatever you want, but tell them she was there and made a phone call and left again."

He spread his hands in a gesture of helplessness. "But I can't prove she ever left."

"Maybe they can," I suggested, and gently closed his door. I hoped I had given him good advice. He could have taken his story to Geof, who would have respected his privacy, but would Ailey protect a man's reputation when his own reputation as a detective was at stake? Without saying a word to another person, I already felt as if I had betrayed Russell Bissell. On the other hand, he might have killed her to keep her from betraying his homosexuality. Or maybe he had lied . . . maybe he'd had sex with her and hated both himself and her afterwards . . .

I realized, sadly, it was a secret that wouldn't keep.

26

I slipped into Beryl's office just as she was putting on the jacket of her gray wool suit. "Miss Cain," she said, and smiled warmly, her large gray eyes expressing her surprise at seeing me there.

"Jenny, please." I stepped farther into her office. "Are you leaving?"

"Yes, I have a couple of sales calls to make."

"Mind if I walk out with you?"

"Not at all." Her smile was like a magnetic force pulling me out of the building after her. "Did Russell fix you up with a prearrangement plan?"

"Just about," I lied. We were outside the front door by now, standing on the steps above the parking lot. "But that's not what I need to ask you about, Beryl. It's about Sylvia, and finding out who killed her."

She stopped in her tracks and looked closely at me, as if seeing whether I were serious, or someone to take seriously. "She was a dear child, Jenny . . . sweet, hardworking, conscientious, and if there's anything I can do to help find her murderer, I want to do it. I can't imagine what I can tell you, or how telling you will help, but ask me anyway."

"Actually, it's about her husband."

"Darryl?" She took my arm, began steering me down the steps. "Let's talk as we walk, I'm running a little late. What can I tell you about Darryl Davis?"

"Did he want the divorce?"

"Lord, no." Her voice was resonant, vibrant, a voice to match her appearance and the strength of her personality. I blessed her silently for being so willing to accept my curiosity without question; maybe she sensed my good intentions, or maybe she just liked to gossip. "It was killing him, I just know it was, because he adored her. But Darryl always gave her whatever she wanted, so I suppose he would have given her the divorce, too."

"Didn't he know about the others?"

She glanced at me. "The other men, you mean?"

"Yes," I said, glad to be talking to another woman.

"Of course he did, but he understood."

"Under*stood?*" I stopped, pulling her to a halt as well.

She glanced at her watch, a pretty, delicate affair with a sprinkling of diamonds on it. "I told you, Darryl let her have anything she wanted, that's the kind of lovely man he is. Maybe it's not the sort of marriage you or I would like, although I don't know . . . put that way, it doesn't sound so bad!" She shook her head, smiled wryly. "But they were different from the rest of us, at least partly because of the difference in their ages, of course. They solved their problems in their own way, I guess." She started moving again, so I did, too. "Sylvia was quite fond of him, really she was, and she was grateful to him for being so good to her. Darryl's a good man, a fine man. But she was young, and pretty, and restless, and well, you know how it is, sometimes it's hard to keep them happy."

"This is my car." I opened the door and got in, not wanting to delay her any longer. "Some marriage," I commented, turning the key in the ignition. Beryl remained beside my window.

"Oh well," she said, and shrugged. "When they got married, everybody said it wouldn't last, that she only felt sorry for him, and she'd grow up, get bored, and leave him. It was

182

inevitable, really, that she would separate from him, like a child from her parent. That's what he really was, Jenny, not so much a husband, as the daddy she never had. And she was a good daughter to Darryl, really she was—taking care of him, cooking for him, cleaning for him—until she figured out he was a grown man and he ought to be able to take care of himself. And, of course, she wanted to be more independent, too.''

I stared at her, thinking how uncanny it was that she had tracked my thoughts exactly. But then it was pretty obvious and just the sort of pop psychology a good barmaid would dispense along with her whiskey sours. It didn't take a psychiatrist to figure this one out. I didn't, however, think I should just swallow it whole. At least, I could check her sources.

"How do you know all this, Beryl?"

"Oh, we talked," she said, and started to walk away. But then she turned back. "You know how it is. She knew I was older, and thought I was wiser." Her chuckle was deep, rich, but there was a sadness to it. This barmaid operated from behind a desk in an office instead of from behind a bar, I thought, and she extended coffee with her sympathy, instead of liquor. I suspected that Beryl Kamiski heard more "personnel matters" than Aaron Friedman, for all his dull, cautious decency, could ever hope to hear. She was saying, "It was pretty obvious to me, Jenny." Of course it was, to any perceptive woman, and to any barmaid who has lived long enough and heard it all before.

I thought of Miss Grant, another perceptive woman, and of her analysis of Darryl Davis's personality. "But it must have been killing him, Beryl, to let her go. Wasn't he possessive, or jealous?"

"Of course he was." Then she added ironically, "But that's fathers for you, they just don't want their little girls to grow up."

"And now she won't," I said quietly.

"No." Then she drew in her breath sharply, and stared at me.

"Thanks, Beryl." I waved, and drove away. In my rear-view mirror, I saw her still standing in the parking lot, staring after me. Like a good barmaid, she had been quick, and sensitive to the nuances of my words and voice. She had figured it out and was appalled; I could see it in her face in the rear-view mirror. I had figured it out, too, but I didn't know the victim or her killer, so I was more emotionally detached from my hypothesis. I was glad, however, to be letting go of it. Now it would be Ailey's job to find enough hard evidence to prove that Darryl Davis had killed his young wife.

"Let me get this straight," Ailey said forty-five minutes later in his gray metal cubicle of an office. I was earlier than I'd told Lewis, but that was fine with me, since I didn't want to talk about Stan Pittman's problems, or Russell's, in front of a reporter. I looked at the cop sitting across from me. Ailey's eyes shone with an expression that was so avid, so hungrily alert that it looked like greed. I was so tired by now that I was having trouble tracking. He said, "She was lonely, unhappy, and she chased all over town looking for a little comfort. And finally, she called her husband . . . like he was her daddy and he'd take care of her, is that it?"

I shifted uncomfortably on the folding metal chair. Coming out of his mouth, my theory didn't sound as plausible as it did in my own head. "It's just a theory, Ailey, but I think it's possible, don't you?"

"Wait a minute." He put up a hand. "So he says to her, meet me at the funeral home, and she goes to meet him, and he kills her . . . because she was leaving him, and he was possessive." He articulated each syllable, like an insult.

"Yes, I think so."

"Why the funeral home?"

"Ask him," I suggested.

"You ever meet him?"

"Yes, at his wife's funeral."

He seemed to wait for me to say something else.

"He seemed distraught," I said.

"Distraught," he repeated, and smiled slightly. The look of triumph in his eyes was growing, and I suddenly had the sense that Ailey was looking into the distance at his own promotion. He looked jubilant to be solving his first solo murder case, even if the lead came through me. I only hoped he didn't get so worked up that he moved too fast . . . it was still only a theory . . . there was still evidence to gather. My worst fears were confirmed when he smacked his palm on his desk and said, "Let's go get him."

"Now?" I stared at him. "Just like that, Ailey?"

"Just like that." He was already on his way to the door, but he stopped, jerked his chin at me. "You want to come, too? Come on."

I went, hoping Ailey was only going to bring the man in for questioning, and not try to arrest him. Alarms were going off in my weary head. Nowhere in my theory had I allowed for the murder of Muriel Rudolph. As we drove out of the police garage, I tried mentally to fit the two murders into one picture. Again and again, from different angles, I tried it, but my brain was fuzzy and the pattern didn't seem to want to fall together. Surely that was only because I hadn't had the time or the mental energy to think it out? But all Ailey wanted to talk about, over and over, were the details we'd already discussed.

"So he gets her to the funeral home," he said as he drove, speaking with an eagerness I'd never seen in him before, "and they go into the morgue. And he comes up behind her and grabs the ends of her hair and pulls them around her neck, and twists real tight and strangles her. Is that how you see it?"

"Yes," I said, reluctantly.

"It would take real powerful hands to pull that off," Ailey said with an enthusiasm that was nearly salacious. "But like you say, he's a big, strong guy. And then he picks her up, without leaving any marks on her body or her dress or anything, and he dumps her into the coffin with Rudolph. Is that how you see it?"

"Yes," I said, irritably. "I guess."

He glided to a stop in front of a neat, modest house on a quiet residential street. Then he was quickly out of the car, with me on his heels. I accept the law that permits an accused to face his accusers, but I would have preferred it in a court of law, not on his doorstep. I followed Ailey up the front steps and waited behind him as he rang the doorbell, then knocked forcefully. After a few moments, a gruff male voice sounded from behind the door.

"Yes?"

"Detective Mason, Mr. Davis. Sorry to disturb you, but it's about your wife's death, sir."

There was a strange, metallic scratching sound on the other side of the door as if he were turning the knob with pliers. When it opened, Darryl Davis stood in the doorway, tanklike, in a blue-and-white seersucker bathrobe, beneath which he was wearing dark blue pajamas and black socks. Like Ailey, he had a broad, impassive face, but the skin was puffy, unhealthy looking, as if he didn't sleep well or eat right. He stood, framed in the doorway, like a Marine drill sergeant, with his hands clasped behind him, staring over Ailey's shoulder at me.

"Will you come in?" He directed it at Ailey.

"No," Ailey said. "We have some new developments in the case. Thought you might like to take a look at them, sir." He had carried a manila file folder from his office to the car; now he thrust it toward Davis. What kind of interrogation technique was this, I wondered.

"This isn't necessary," Davis said.

"Here." Ailey pushed the folder until it touched the belt of the seersucker robe. The older man brought his arms out from behind his back to grasp the folder. It was all I could do not to gasp—at the ends of his wrists, where his hands should have been, were steel claws.

He saw me staring, and said tersely, "Beirut."

Mason turned ostentatiously toward me to say with false regret, "Sorry, I thought you knew. Mr. Davis was wounded in that terrorist attack on the barracks in Lebanon a few years back."

It clicked then: the retired Marine who always kept his hands behind his back, and the former nurse's aide at the veterans' hospital. That's how they had met, of course, this older man

186

and his pretty, young wife. Some of Beryl Kamiski's words took on a different meaning for me now. I nodded, tried to smile, finally settled on lowering my gaze to the cement at my feet. Mason had turned back to face the man who stood, straight and still, in the doorway, the folder clasped in the pincers of his claws. "Well, we'll push off." Ailey nudged me back down the stairs.

"I don't want this." Davis pushed the folder against Ailey.

"You don't?" The detective's expression and voice were all innocent surprise as he took back the case file. "Okay. Sorry to disturb your nap, sir."

"I don't sleep." Davis closed his front door.

We rode back to the station in silence.

Once out of the car, Mason stared across it at me. Now he allowed the triumphant smirk to travel from his eyes to his mouth. "Let me give you a piece of advice," he said. "Livin' with a cop don't make you one."

I stared back at him.

"I expect you'll be staying out of my business from now on, wouldn't you say so?"

I turned away, and walked back to my car.

In that night's paper, there was a Lewis Riss byline over a story that detailed the arrest by Detective Ailey Mason of one of Sylvia Davis's lovers for her murder. He was a man who was old enough to be her father.

"We believe our suspect, Stanley Pittman, Sr., had sufficient motive, which was to protect his personal reputation and that of his businesses," Mason was quoted as saying. "As owner of the funeral home in which Miss Davis was killed, he also had means and opportunity to commit the murder.

"We made the arrest," Ailey continued, "based on an anonymous tip we received concerning a phone call the deceased is alleged to have made to the accused shortly before she was killed. It was this information that allowed us to piece together the leads we had already painstakingly gathered in our exhaustive investigation concerning the events leading up to the murder. We were, of course, already close to the point of making an arrest, but we're always grateful when conscientious citizens come forward in this way to assist the police."

At the end of the story, readers were asked to call the police hot line if they had any information about the whereabouts of John L. Smith, nineteen, who was wanted by the police for questioning in the Davis/Rudolph murders.

27

I spent a quiet weekend, as alone as possible: catching up on my sleep, cleaning house, visiting my mother in the psychiatric hospital where she is a resident, watching TV, reading, playing chess with my personal computer, avoiding the phone. Lewis left a couple of messages on the machine—first, to tell me that Ailey was gloating all over the police station over the humiliating trick he'd played on me, and, a second time, to offer comfort, either physical or chemical, or both. The only calls I returned were from Geof. From his hotel room in Philadelphia, he told me that I'd been more helpful than Ailey let on with his coy speech to the newspaper about anonymous sources.

"Did he tell you much about it?" I asked him.

"Enough," he said. "Jenny, don't be so hard on yourself. You came up with some extremely useful information, and you got people to talk to you who wouldn't talk to us. Do you think that Ailey and I never come to dumb conclusions about cases? Listen, feeling foolish is a common disease, but it's not fatal."

"Yes, but *being* foolish can be fatal to oneself, or others."

He didn't say anything.

"Well?"

"Yes," he agreed, in a reluctant tone. "Especially, in police work. Listen, if you're feeling that bad, why don't you fly down here for the rest of the weekend and let me massage your ego, and other parts. . . ."

"No."

"Why not?"

"Because."

"Well, now there's a reason."

"You wouldn't want me, I'm wearing a hair shirt."

"You're right, it's damned uncomfortable to make love to a woman in a hair shirt. How long are you going to play martyr, Jenny? I'd like to know so I'll have some idea when it's safe to come home."

"By that time, I may have gone to live as a hermit in a cave, where I will be less of a menace to innocent people. Geof, did Ailey tell you about our visit to Darryl Davis?"

"Yes." There was reluctance in his tone, and disapproval, and I sensed he still didn't want to discuss the case. Ailey's case. But he said, "I love you."

"And we all know what reliable taste you have in women."

"Hey," he said.

By Sunday, I had worked myself into a real funk, which did not even lift when I went to work, like a regular human being, on Monday morning.

"Jenny!" My secretary's eyes were round with dismay and excitement. "Isn't it awful about Mr. Pittman? Who would ever guess that that funny little man was a murderer?"

"I wouldn't have," I said. "What else is new, Faye?"

"Well, Derek called in sick," she informed me. "And Marv's got a dead battery, so he won't be in until later, either. But you'll be glad to know I got all these done for you, and early for once." She patted a stack of documents.

"These?" I frowned at them.

"The agenda for your board meeting this afternoon," Faye said patiently, as to a forgetful child. "As far as I know, they'll all be here; at least, I haven't had any calls from their secretaries to say otherwise. Jenny, what do you think I ought to fix at that time of day . . . regular coffee or decaffeinated?''

"Board meeting?" I picked up a copy of the agenda and read it as if I hadn't written it myself several days previously. The top item under Old Business was: "Union Hill Cemetery Investigation Progress Report by J. Cain, Exec. Dir."

I walked past Faye into my office and slumped into my chair. "Mr. Chairman," I rehearsed silently. "I regret to report there is no progress in the investigation into the matter of the bodies that are missing from Union Hill Cemetery because your executive director has wasted her time chasing down blind alleys, barking up wrong trees, making a nuisance of herself at police headquarters, interfering in people's private lives, and accusing the wrong man of murder. What is that you say, Mr. Chairman? You're tired of Hector? Oh, you wish to fire the director. Is there a second to the motion? Gentlemen, please, one at a time!''

Faye appeared at the door with a calendar in her hand. "You seem tired this morning, Jenny," she said kindly. "Would you like me to run through the day's appointments with you?''

I nodded, and Faye came in and sat down across from me. "In twenty minutes, you're talking to a grant applicant." She read from the calendar while I stared at the cloudy day outside my windows. "It's that woman with the idea for a carnival to benefit battered children. And then you have an appointment with a lawyer who wants to know how we handle bequests to the foundation. And after that, I told the director of the city mission that he could see you, because they had to serve extra people during that cold, wet spell, and they're running low on food money this week, and . . .''

The phone rang. When she saw I wasn't going to get it, Faye reached over my desk to pick up the receiver. "Port Frederick Civic Foundation," she said in a cheerful voice.

I hadn't noticed before, but the leaves were budding on the trees below my fourth-floor window; soon, the roofs of the smaller buildings would disappear from my view. Then I'd be looking out on a sea of green leaves, punctuated by stretches of pavement and by the few buildings downtown that are taller than the trees. Soon, it would be just me and the birds in the tops of the trees.

"I'll get her," Faye said, and held the phone out to me.

Do birds nest in downtown trees, I wondered. Maybe they're put off by the automobile fumes and the heat rising from the asphalt, not to mention all the pedestrians. I tried to remember when I'd last seen a sea gull downtown, and couldn't do it. I tried to care about whether there *were* any birds downtown, and I couldn't do it. I tried to care about the fact that I couldn't seem to care about whether there were any birds downtown and couldn't do that, either. Like Marv, I had a dead battery.

"Jenny?"

I looked at the phone in Faye's hand, then reluctantly took it from her. "Yes?"

"Jenny?" inquired a male voice, sounding doubtful.

"Yes, Stan. Oh." I sat up straighter. "Hello, Stan."

"Are you coming over to the funeral home this morning to work on the Union Hill business, Jenny?" He sounded even more depressed, if that were possible, than I. There was a note of pleading in his voice, as well.

I told him I hadn't planned on it.

"Oh," Stan said.

There was a pause while I struggled to think of something tactful to say to him. Finally I said what I should have said immediately: "Stan, do you want me to come over there now? I've had some experience with this sort of thing, as you know, and I'd be glad to come over and talk to you about it, if you . . ."

"Would you?" He sounded pathetically grateful.

"I'm leaving right now," I promised him.

Faye offered to make the necessary calls to postpone my meetings, and I left the office. My battery wasn't entirely recharged, but at least it was hot-wired by an old friend's troubles.

"He's still in jail?" I stared across Stan's desk at him. "Why, Stan? Didn't they set bail? Was it too high? There are bondsmen, you know, who . . ."

"Dad wouldn't pay it."

"He wouldn't *pay* it?"

"You know Dad." Stan slid down in his chair as if somebody had pulled him down by the ankles. He sighed again. "He says he'll sit there until hell freezes over before he'll pay them one red cent, and if the family makes his bail, he'll personally see to it that we're all buried alive in airtight caskets. He says they're all a bunch of goddamned dumb bunnies, and when he gets through suing them for false arrest and defamation of character, they won't have a rope to hang a horse thief."

"Well."

Stan rolled his head on the rim of the chair until he could see me from a sideways angle. "What am I going to do, Jenny?"

"Try to prove he didn't do it, I guess."

His eyes slid away from mine and found a focus at a point on the edge of his desk.

"Stan?" I felt a little nauseated. "He didn't do it?"

"Which?"

"Oh God." This time it was I who sighed. "Well, let's take it one step at a time. He did have an affair with Sylvia Davis."

"Yes." Stan's eyes remained fixed on the point on his desk.

"And you were being blackmailed by the Jackal."

He looked surprised at my knowledge, then his glance slid away again. "I was looking forward to finally being able to fire the little bastard, but he's disappeared. I'm beginning to think there's no justice, Jenny."

"How long had he been blackmailing you?"

Stan's cheeks turned pink. "Several months."

"How much did you pay him?"

The cheeks grew pinker. "A thousand a month."

"Goodness."

"Yeah, and the kicker is that it was only a short fling, and it was over months ago." He laughed, a sound full of bitter irony. "I guess the lesson here is that lust may come and go, but extortion lingers on."

193

That surprised me. "I thought you told Sylvia, at the office party, that she had to break off the affair."

"Huh? Oh. No, I just told her about the blackmail, that's all. I wouldn't pay anymore, and I thought maybe she'd make him quit. Don't know why I didn't think of it before. Too embarrassed, I guess, didn't want to upset her. She was an awfully good secretary, you know . . . reliable, conscientious, honest as the day is . . ."

It was too much, and I raised a hand to stop it.

"Why did he blackmail you, instead of your dad?"

"Because," Stan said bitterly, "he knew my dad would just explode like Mount Saint Helens and fire him, and probably Sylvia, too. And what he wanted was the money, of course. Oh, he knew the real sucker . . . more worried about my company's image and my family's reputation than about little things like truth, justice, and breaking the law. Part of the deal was that I couldn't tell my dad."

"Did you?"

"God, no."

"But if your father didn't know, he didn't have any reason to kill Sylvia! Anyway, why kill *her?* She wasn't doing him any harm, she didn't even know about the extortion. If he was going to kill anybody, it should have been the Jackal."

"Yeah!" He brightened, but only momentarily. "Yeah, but there's only our word on it, and who's going to believe us now?"

"Did Sylvia call your dad that night, Stan?"

"He swears she didn't, and my mom says the phone never rang. And he didn't leave the house all night, not until his regular time to go to work in the morning."

"Well," I said brightly, "that's an alibi. Does he have a witness to any of that?"

"Sure."

I waited.

"Mom."

We held each other's eyes for a long, defeated moment. I looked away first, embarrassed at having nothing helpful to offer in the way of advice. We sat for a few moments in a mutually depressed silence until I broke it with a question that had been bugging me for some time.

"Stan," I said, "why did you go ahead with that office party, in spite of the fact that one of your employees had recently died?"

"Oh, you know how it is. Those things have a life of their own. I mean, once you've bought the dip, you might as well go ahead and dunk the chips. And to tell you the truth, nobody liked John Rudolph much anyway, except Sylvia, and his wife, I guess. He wasn't anything special, Jenny, just this horny little guy who died, that's all. I know it sounds callous, but I don't suppose we thought much about him at the party."

I accepted the answer. But it did seem to me that for such an inconsequential man, John Rudolph had surely gone out of this world dramatically, and now his wife was dead, and his lover, too. As we sat there in silence again, my brain began playing games with the words . . . *inconsequential, sequential, consequence, sequence, essential, quintessential, consequential* . . . as if once I had scratched the word *inconsequential* it split open and other words poured out. Stan interrupted the flow of irrelevant words by voicing painfully relevant ones.

"So what happens next, Jenny?"

"Didn't your lawyers tell you?"

"Yeah, but make me believe it."

I told him, and he seemed to believe it.

28

Stan went back to work, what little of it there was after the news of his father's arrest. For my part, I didn't want to go back to work, but I didn't want to go home, either. I didn't even want to talk to Francie.

I slipped out of Stan's office while she was on the phone, and then out the back door to the memorial park. Over the weekend, the spring rains had started again; now the first cold sprinkles of the day fell on my hair and shoulders. The sky above was gray as a slate tombstone; my mood below was more the color and weight of lead. It seemed the appropriate moment for a walk in a graveyard.

I started off around the memorial park, toward the entrance to Union Hill Cemetery, not even caring if I got wet and chilled. The sprinkles stopped, however, thus aborting the particular route of martyrdom that would have sent me to a hospital with pneumonia. Regardless, I trudged on.

At the gate, I paused to survey the full expanse. And then I marched from stone to stone, reading some of them again, thinking about none of them. The holes in the ground still lay open like doors to dark apartments waiting for the residents to return. Down one long, uneven row I went, then up another, until I worked my way through the entire cemetery, covering even more ground than I had a few days before.

I came up against the outermost edge of the cemetery and leaned against the fence. I looked down. The ground sloped away to a flat place, and then down a cliff to the ocean. I hooked the toes of my shoes in the holes in the fence, hoisted myself higher, and leaned over for a better view.

There were three flat rocks lined up at the edge of the flat place. They looked as if they had been placed there deliberately, rather than having simply been washed up by nature, so I climbed over the fence and scrambled down to inspect them.

When I got close, I saw that the rocks were pushed firmly into the ground and spaced about two feet from each other. Affixed to each one was a piece of tin, like a pie plate, which somebody had flattened and cut into an oblong. On the tins were crudely hammered names and dates, evidently of birth and death, Esther, 01–39; Roland, 52–39; Susanna May, 39–39.

As I stood looking down at "Esther," I realized my feet were sinking ever so slightly into the damp earth. I moved in front of "Roland." Again, the ground beneath my feet felt spongy, giving. Curious now, and paying attention, I stepped in front of the last tin marker.

"Graves," I said aloud. And they weren't empty. Whoever had been buried in them was still buried in them.

The Jackal had been right when he said some of them were still here, waiting for me to find them. But who were these people? And what did their presence—their bodily presence—mean, if anything?

I walked briskly to the cemetery gate, and from there to my car.

"They were victims of the Great Depression, Jennifer."

Miss Grant's eyes were moist with sympathy as she passed a plate of buttered English muffins to me. A cup of English Breakfast tea sat on a table by my elbow, raising thin curls of steam into the cozy room.

"Do you mean, Miss Grant, that they died during the Depression and couldn't afford gravestones?"

She finished chewing and swallowing before she spoke. "My dear, they couldn't even afford a grave or a burial, and certainly not a tombstone. They were given those plots for free by Spitt's father, which was a fine and noble thing to do, but I'm afraid the Pittman generosity did not extend to a proper grave marker, and so the poor things had to provide their own from whatever materials they found to use."

"Who were they, Miss Grant?"

She named an old and perpetually impoverished family of the town. I had been to school with several of them; she had taught almost all the living ones.

"They're still there," I said, "in the cemetery."

"Yes, dear."

"That should mean something, shouldn't it?"

"I don't know, dear." She smiled encouragingly at me, as if I were taking an examination she was sure I would pass. "Should it?"

I asked her why she hadn't included their names among her records, and she gave me the perfectly reasonable answer that they were not really part of the cemetery proper. Before I left her apartment, I also asked her opinion of the arrest of Spitt Pittman for the two murders.

"Oh, well. It's absurd, of course. Except . . ." Creases appeared between her eyebrows. "It would be so like Spitt to try to economize in that way."

"Economize?"

"By burying two bodies in one coffin." She pursed her lips and shook her head in a disapproving fashion that would have done nothing for Stan's peace of mind.

Damn it, it had to mean something.

One hundred and thirty-three bodies gone, three remaining.

For lack of any better ideas, I drove back to Harbor Lights. I entered through the public wing, which was conspicuously empty, since people don't like to think their friendly funeral director will hasten them to their graves, and then I slipped back into the cremation-urn display room. Again, I pulled out the cardboard boxes and began to pore over the archives, hoping something might trigger an intelligent, even original thought.

I was reading through the newspaper death notice for Erasmus Pittman for the fourth time when the coincidence really struck me. The old man had died and been buried in Union Hill Cemetery on June 30, 1886. And the last time that cemetery was used, excepting those Depression graves, was 1886.

Quickly, I ran my finger down the list of "Dates of Death" in the record compiled by Miss Grant. There was none later than June 30, 1867. He had, indeed, been the last person to be buried in his own cemetery. Why? For sentimental reasons? That seemed highly unlikely. There was remaining acreage that might have been put to profitable use, and God knew, the Pittmans were nothing if not profit minded. If they hadn't continued burying people in that cemetery, there had been a reason.

"But what, damn it, what?"

I slammed the record shut, leaned back against the sofa, put my feet up on the coffee table, closed my eyes, and let everything I had read and observed float through my consciousness. After a few moments, I got up and stalked out of the room, back to Stan's office, no longer caring who saw me.

"Stan." He looked up from the telephone he had been about to dial and replaced the receiver. "Your family gave Union Hill Cemetery to the historical society in . . ."

"Nineteen fifty-two."

"Why didn't you use it before that?"

"What do you mean?"

"Well, there was room for more graves. Why not use it?"

"We couldn't, Jenny."

"Couldn't? Why not?"

"Well, because of the terms of the will, my grandfather's will. He left the property, along with everything else, to my father, along with the proviso that the cemetery remain inviolate, protected, never to be used for profit again. As my father said, they were patriotic, my ancestors."

"Yes," I said.

Maybe, I thought.

I walked slowly to the cremation-urn display room thinking: it was the sons, Americus, Honor, and Justice, who did it, who stopped the use of the cemetery upon their father's death. But why? Why? On my way down the long hall, I stopped to stare at each of their pictures in turn. Why, fellas? Why did you do it?

They didn't reply.

Neither did their brothers-in-law, the liveryman, the upholsterer, the smithy who ran the forge, the . . .

Where was the sawmill owner, the man who had married the other Pittman daughter? He was a natural to join the firm, but his portrait wasn't on the wall.

I trotted back to my cozy den to look him up.

Yes! Here he was, mentioned in the death notice for his wife, in 1848.

"In this city, the 21st instant, Mrs. Sarah Clark, wife of Mr. Benjamin Clark, the proprietor of the local sawmill, in the 25th year of her age, in childbirth, infant not surviving. She was a dutiful wife, an affectionate daughter to Mr. Erasmus Pittman and his wife of this town . . ."

It was the year the cemetery opened. Upon checking back through Miss Grant's record, I saw that Sarah Pittman Clark was the first person to be buried in Union Hill Cemetery.

I ran my finger down the long lines of names in Miss Grant's record of burials to see if I could find Benjamin Clark, not quite sure what I was looking for but figuring I should take this investigation of his life and times to its logical end. And there he was, having died in 1880 at the age of sixty, from "surgery in Boston." Miss Grant had compiled quite a bit of information on Ben, listing the names of his parents, his children, and his wives, and the dates of his marriages. It looked as if Ben had remarried a few weeks after Sarah died. Now that was interesting, or was it? I thought about looking up a few of his descendants to inquire about him but decided that might require more effort than it was worth.

Instead, I went "Christmas shopping."

It's a method I use for last-minute shopping when I have a long list and no time: I enter a department store with my gift list and an iron determination to match every name on that list with a gift from that store before I depart. It always works and has the added bonus of including gift wrapping. In the same way, I made up my mind not to leave that room until I had figured out why the Pittman boys had closed their cemetery, and what a missing portrait had to do with it.

I opened my eyes once, to pore over the ledgers from the Pittman businesses. Then I leaned back and closed my eyes again. My shopping was nearly done.

The next time I looked up, I knew.

As I walked one last time down the corridor to Stan's office, I winked at one of the paintings.

"I'm on to you, you old rascal," I whispered.

I could have sworn he winked back at me.

Then I requested the pleasure of Stan's company to the foundation board meeting, which would begin in half an hour. He was, he told me, exhausted and embarrassed, and he didn't want to go.

"I think you'd better," I advised him.

29

I was right on time for the board meeting, with Stan in tow like a reluctant barge being tugged against the current. I hadn't been able to tell him much on the drive over, because I was still feverishly working out in my mind exactly how to present my conclusions so they would make as much sense to him and to the rest of the world as they did to me.

I flung open the door to the office. When it flew back and the knob hit the wall with a bang, I knew I was chugging along on all cylinders again.

"Hi, Faye!"

"Regular coffee," she replied.

I pulled Stan into the conference room after me.

My bosses, the foundation trustees, were characteristically even more prompt than I. Officially, there were five of them, appointed to life terms, but the only young one among them had departed for Colorado some time before, leaving only the four remaining members to conduct business. They were powerful, intelligent, and demanding, and not one of them was a day under sixty-five years of age.

When Stan and I walked into the conference room, they were already seated in our donated antique chairs around our donated antique conference table, flipping through the pages of their copies of the agenda. Clockwise, from right to left as I viewed them, they were: Jack Fenton, chairman of the board of First City Bank; Roy Leland, chairman emeritus of United Grocers; Pete Falwell, president of the Port Frederick Fisheries; and Edwin Ottilini, senior partner in Owens, Owens, and Ottilini, Attorneys at Law.

Four pairs of shrewd eyes set in four lined and tanned faces looked up. I smiled, nodded to them. Four nods returned my greeting. And then they took in the presence of the young man behind me.

Pete Falwell stood up. Moving with the quickness of a senior tennis champion, he went at once to Stan's side to wrap one arm around the younger man's shoulders and shake hands with the other. "Good to see you, Stanley," Pete said strongly. "Couldn't believe what I heard on the news this morning. Still don't believe it. Never will believe it. You give my best to your mother and father, and you call me if there's anything I can do to help your family, you hear me?"

"Thank you, sir," Stan said in a faint voice.

There were similar murmurs from the other three trustees, but they were looking over at me with an obvious question in their eyes: "What's he doing here?"

"I invited Stan to participate in our meeting because of the first item on our agenda," I told them. "Do you all have coffee? Yes? Well, I'm ready to start whenever you are, gentlemen." I ushered Stan into an empty chair and then took my own place at the end of the table opposite the president of the board, Edwin Ottilini. The arrangement had always secretly amused me, making me feel like "mom" at a family gathering with "dad" and all the "boys."

"Dad" called the meeting to order, called for the reading of the minutes of the last meeting, then quickly turned things over to me by saying, "And now our director will tell us how she has solved the mystery of the missing bodies in Union Hill Cemetery."

Although Roy Leland leaned forward in serious anticipation, an amused chuckle made the round of the other trustees, who appreciated the unlikelihood of Edwin Ottilini's suggestion.

"Oh, they're long gone, Edwin," Pete Falwell said.

I rose to my feet. "Yes, they are."

At the serious tone in my voice, the chuckles dried up. A slow smile began to spread across Roy Leland's face. Stan looked only mildly interested, however; he wore the jarred, tired look of a man whose shock absorbers are all worn out.

"Jennifer knows," Roy said in a stage whisper.

"No," said Edwin Ottilini. Then, "Really, do you, my dear?"

"Yes," I replied.

"Where are they?" Pete Falwell demanded, slapping a palm on the table. "Where's my great-grandmother?"

"I'll get to that," I promised him.

And I did. But first, I had to start at the beginning.

"Spitt Pittman's grandfather was a man named Erasmus Pittman," I began. "Like most of the men who became American undertakers, he was a carpenter and cabinetmaker who also happened to make coffins. It was a natural and easy progression for these men to go from making coffins to handling funerals and burials.

"But Erasmus was also the sexton of the largest, most important church here in Port Frederick. And that gave him even more control over the burials of his fellow citizens. In fact, as the sexton, he was paid fees to bury people in the churchyard. So by the 1830s, when he was middle-aged, Erasmus made their coffins, helped prepare their bodies, and buried them. Undertaking was a profitable and growing business for him.

"But he and the town had a problem: the conditions of the church graveyards all over England and America had become shameful. They were so horribly packed with bodies that sometimes the burial mounds literally climbed up the sides of the churches. Dogs unearthed the bodies, looking for bones. The sights and smells of the graveyards were hideous, and they were so unsanitary that they posed a clear and present danger to the health of the living. In fact, in Boston there was an outbreak of plague that was blamed on the unspeakable conditions of the graveyards. Several thousand people died in Boston that year, and other towns and cities began to appreciate the dangers and to lobby for new graveyards to be located in rural areas outside the city limits.

"By then, even little Port Frederick wanted a new cemetery. But Erasmus objected, because he would lose the burial fees. Finally, however, he seemed to recognize the writing on the tomb, and so he devised a plan that would profit both the town and himself. He offered to open a new cemetery on a plot of land he owned at the edge of town, the place we now know as Union Hill. He offered to sell burial plots in the new cemetery, in lieu of taking burial fees. Well, he was a bit ahead of his time in regard to small towns, but he wasn't the first by any means to propose such a scheme, the forerunner of our modern cemeteries.

"At any rate, the town agreed—by that time, they would probably have agreed to anything, just to get the cemetery moved—and he was in business.

"In fact, he was in lots of businesses. Erasmus, you see, had three sons and three daughters. The sons were Americus, Justice, and Honor . . ."

Across the table from me, a twinkle appeared in Edwin Ottilini's eyes, but with Stan at the table, the old man was far too tactful to smile outright.

". . . and they joined their father in the undertaking business. The daughters married well and handily: one married the owner of the livery stable, a business that was obviously useful to Erasmus; one married a man who did upholstery, and who also just naturally joined the Pittman carpentry and undertaking firm; and the last one married the owner of the local sawmill. Now that was really convenient, because he could furnish all the lumber to the Pittman enterprises at a healthy familial discount. As you see, Erasmus had all the corners on the burial business."

I paused to gather my thoughts and check my notes. No one seemed impatient for me to get on with it; even Stan was observing me now, if only with a passive, detached sort of curiosity. For all the animation he showed, I might have been talking about somebody else's family, which he no doubt wished I was.

"And then Erasmus hit his first and only patch of bad luck," I continued. "Right as the new cemetery opened, one of his children died. She was Sarah, the daughter who was married to the sawmill owner, a man named Benjamin Clark. Sarah died in childbirth, leaving no other children. I found her death notice among the old newspaper clippings that Miss Grant had collected. Interestingly enough, a few weeks later, Benjamin remarried. There doesn't seem to have been any question of foul play in Sarah's death, so the husband's actions were only suspicious from a diplomatic point of view. It was, perhaps, not entirely tactful of him to marry again so soon."

One or two of the trustees evidently felt it safe to smile, and did.

"Soon after that, Port Frederick lost a citizen to the grippe, and that man became the second to be buried in Union Hill Cemetery. You will not, however, find his remains there today. In fact, I don't think we'll ever find them, or the remains of any of our ancestors who were supposedly buried there."

A restive murmur circled the conference table.

I raised my volume slightly. "You see, when Erasmus lost his daughter, and the son-in-law remarried, he also lost access to all that cheap lumber at the sawmill. With the opening of Union Hill, he was going to have to purchase all his lumber at full retail price." I felt my own excitement growing as I got closer to the end of my story. "In going through Erasmus Pittman's old accounting ledgers, I discovered that after his daughter died, he began to purchase considerably less lumber than he used to, and yet his woodworking businesses continued to grow. In the years following the opening of Union Hill, he did an increasingly large trade in furniture and, of course, coffins."

I looked around at each of the men in the room.

"So where was he getting the lumber to fill all those orders for all those chairs and tables and bedsteads?" I inquired rhetorically.

"Who cares?" Roy Leland shifted his massive body in the vulnerable old cherry-wood chair, which, like so much antique furniture in Port Frederick, had been constructed more than a hundred years before by the Pittman boys. The big man cried out impatiently, "What I want to know is, where's my great-great-granddaddy's coffin?"

"You're sitting on it, Roy," I said.

30

"Grandfather?"

Roy rose a few inches from the seat of his chair and remained there, stuck in space, as if he were afraid to sit back down again. Finally, gingerly, he lowered himself. The other men peered at their own chairs with suspicion and at me with even greater doubt. Only Stan looked at me with absolute and awful comprehension in his eyes.

"I'll admit I can't prove it," I told them, "but here, in as few words as possible, is what I'm convinced happened to our ancestors: when they died, their relatives bought plots in Union Hill Cemetery from Erasmus, and they also arranged for him to make the coffins, transport the bodies to the cemetery, and bury them."

"And he didn't?" my favorite banker, Jack Fenton, spoke up.

"And he did," I replied. "Briefly. Just until their backs were turned, I suspect, and then he brought the coffin back to the surface again and had his boys fill the grave with dirt. Then, probably at night, he transported the coffins back to his shop where he removed the bodies so that he could reuse the lumber! And from all those coffins, he constructed many of the heirlooms we have today in our houses and offices."

"If he was so damned smart," Roy said, as if he'd caught a flaw in my reasoning, "why didn't he just use the same coffin over and over?"

"Because they were measured and made to order, Roy," I said. "A family might have wondered why he had supplied a six-foot coffin for their five-foot grandmother, not to mention that her coffin would have had nail holes where the custom hardware had been attached to carry the previous occupant."

"But the expense of all that transportation!" the banker objected.

"No expense, Jack," I rebutted. "It was only a horsedrawn wagon, after all, and his sons did the hauling. His expense was not in labor, but in material."

"All right, all right." Roy acquiesced in a voice that seemed weak for so large a man. "So we know what happened to the coffins. But what did he do with my great-great-granddaddy?"

"I don't think we'll ever know for sure, Roy. But he might have cremated him. Or taken his body out to sea and, well, dumped it." Upon seeing the look on Stan's face, I added quickly, "With maybe a little ceremony or at least a prayer, of course."

"Stanley?" Jack Fenton looked, for the only time since I'd known him, bewildered. "Is this possible, Stanley?"

My old school chum raised a haggard face and haunted eyes. "My dad has a favorite hymn," he said slowly. "It was his dad's favorite, and his father's before him. It's even engraved on the tombstone of Erasmus and Seraphim Pittman." A tiny, tired smile began to play at the corners of his mouth. " 'Saving Grace.' "

I desperately fought the urge to giggle.

"Oh, yes, Roy, God help me," Stan said mournfully. "It's more than possible, it's probable to the point of certainty. Nice work, Jenny." The tiny smile grew into a wry grin.

At the opposite end of the table, Edwin Ottilini cleared his throat. "But if the practice was so successful, why did they stop it?"

I spoke up again. "Probably because the three 'boys' were afraid somebody would catch them at it, or maybe they didn't approve. But," I glanced with sympathy at Stan, "it's also true that by the time Erasmus died, metal caskets were taking over the market. There wasn't nearly as much demand for wood anymore."

Only Stan laughed openly, but it began as a weak, rather helpless-sounding chuckle.

"Well, I don't see what's so damn funny," Roy Leland said. "We own one of those beds your great-great-granddaddy made back in the Civil War, Stanley, and a dining-room table, too. Dammit, boy, all these years we been sleeping in somebody's casket and eatin' off somebody's coffin! It ain't funny!"

Stan groaned. He put his head in his hands, and I had an awful, sinking feeling he was going to cry. Instead, the weak chuckles grew into a cascade of laughter. Finally, he had to wipe his eyes with the handkerchief Edwin Ottilini passed down the table to him.

I gave the "boys" and myself a little extra time before I went on to the next order of old business.

It was late afternoon when the meeting finally adjourned.

"Jenny." Stan pulled me to one side of the conference room while Pete Falwell waited to give him a ride. "Do we have to tell the police about this business at Union Hill?"

I thought about it. "Well, the statute of limitations is sure to have run out on whatever crime your ancestors committed. And there's nobody to arrest anyway."

"What about the newspapers?"

"That's up to you, Stan."

He stuck his hands in his pockets. "The timing couldn't be worse, Jenny."

I couldn't argue with that.

"Maybe somebody who was here at the meeting will tell the paper," he suggested.

"I doubt it."

Stan stared down at the carpet, as if the answers were woven into the pile. "Nuts," he whispered.

I thought that pretty well summed things up.

He released a huge whoosh of breath through his mouth.

"Some families have skeletons in the closets, you know? Mine, we *ought* to have skeletons, but we don't! Well, I don't know what to do, but I do know I've got to get over to the jail to see my dad. Maybe he'll have a suggestion or two."

"I'm sure he will," I said.

Stan tried to smile, then said in wistful tones, "Actually, it's rather peaceful with Dad in jail. I'll be kind of sorry when he gets out."

I patted his arm, and again, he tried to smile. It was that brave effort, more than anything, that erased my sense of triumphant discovery, drained my energy, and ruined my day.

Before I left for home, I called Miss Grant to give her the "good news." In amazed tones, she repeated almost every sentence I said to her, so that by the end of our conversation I had begun to worry about her hearing.

"Thank you so much, my dear," she said at the end of my recital. "I've been so worried there would never be an adequate explanation, as I've been telling Lewis."

"Telling Lewis?"

"Your friend Mr. Riss, dear. We were just sitting here, relaxing and chatting over a nice cup of tea when you called. But my, you should see him now, taking notes like anything!" She laughed fondly. "Do you have anything you wish to say to him, dear?"

"Yes," I said grimly. "But it'll wait."

31

By the following weekend, Geof was home again, but busy catching up with things at the station, so I didn't ask him to accompany me on my regular Sunday trip up to the hospital to see my mother.

It was a dreary ride in a dreary month, through landscape as unadorned as a hospital room and as gray as linens from a hospital laundry. The hilly, curving roads were slick enough to cause unwary drivers to skid off the road, like the mind of a mental patient slipping off its track.

I had avoided thinking about the case all week, but now that I faced miles of empty road, I let myself consider the evidence against Spitt. His fingerprints were all over the morgue and on John Rudolph's coffin, as well. But so what? It was his funeral home. But he had access to the funeral home at any time of the day or night. Again, so what? So did Stan, and some of the employees probably had keys, possibly even Sylvia. But then there was the phone call from Russell's house . . . except we only had his word on that, and his opinion of her state of mind. So all the police really had against Spitt was opportunity, access, no believable alibi, fingerprints, and a motive.

"Damn," I said to the empty road.

Put that way, it didn't look so good. It looked terrible, in fact. And the defense was going to have its work cut out in trying to make a temperamental, philandering, tightfisted old son-of-a-gun in an unpopular profession look innocent. The publicity that Lewis was giving to Union Hill Cemetery wouldn't help the cause, either, suggesting, as it would to some people, a lack of moral fiber, almost a genetic defect, in the Pittman family.

I turned onto the gravel drive that wound through the forbidding stone gates of the Hampshire Psychiatric Hospital. My mother's room was on the fourth floor, the fifth door to the left of the elevators.

"Hi, Mom."

She was lying on her left side, so I kissed her right cheek, then her forehead. At the sound of my voice, her eyelids fluttered over her beautiful, Swedish blue eyes, but that was the only response. Illness had wasted the flesh from her tall, willowy body, leaving the flawless skin pasted to her bones so that she looked like an outline of herself. She wore a soft pink nightgown, tied under her chin, and she lay on soft, pastel cotton sheets, one of several sets that I had brought from home. The nurse's aides were nice about accommodating my small efforts to make her more comfortable. It was probably useless, though, since the chemical imbalance that had disintegrated her brain had long since rendered her oblivious to the fabric content of sheets. But maybe, just maybe, she was still vaguely aware of the content of love, and so I kept coming, kept chattering to her as if she could hear me, kept holding her thin, cool hands in my own warm ones. I pulled up a chair beside her bed and took one of those cool hands and began to massage her fingers, one by one.

Maybe if I approached the crimes from another angle . . .

"Mom, let me tell you about a woman I never knew."

Her hand, within mine, twitched, was still again.

"She was twenty-six years old, this girl, and she was married to a much older man. They met in a veterans' hospital when she was a nurse's aide and he was there for treatment. You see, he was a Marine, and he lost his hands during a

213

terrorist attack on the Beirut, Lebanon, Marine barracks a few years ago.''

I thought, what gibberish this would seem to my mother if she could hear it. She had withdrawn from reality years before there were such things as terrorist attacks on peacekeeping forces in Lebanon.

''I don't really know why she married him, I can only guess that she treated him kindly in the hospital, and he fell in love with her, and she appreciated his maturity and the stability he offered to her.

''But the marriage didn't work out for her, Mom. She drank too much and maybe took a few drugs, but she was mainly addicted to men. It's a funny thing, though; everybody seemed to like her anyway. It wasn't just that she was pretty to look at, but she also had a sweet, lively personality, and everybody talks about what a hard worker she was, how conscientious she was, and honest. She was a funny mixture, really, of the ethical and the unethical, the moral and the immoral, the legal and the illegal.''

For a few moments, I kneaded my mother's fingers in silence, hardly aware of my own actions. I was thinking that Sylvia's contradictions were not so unusual, not if you stopped to think about it. Most people, after all, were a mix of good and evil; we all had our spots of vulnerability to temptation, a thin place in the fabric of our morality where only a little pressure might cause a break in the weave. For Sylvia, that weak spot was sex. But for somebody else, it might be money. Or flattery, or rich food, or cocaine, or prestige, or nice clothes, or pride. Sylvia probably never even took home a single Harbor Lights pencil that didn't belong to her, but she couldn't resist a willing man. Another person might be faithful to his wife but never think twice about quietly going home with too much change from the grocery store. Everybody had a different weak spot. I wondered, very briefly, what mine was.

''Spitt's a good example, Mom,'' I said.

''He's like Sylvia in that his temptations lie in the corporeal realm—food, drink, women. In that, you might say they were alike, but I do think he's a basically honest businessman. Oh, he may hang fake pictures of his ancestors, but I'd be surprised to find out that Spitt ever stole a penny from anybody. And heaven knows he probably demands a scrupulous accounting of every penny that his employees spend! I suppose that's one of the reasons Sylvia was able to keep her job, even after their affair. I mean, she was conscientious about that sort of thing, just the quality Spitt would want in an employee, especially in a business like his where transactions are conducted in . . ."

My hands froze on my mother's fingers.

". . . cash."

Something, some message, was whispering its soft, sinister way from the deeper recesses of my brain. I felt my eyes look down and to the right, my lashes lower, my mouth open slightly, as if I were trying to cavesdrop on a whispered conversation behind me. Why did I feel as if I were at an intersection where two paths crossed and that I should stop, look, and listen?

Sex, sex, and more sex, Ailey had said to me.

Cash, cash, and more cash, I said to myself.

My pulse was yammering in my ears sufficiently to drown out the whispering in my brain, but maybe I had heard enough already. I had uncovered the Erasmus Pittman scam by comparing his receipts and accounts and then determining that he wasn't purchasing enough raw materials to account for the number of products he was selling. Receipts and accounts. Supplies and sales. Cash. What if somebody at Harbor Lights wasn't supplying the customers with what they paid for? And what if Sylvia found out about it, just as I found out how Erasmus had cheated his customers? Only, I made my discovery from the safe distance of a century later, while Sylvia—pretty, sweet, conscientious Sylvia—was right there in person to point the accusing finger.

Could history repeat itself? There was World War II, wasn't there? There were once again American advisors in distant agrarian countries, weren't there? History repeated itself every day.

215

But how had it been accomplished?

And how had Sylvia discovered it?

I had the feeling, stronger than ever now, that somehow or another, it all came down to John Rudolph. She had been his lover, and she had been killed. Muriel was his wife, and she died, too. And I mustn't forget that John himself was dead. Was he, had he always been, the link?

John Rudolph . . . funerals . . . and cash.

"Good afternoon, Miss Cain."

A nurse walked in with my mother's supper: glucose in a clear plastic bag which she hooked up to the feeding tube that led into a needle in my mother's arm. I watched her perform her questionable miracle, then kissed Mom goodbye. I had a powerful hunch, and it was going to drive me immediately to the offices of the *Port Frederick Times*. Lewis would be there, working on Sunday, or I didn't know my ambitious reporter.

He was, and when I walked in, he looked up in surprise.

"You've left him . . ." Lewis grinned, and opened his arms as if to welcome me into his embrace. "And come running to me."

I was already talking as I walked over to his desk. "Lewis, do you keep other newspapers on file around here?"

He dropped his arms, folded them over his chest.

"Why yes, I'm fine thank you, and you? Yeah."

"The Wall Street Journal?"

"Sure." He had tilted his head by now, and was giving me a reporter's inquisitorial stare. "Should I be taking notes?"

Other than the weekend guard in the lobby, we were the only workaholics on the premises, so I talked freely. "Lewis, I want you to get me a copy of last Wednesday's *Journal,* all right?"

"If you say so." He went after it, returning in a few minutes, which I spent drumming my fingers on the top of his computer monitor. When he returned, he held up the front page for me to see. "Which story?"

I scanned it, looking for news about the funeral industry.

"This one," I said, and handed it back to him. "Here. Why don't you read it aloud, so we'll both know?"

"Sure." He folded the paper back. "And after that, boys and girls, Uncle Lewis will read to you all about Brer Rabbit and the Three Blind Mice, since Uncle Lewis doesn't have anything better to do on a Sunday afternoon, right? Draw up a rug, kiddies, here goes. . . ."

He read to me the *Journal's* report that prearrangement salespeople in Texas had been caught skimming off their client's contracts. When customers paid in cash, the salesperson simply falsified the contract and pocketed a little money off the top. Other times, the salesperson convinced gullible customers to make out their checks to him, and again, skimmed some off the top for himself, then made out contracts for less money. Or, he offered to write the check for the down payment himself—so that a customer who could not otherwise afford a contract might take advantage of a "special deal"— and to bill the customer later. That, of course, allowed the salesperson to "buy" a contract for lesser amounts than the customer ordered and to skim when the customer wrote a personal check to pay him back. They were easy scams, the *Journal* pointed out, and possible not just in the funeral industry, but in any business that depends to a great extent on the inherent honesty of its salespeople. The paper went to some pains to point out that the "vast majority" of prearrangement companies dealt honestly with their customers. But if the story had an editorial slant, it was "buyer beware."

In the reading, Lewis's voice had grown increasingly sharp, alert, interested. When he finished, he looked up at me and said, "Now, little girl, you will kindly tell your Uncle Lewis why you had him read that particular story to you, hmm?"

"I think somebody at Harbor Lights has been pulling those scams, and Sylvia Davis found out about it," I said, "and that's why she was killed."

Lewis let out a long whistle. "Jesus."

I pulled over a chair from another reporter's desk and sat down in it.

"Well," Lewis said, "what do you . . . ?"

I held up my hand. "Wait a minute, Lew, let me think."

He complied, uncharacteristically, without argument. What I was thinking was that all I had was another theory, but no evidence. I could lay it on Geof, but he would politely, insistently, and correctly suggest that I take it to the police officer in charge of the case. And why should Ailey Mason pay attention to any hypothesis of mine? I didn't have any more credibility with him than he did with me, possibly even less since the Darryl Davis fiasco. What I needed this time, instead of running to the nearest cop with my latest, possibly harebrained theory, was evidence. Inarguable, irrefutable, direct evidence.

"Lewis?" I looked up.

"Still here," he said. "Older, but still here."

"I think you need a funeral prearrangement plan, Lewis."

He cocked an eyebrow. "Is that a veiled threat of some kind? The only reason people arrange for funerals is if somebody's gonna die. Do you know something I don't, Cain?"

"I know that you and I need to set up appointments for tomorrow to take out prearrangement contracts for ourselves, or for our parents, or anybody else, it doesn't matter who. And when they ask us for a down payment, we're going to pay them in cash. You see?"

He was nodding. "Plainly. How much cash?"

"I'm not sure, but we may each need several hundred dollars before the job is done." I looked him up and down, taking in the unshaven cheeks, the missing button on his shirt, the ratty cuffs on his jeans. "Do you have that much on hand, Lewis?"

"Sure." He grinned, and combed his hair with his hand. "See, I got this sock full of cash, thought I'd need it to purchase a bit of the evil weed, but it seems I came into a fortune in mind-altering substances. I got cash to burn, Cain. I might even smoke some of it."

"I wouldn't." I smiled back at him. "It has probably been salted with arsenic by the DEA. Now about our appointments. I'll set up meetings for myself with the prearrangement-sales manager, with Stan Pittman, and with Spitt, if he's out of jail yet."

"He is," Lewis informed me.

"Good." I pointed at him. "You take Aaron Friedman, just to see if he ever sells plans, and Russ Bissell, and the other prearrangement salespeople. I don't imagine there are more than a couple of them, and you can get their names from the secretary at Harbor Lights, a friend of mine by the name of Francie Daniel. What do you think, Lewis? Sound okay to you?"

He was looking down at the floor, and frowning. I thought maybe he'd detected a flaw in my plan. "Listen, Cain. When you prearrange your funeral, you can pick your own flowers and music and crap, right?"

"Right."

He looked up. "You think they'd let me pick Springsteen?"

"Springsteen on a pipe organ?" I pretended to consider it. "Gee, I don't know, Lewis, which song did you have in mind?"

" 'Cover Me,' " he said, and grinned.

We used the phones at the *Times* office to make our appointments. Amazingly, everyone we wanted to reach was available to answer the phone, even Spitt, who had indeed been released on a bond that he swore to me he would never pay back to "that dumb bunny," his son. Everyone we wanted to see was also available to see us when we wanted to see them the next day. I wondered if we should take that as a good omen or just sheer dumb luck.

To justify the unseemly urgency of our Sunday calls, I told each person on my list that "my mother has taken a turn for the worse." Lewis claimed that a beloved uncle was at death's door and demanding that his funeral be arranged so he could die in peace.

"God will get us for this," Lewis predicted after he hung up from his last call. "If my uncle gets sick and dies next week, I'll never forgive myself."

"I didn't know you were superstitious, Lewis."

"Jenny, Jenny, there's so much you don't know about me." He rolled his chair closer to mine and leered intimately into my face. "Wouldn't you like to get to know me better, Cain? I am not merely the callow, shallow reporter you see salivating before you. No. Beneath this hairy chest there lie fascinating depths for you to plumb to your heart's content when, as they say in the movies, this is all over."

"Lewis . . ." I breathed it seductively.

He rolled closer. "Say it, Jenny."

"When this is all over . . ." I placed my hands on his knees. ". . . this will all be over." I shoved hard. Lewis rolled across the aisle and banged up against his own desk.

"Damn! I'm on a 'downbound' train with you."

I stood up and began to gather my purse and coat. "On the other hand, Lew, if you're a good boy, maybe I'll help you win a Pulitzer Prize for investigative reporting of fraudulent practices in the Port Frederick funeral industry. And tell the truth, Lewis, which would you rather have—me or a Pulitzer?"

He grinned and walked me to the door.

32

I met Stan for breakfast the next morning at the Sunnyside Up and Cup, a local café with smiling sun faces on its menus and "bottomless" coffee mugs and tall red vinyl booths where one might talk to one's companion in relative privacy.

He ordered poached eggs, which nearly ruined my appetite for my two-egg cheese omelette (cooked well, not runny) with onions, green peppers, and extra cheese. Worse, he only picked at them, so I had to endure having those two rheumy egg eyes gazing reproachfully up at me as he gradually blinded them with his fork. King Lear came unfortunately to mind.

"I don't do much prearrangement work, Jenny," Stan said right off, repeating the caveat he'd offered on the phone the day before. "It doesn't seem fair to take the business away from our salespeople. But now and then I'll do it for friends, the same way Dad and I will handle funerals if somebody makes a special request."

"I appreciate it, Stan."

He peeled the paper top off a little white tub of Half 'n Half, poured the cream into his coffee, and then began to stir it as methodically and seriously as if it were his mission in life to mix that coffee with that cream.

"Feeling low this morning, Stan?"

He shrugged. "I paid Dad's bail. I think he may disinherit me for doing it." He looked up at me with eyes that were as lugubrious as the yolks of his poached eggs. "Do you want me to give you the whole spiel on prearrangement, Jenny, or do you kinda already know what you want?"

"If there's anything I can't stand," I said, "it's high-pressure salesmanship."

He looked blank, then smiled.

"I'll tell you what," I said then. "Let me describe to you what I want, and then you tell me what it will cost. And then I'll give you a down payment, and we'll be done."

"If there's anything I can't stand," he said, "it's an indecisive, wishy-washy customer who doesn't know her own mind."

I laughed, and then launched into a fictitious description of the funeral of my dreams. It didn't take long for him to fit it nicely into one of his company's available plans, and to affix a price to it.

When I pulled out the down payment in cash, he raised his eyebrows slightly but didn't demur. Instead, he rummaged to the bottom of his briefcase, pulled out a pad of receipts, and wrote one out to me in the amount of $250.

"Thanks, Jenny."

"Thank you, Stan."

From the cash I had given him he extracted, in a preoccupied, absentminded sort of fashion, a five-dollar bill and two ones—added change from his pocket—and left it all on the table to cover food and tip.

Back in my car, I wrote a note to myself: If he didn't do much prearrangement, why would he carry a cash-receipt pad around with him? And why would he pay for breakfast with the cash I had given him on account, a loose practice at best, and without even making a note of the amount or asking for a receipt from the waitress?

I called Francie Daniel from my office.

"Francie," I said, "would you quietly look through your

222

files and find out for me which salesperson handled the prearrangement account for John and Muriel Rudolph?"

I hung on the line while she went to look.

"I'm sorry," she said when she returned, "I can't find it anywhere."

No, that would have been too easy. I sighed, even though I had not expected her to locate the file.

"Do you want me to ask around?" she inquired helpfully.

"No! Thank you, but don't do that! And Francie, the salespeople will be turning in several contracts and cash down payments today and tomorrow from me and from that reporter, Lewis Riss. Will you please call me, privately, the minute you get them all in?"

She agreed to do so.

I met Beryl Kamiski for lunch at the restaurant of her choosing, the Sailors Three. A waiter in black slacks, white shirt, black tie, and a long, immaculate white apron brought us each a serving of Beryl's recommendations: Crab Louis salads and glasses of a superior domestic white wine.

"Exceptional," I said after my first bite.

"Good." Beryl wore a stylishly cut black silk suit with a mauve silk blouse and tie. Instead of the usual prim bow—the kind that says I-may-be-here-on-business-but-by-God-I'm-still-feminine—she had unbuttoned the top three buttons, laid the collar open, and flipped one end of the tie over the other in a loose, casual knot at the bottom of the V. It just covered what would otherwise have been a generous peek at her generous cleavage.

She smiled at me, and I felt as if I had known her for years.

"I'll tell you a secret, Jenny," she said in the brisk, intimate way she had of speaking. "This business teaches you to appreciate life. There's nothing like a funeral to make you glad you're alive, you know? I don't mean to sound egotistic, but I probably enjoy life more than most people I know. I love good wines, good food, I love handsome men, nice clothes, really good music—Frank Sinatra, Tony Bennett, none of this modern junk. I love vacations in Las Vegas, Hawaii, Dallas, all the really nice places. I like to dance a lot and drink a little, and God, I love to sell things, and I love to talk, talk, talk.''

When I smiled, she chuckled at herself. It was a deep, rich, smoker's laugh that attracted attention. The male glances lingered for several seconds. She was a large, handsome woman with an air about her of having lived a ripe, sensual life, of knowing secrets, and of maybe even being willing to share one or two of them. There was something common about Beryl, but she had dolled it up, toned down the sass with a little class. I suspected that she moved as easily among the gentry as among the peasants.

She put down her glass of wine, leaned toward me, looked me straight in the eye. Her own eyes were large and gray, laugh lined, life lined, and there was a shrewd knowingness in the depths of them. I felt she was either going to tell me a very funny dirty joke or something deadly serious.

"I'll tell you what I know, Jenny," she said in a low, vibrant voice. "Life is no laughing matter. Oh, these comedians who laugh at life and death, what do they know about the pain of losing someone you love? Nothing! They don't know anything about it! But I," she tapped the flesh of her chest with a long, pointed, red fingernail, "I've lived and loved, I've loved and lost. I've seen more funerals than the average person sees in three lifetimes, and I'll tell you something. . . ."

She leaned closer.

I leaned closer.

"There are some funerals that provide a sense of comfort, and some that don't; some funerals that ease the pain, and some that don't; some funerals that allow the survivors to celebrate the joy of the life of their loved one, and some that don't."

"Which ones," I said, "don't?"

"The ones that are planned at the time of need, Jenny."

"Time of need?"

She looked to her right, to her left, leaned forward.

"Death, dear."

224

At which point I knew we were off and running. Well, I thought, as she sold me on the benefits of a top-of-the-line funeral for my sister, there are all kinds of sales approaches. Hers was magnificent in its way—illogical, yes, but dramatic, theatrical almost, and probably highly effective with many different types of people. The fact that I kept wanting to laugh in no way negated the fact of the power of her personality, and thus of her presentation. The woman was a saleswoman par excellence. It was only dried-up old MBA's like me that she would have a hard time convincing.

On this day, however, I was an easy sell.

Like Stan, she raised her eyebrows over my display of $250 in bills. "Cash, dear? I don't think I have a receipt pad with me. Let me check." Like Stan, she rummaged through a briefcase, but unlike him she came up empty-handed. "Will you trust me to mail you one?"

I said I would.

She picked up the tab on her American Express Gold Card and slipped the blue copy in her briefcase. "It's a shame about Spitt," she said on our way out the door together. "But I absolutely refuse to believe he did it, so I know he'll get off. Between you and me, though, it's been awful for business. Do you know, for a second there the other day, I thought you thought that Darryl Davis did it. Isn't that silly?"

"Really," I said.

Back in my car again, I added to my notes: If she couldn't give me a printed receipt, why not at least scribble a temporary one on a piece of scratch paper?

I found Spitt at home in his wood-paneled den.

His wife—a small, pleasant-faced, white-haired woman in a black dress—led me into the den in the manner of a nun ushering in a penitent to see the Pope. "He will see you now, dear," she said. "Thank you, Reverend Mother," I was tempted to reply.

Spitt had his slippered feet up on the footrest of a brown leather recliner, and from that throne, he waved me into the room. I went, with some trepidation when I saw what awaited me there: a wild hog snarled down at us from the west wall; on the south wall, the head, neck, and shoulders of a creature that used to be a goat or a sheep—for some reason I couldn't immediately think which—hung from a wood plaque; to the east, there was a stag; and to the north, a doe. I tried to look her in the eyes, with the vague notion of apologizing to her for my species, but found I couldn't do it: she was cross-eyed—definitely, for all eternity, cross-eyed. I wondered if the fault were nature's or the taxidermist's. God, I thought, how would I like to have my own slightly bowed legs glued to a plaque and nailed to a den wall for future generations to view?

"Sit down, girl," Spitt commanded.

"Gee, Spitt, what a nice collection of dead heads."

"Trophies." He glared at me. "They're called trophies."

I sat down uneasily among the quick and the dead on a sofa that was upholstered in a tartan plaid fabric rough enough to sand wood. Curtains of a similar dark plaid hung at the four windows. There were a television, a poker table, and four chairs and a couple of beanbag chairs, probably for the grand-kids. The only hint of a feminine influence in all that aggressive masculinity was a little basket of pink fluff and crochet needles, tucked back into the corner of the seat of a brown leather armchair.

"Why do you want a prearrangement plan from me? I got people to handle that sort of thing, don't do it myself much anymore."

It was obvious that Spitt might be as free as a bird, but he was not as happy as a lark.

"You know more than they do," I said. "It's for my mother, Spitt, and you're closer to her generation. I just think you'll have a better idea of the right and proper thing for me to do for her."

He plucked at his lower lip as he continued to regard me, but any suspicion seemed to have melted from his eyes. Instead, I sensed in him a certain gratified pleasure at my words. Bull's-eye, I thought.

But half an hour later, when I opened my purse to pull out the cash, he shook his head and frowned at me again.

"What do you think I'm trying to do?" he said. "Pull a fast one on Uncle Sam? Hell, I'm in enough trouble over this murder business. You don't have a check, do you? I'd sure as hell rather have a check."

"No, I'm sorry."

He took my cash then, but with evident reluctance.

"Get my wife to write you out a receipt before you leave," he commanded, and I swore I would.

But when I walked to the front door, I found that all she had to offer me were doughnuts.

"Oh," Mrs. Pittman said, her little mouth opening into a circle to match the word. "You're not leaving so soon, are you, dear? I have coffee on and some nice, fresh doughnuts. Won't you stay for a buttermilk doughnut?"

"I'm sorry," I said. "Spitt asked me to ask you for a receipt for a cash payment I gave him, Mrs. Pittman."

"A receipt?" She looked suddenly flustered. The hand that wasn't holding the plate of pastries came up to her cheek. "Oh my, I wouldn't know how to do that, dear."

"It's very simple, you just . . ."

"Oh, no." She clung to her plate with both hands and shook her head back and forth. "I don't know anything about business, why I know I'd get it all wrong, and Spitt would have a conniption fit, oh my dear, no, no."

And that was that, except that she forced a buttermilk doughnut on me as I walked out the door. I thought about giving her a receipt for it, but I didn't want to upset her.

33

"Friedman doesn't do prearrangements," Lewis told me a few minutes later over the phone, when I called him from my office. "Like some people don't do windows, he doesn't do prearrangements. He wanted to foist me off onto Russell Bissell, so I let him do it."

"And what about Bissell, Lewis?"

"Men as good-looking as he is shouldn't be allowed loose on the streets, that's what. Do you have any idea what seeing him did to my ego, Cain? It's still lying out there in my car, flattened, gasping for air, wouldn't even come back into the office with me."

"That must be a relief to everyone."

"They ought to just pour cement over the guy and stick him up on a pedestal in a public square. For him, I might even consider a sex-change operation."

"What about the prearrangement operation, Lewis?" I spoke in patient tones.

"He gave me a receipt for the cash."

"Well, that sounds on the up-and-up."

"Except . . ." He drew out the syllables.

"Except?"

"You know how some people make ones that look like

sevens? He does that. I gave him a down payment of seventy-nine dollars, and he wrote out a receipt. And what I saw when I looked at it later was that the number could look like seventy-nine or . . ." Again, he drew out the word.

"Nineteen," I said. My pulse quickened. "That's very interesting, Lewis. What about the other prearrangement salespeople?"

"There are only two on staff right now, and they're both part-timers. I didn't even bother with them, Jenny, because one of them's too new to be our man, and the other one has been on maternity leave all month."

"That's sweet of you to think that pregnant women don't kill people, Lewis, but wouldn't she be a perfect suspect, with all that time on her hands?"

"It's her ninth month, and she's expecting twins."

"I see what you mean," I said. "Well, I guess now we wait for them to turn in their contracts and cash to Francie Daniel. Then we'll ask her to tell us if one of them turned in less cash than we doled out. Do you realize we might have our answer as soon as tomorrow, Lewis?"

"In the meantime?"

"I have one more appointment," I told him. "I'm hoping to learn something more to support my hypothesis."

"You know, there's a certain cold-bloodedness about you, Cain," Lewis said unexpectedly. "Maybe that's what makes you so sexy. I mean, you're all smiles, all kind of warm and sunny, you know? But there's something calculating about you."

I hung up soon after that, in order to make my last visit of the day. And so I wouldn't have to think very much about his last statements. I preferred to think that the quality to which he referred was called intelligence, and that it was sometimes necessarily accompanied by a certain emotional detachment. That trait in Geof went a long way toward making him a good cop, but did it do either of us any good as people? I was over thirty, never married, childless. He was over thirty, twice married, childless. Could these facts be attributed to fate, good luck, bad luck, practicality, or . . .

It was nearly five o'clock when I left for John and Muriel Rudolph's home on Brooklyn Terrace.

The eldest child opened the door of the mock-Tudor condominium with the early annuals blooming out front. She was a thin girl with pale skin and light brown hair, and she was wearing a green-and-white striped dress that looked too old and too small for her. Her mom's, I suspected.

I introduced myself, vaguely, as someone who was investigating her parents' deaths. I was awfully sorry to intrude, I said—sincerely—but I wondered if I might ask her a couple of important questions.

"I guess so. I'm Angie," she said, with an air of being upfront about things. I guessed her to be fifteen, although her blue eyes, if taken out of context, could have passed for those of an older woman. She ran thin fingers through her clean bangs, then tucked a strand of loose light brown hair behind an ear. "Would you like to come in, Mrs. Cain?"

"Hello, Angie. Please call me Jenny."

She held the front door open for me and stood courteously aside to let me enter. As I stepped into the little front hallway, there was an awful crashing sound from the floor above us, followed by a high-pitched scream and a couple of dull thuds. It startled me so that my head jerked, my mouth fell open, and I reached out with one hand to steady myself by touching the wall. The only other time I had been in this house, I had witnessed the aftermath of a murder; for a moment, I was afraid someone else was being killed.

Angie reacted by pursing her lips.

"Excuse me," she said in a high but steady voice. She walked to the bottom of the stairs that led to the second floor and placed her left hand on the bannister. "Jimmy!" she yelled up with such unexpected force that I jumped again. "Andy! If you don't settle down this instant, I'll make you eat the noodles without any spaghetti sauce on them!"

From just over my head, I heard a child say, "Yuk."

Another small voice yelled back, "I'll put the spaghetti up your nose!" But that was followed by a squeal and giggles, and then a chant of, "Spaghetti up your nose, spaghetti up

230

your nose!" The noise diminished to a dull rumble that fell approximately in the decibel range of a moving roller coaster. It seemed to satisfy their sister, though, and I thought at least we would be able to talk above it.

"Won't you come into the living room?" she asked.

I followed her into that room which her mother had maintained so neatly, and sat down on one end of the sofa. Angie disappeared into the kitchen for a few minutes. When she returned, it was with two cups, two saucers, two spoons, two white paper napkins, and a package of Oreo cookies. She placed them on the coffee table, then disappeared again. This time, she came back with a pot of coffee on a brown plastic tray, along with a large jar of Cremora, a box of sugar cubes, four pink packets of artificial sweetener, and a round plastic dinner plate.

"Oh, Angie," I said, "you don't have to . . ."

She smiled graciously at me, as her mother might have done, and began to lay out the Oreo cookies in two circles on the dinner plate, making a smaller circle inside a larger one, with a single cookie in the center. The edges of the cookies rested on each other like dominos. When she finished, she wiped her hands together, then sat down a couple of cushions away from me on the sofa. Angie crossed her ankles and folded her hands in her green-and-white-striped lap.

It was those cookies, displayed so carefully in a child's imitation of the perfect hostess, that got me. A painful lump of sadness lodged in my throat, like a lozenge that wouldn't dissolve.

"Thank you, Angie." I coughed in an effort to clear my throat of the lozenge and my voice of pity, only to feel a prickling of tears behind my eyes. Quickly, pretending busyness to cover my dismay, I broke the outer circle of dominos by taking an Oreo. Then I placed a napkin on my lap and began to munch the cookie.

She ran her fingers through her bangs again and tucked another strand of hair behind her ear before asking: "Will you have some coffee, Jenny?" At my helpless nod, she began to pour and to chatter as she must have thought a good hostess should: "Aunt Janie's living with us now, but she's at work till five-thirty. I get the boys' suppers and see they get started on their homework and all, and try to keep them from absolutely, you know, tearing the house down!" She smiled at me, inviting me to join this motherly amusement of hers.

I tried. "I'm sure you're wonderful with them, Angie."

"Well, they're certainly a handful," she said, just as her mother must have done many times. She passed me a cup of coffee, and a wave of it splashed over the edge onto the saucer. She flushed and jumped up from the sofa. "Oh, I'm so sorry. I'll get something . . . ."

"No problem." I emptied the liquid in the saucer back into the cup and began to sip the coffee. "It's excellent."

Slowly, she sank back onto the cushion.

"You said there was something I could help you with, about Mom's . . . about Mom's . . ."

Her lips formed the letter *m* to begin the word *murder*, but the rest of the word refused to come out, and then she couldn't even get out the word *Mom's*. She began a dreadful, helpless humming on the single letter. The expression in her eyes grew frantic, frightened. I scooted closer to her on the sofa and grabbed one of her hands from out of her lap and held it tight. With my free hand, I began to stroke her shoulder, in small circles like the Oreos. And then I began to talk in as plain and practical a voice as I could manage, no sugar, no syrup.

"Yes, you *can* help," I said. "You can help in a way that probably nobody else can, Angie. Just as you're helping to take care of your brothers and to keep this house so nice and clean, and to feed the boys and make sure they're warm and safe, and get them off to school. It's a huge responsibility, I know, and it's very difficult . . ."

I just talked, not even sure what I was saying, but eventually I got around to this: "What I need to know, Angie . . . I realize it's a funny question, but it's important . . . is what your mother thought of your dad's funeral service. Was the coffin the one she expected, did they sing the right songs, were there the correct number of limousines, that sort of thing. I just wondered if she said anything about it to you."

She had stopped the dreadful humming and her rigid hands and shoulders had begun to relax. When she spoke it was in a nearly normal voice.

"Gosh, no! She was really upset, because after the service she realized it hadn't been what she and Dad had wanted at all! See, when Dad died, she told the funeral home to take care of everything, and then she was so mad when they didn't do it right. Like, she and Dad wanted this coffin that's called the 'Majesty,' and instead they got something a lot less pretty. And they'd wanted . . ."

"They had bought a prearrangement plan?"

"Yeah! That's what Mom called it! And, see, they'd said they wanted . . ."

I let her go on to describe to me the differences between the funeral John Rudolph thought he bought and the one he got.

"Was she going to complain about it, Angie?"

"Oh sure! She was so mad she was going to tell some newspaper reporter even, and show him the contract and all."

"Contract? Do you still have that contract, Angie?"

When she got up, saying she was going to look for it among her father's papers, I knew she wouldn't find it. There had been no prearrangement papers in the estate-planning file folder that I had leafed through the morning of Muriel Rudolph's murder, no sign of any materials like the ones Russell had given me to keep the night we had dinner together. My best guess was that she had taken the file out that morning to show the prearrangement contract to Lewis. Her murderer had recognized its incriminating import—would probably have searched for it if it hadn't been so easy to find—and had stolen it.

That is why the murderer had come to visit her that morning, because of her words the night before: "It was wrong, Stan, it was all wrong!"

It was her husband's funeral she had been referring to, not Sylvia's sex life, and that's what worried the killer. If Muriel complained, the record would be checked, and then probably other records, until the house came tumbling down.

233

And why the list of names on her napkin?

Judging from the other words she had written—*party* and *bitch*—she probably had been thinking about her husband's lover that morning, and maybe she was making bitter guesses about Sylvia's other lovers. Maybe she was going to show that list to Lewis, as well as complain about the funeral. Or maybe if I checked I would find it was only a list of her husband's pallbearers.

When Angie returned to the living room empty-handed, I had a last question for her: "Do you know who sold that prearrangement policy to your parents?"

"No, gee, I'm sorry, I don't know."

Just before I left, the boys came down the stairs. The younger one was walking on the heels of the older one, who was yelling at him to "stop it right now! Angie, make him stop it right now!"

They were handsome little redheaded fellows, maybe five and seven years old, who ignored me completely. There were dark circles under their eyes, and there were tired, whiny notes in their voices. They were too thin, like their sister.

"Angie," I said, drawing her attention away from the boys. She was standing straight and ladylike once more, so I didn't try to touch her again. "I have a good friend who's a cop. Maybe some Saturday, the boys would like to ride around with him in the police car."

"Oh boy!" the youngest child exclaimed. There was a desperately eager expression in the blue eyes he raised to me. I wanted to grab him and to hug him tightly until the desperation eased away. I wanted to embrace them all, but I was a stranger who would only repel and frighten little boys.

Feeling angry and helpless, I left.

I worried all the way home about whether she would fix a green salad to go with their spaghetti. And what about milk? Did they drink enough milk? But sometimes dark circles under the eyes are a sign of milk allergy . . . could they be allergic to milk products? I had better tell Angie to check it out with their doctor.

They have dark circles under their eyes because they are

234

grieving and not sleeping, I reminded myself as I pulled into Geof's driveway. And they have aunts and uncles and cousins. They are orphans, but they are not alone; they have family who will take care of them, and it is none of my business.

Since Geof wouldn't be home from the station until very late, I had my spinach salad, cherry pie, and white wine supper alone. After considering how few calories there are in spinach, I added a dollop of vanilla ice cream to the pie. While I ate, I looked up milk allergy in a health dictionary, but only because I was curious, that's all.

It took me a long time to get to sleep that night, possibly because of the ice cream, but more likely because I was anxious about what sort of report I would get from Francie the next day. My dreams that night were restless, foggy ones, but I finally slept deeply and was barely aware of Geof's kiss on my cheek when he slid into bed beside me.

34

I was acutely aware of his presence, however, when he walked into the kitchen the next morning. I looked over my shoulder and saw that he was fully dressed in a business suit but still yawning. I opted for a flippant greeting, to cover my sudden attack of nervousness.

"Hey, sailor . . . cuppa coffee for a kiss?"

"Such a deal." Geof yawned widely again. " 'Scuse." He walked over to me and held up his end of the bargain. Then he accepted the cup I gave him, carried it to the kitchen counter, and sat down on a stool. From that perch, he observed me with a fond expression. Immediately, guilt poured over me as if I were taking a shower in it. And it only got worse when he said, in a lazy, intimate, lovers-in-the-morning sort of voice, "It's nice to see you when we're both awake. We've got to keep meeting like this. So what's on your schedule, Jenny? What's up at the foundation today?"

Oh, I thought wildly, nothing at all. I'm just busy playing cop, just kind of casually waiting around to hear the trap spring on a murderer, but other than that, really nothing special. Why? Do you want to have lunch?

"Oh, nothing much." I smiled, shrugged, turned quickly away to stick two slices of bread in the toaster. So what now,

I inquired sarcastically of myself. Now that there is time and opportunity to tell him, are you going to do it? Behind me, Geof began to talk about the seminars in Philadelphia and about the cases he was working on at the station. It had been easy for me to avoid the issue the last couple of days, but now, faced with the man himself—the *police*man himself—it was impossible to dissemble. I couldn't possibly lie to him, or even chatter on about the weather or business as if matters of life and death weren't pending. By keeping important secrets from him, I was creating a distance between us that would only lengthen if I didn't close it at once. My excuse for not telling him that he would say it was Ailey's case— seemed pretty weak to me now; I suspected it was, at least partly, pride and the fear of looking foolish (again) that had propelled me along this far without consulting him. But as Ailey had said, living with a cop didn't make me one. Who did I think I was, playing private investigator without a license? I had ideas and information that belonged in police hands, and the hands of a policeman were wrapped around a coffee cup right across from me. The toast popped up. I buttered it, cut it in half diagonally, put it on a plate, and turned around to hold it out to him.

"I'll trade you this toast," I said, "for a little forbearance."

He raised his eyebrows but reached out for the plate.

While he ate slowly, I gave him a complete rundown on my activities in the last two days. At no time during my recital did he express, vocally or facially, a judgment, so that my nervousness, my dread of once more having dived headlong into an empty pool, only increased as I talked. When I finished, I waited apprehensively for him to comment, still having no idea what he was thinking, either of the theory or of the woman behind it.

"You'll have to take this to Ailey." He spoke in a surprisingly mild, noncommittal tone as he brushed crumbs from his mouth, then off his fingers, then off his lap with a napkin. "I guess you know that, though, or you would have told me sooner."

I turned away from him, fiddled with the cream pitcher, the

sugar bowl, and my coffee cup, before finally saying, "Geof, my face is still burning from the last time I took one of my ideas to Ailey."

"Damn him."

I looked back at him, startled. His expression had turned hard, further unnerving me. "Nothing like that will happen again, Jenny," he said in a voice that was tough enough to make any suspect confess to any crime. "You know, I've kept my nose out of this case, I've kept my mouth shut, I haven't wanted to criticize his conduct of this case. But the way he treated you, not to mention Mr. Davis, was unconscionable, and it won't, by God, happen again."

His anger gratified me more than I would have thought possible. "I'm incredibly glad to hear that," I said with a certain wryness, "but please don't ask me to tell him yet. Let me wait long enough to get the news from Francie, and then maybe I'll have evidence for him, not just ideas."

"I don't know. Well, by tonight, you've got to tell him, otherwise you take a chance of jeopardizing an ongoing investigation."

"I don't see how." I couldn't help but object. "He thinks he already has his man. He's not investigating any other possibilities."

"No, *he* isn't."

I gazed at him in surprise. "You don't think Spitt did it!"

"Let's just say I'm keeping an open mind." I watched him drain his coffee cup, waited for him to say more. But when he had swallowed the last drop, he looked up, noticed me observing him, and only smiled.

"Well?" I demanded.

He shrugged. "It's still Ailey's case."

But cracks were beginning to appear in Ailey Mason's credibility in the eyes of the senior detective. That was enough to satisfy me for the time being, so I didn't press him. At least, not figuratively. I did, however, walk over to him, put my arms around him, press my chest against his, and peer into his brown eyes. "Are you stunned by the sheer brilliance of my deductions? Are you very annoyed?"

He smiled, kissed the side of my face. "I don't know yet," he said, without indicating which question that reply was meant to answer. He kissed the edge of my mouth, touched my lips with his tongue. "Ask me later, after you find out if you're right." He pressed his mouth full onto mine, so that his words whispered seductively into my open mouth. "Will you call me as soon as you get the report from Mrs. Daniel? And will you talk to us before you talk to that reporter?"

"Oh, you silver-tongued devil, you." My own mouth began to reply actively to his probings. "You know that right about now I would do anything you wanted. And, by the way, thanks for the forbearance."

"You ask a hell of a lot for two pieces of buttered toast." His hands were moving under my suit coat. "Is there anything else in this deal for me?"

"Ask me later," I whispered.

"No," Geof said urgently. "Show me now."

We were a little late getting to work that morning.

When I did finally reach the office, I felt better about life in general and my investigations in particular. At least now there was a competent, intelligent policeman who had heard my theory and hadn't laughed at it, hadn't demanded that I stop at once, as he had every right to do if he thought I was nuts. I knew he would also have asked me to cease and desist if he thought there was any danger involved, but it was clear that from here on, the investigation was a dry, safe matter of paperwork. The salespeople would turn in their cash and contracts to Francie, she would report her findings to me, I would turn them over to Ailey. No knives, no guns, no physical jeopardy, just paperwork. Clean and press, as the weight lifters say. In and out. I would be out of the case, and safely out of harm's way, when the time came to confront and arrest a killer.

"And if it turns out to be Spitt, after all?" I asked myself. I would turn in my badge.

The workday went surprisingly fast, but then I had a lot of lost time to make up for, phone calls to return, letters to dictate, applications to read, meetings to attend. I worked myself and the staff frenetically in an attempt to take my mind off the phone call I was expecting at any minute of the day from Francie. By 4:55, Faye, Derek, and Marvin were staggering from my desk to theirs like marathon runners on their last lap.

"Go home," I suggested. "You deserve it."

Derek looked pointedly at the clock behind my desk. "Golly, a whole five minutes early." He grinned, and said to the other two, "Come on. Let's get to our bunks, so the next shift of slaves can take our places at the oars." With the quick steps of someone who's escaping, Derek fled through the front door of the office, letting it slam behind him.

" 'Night, Jenny," Faye waved on her way out.

"You'll get your expense vouchers in to me, won't you?" Marv inquired, and when I promised I would, he, too, waved good-bye and departed.

It was 4:57.

The Harbor Lights offices closed at five, like ours.

I stared at the phone and drummed my fingers on my desk. Four fifty-eight.

What if I were wrong? Or what if I were right but the killer were clever enough not to cheat on this particular contract? Maybe he wouldn't, thinking it would be too risky to try it with a customer like Lewis or me, who might be too savvy about business. Or maybe I was right, but some of the salespeople were slow in turning in their contracts, so Francie didn't have a complete report for me. Damn, I had been through so much in this case—being there when Sylvia was discovered in the coffin, seeing the body of Muriel Rudolph, enduring the humiliation of picking the wrong suspect—and I wanted it to end, now, here. Please, I pleaded with the phone, ring now with the news I want to hear.

The phone rang.

"What do you hear?" asked Lewis, for the fifth time that day. "How's my Pulitzer coming along?"

"I'm still waiting," I told him.

"Good-bye," he said, and hung up.

The phone rang again, and I grabbed it.

"Jenny?" said Geof. "Are you coming down to see us?"

"Nothing to report yet," I said, "but soon, I hope."

"What time do they close up shop?"

"The funeral home?" I stalled. "Oh, the usual, I suppose."

"Like now." I heard amusement in his voice. "Look, if you don't hear anything from her by six, you probably won't today. But come on down here and talk to Ailey anyway, all right?"

"All right." I tried not to sound grudging. " 'Bye."

Four fifty-nine.

At 5:00, I couldn't stand it anymore and called her.

"Harbor Lights," Francie answered promptly in her usual cheery voice.

"It's Jenny," I said. "Do you have the contracts?"

"Oh!" Her voice became an excited whisper. "All of them! Just now! Yes!"

And then she put me on hold.

"Damn," I said to the unresponsive receiver. And then, a few minutes later, tentatively: "Francine? Francie, are you there?" Well, I had waited all day, I could wait another minute or two. But even after that time, she didn't return to the phone. "Francie?" I said into the silence that was beginning to seem ominous.

Maybe we had been disconnected and she was trying to get back in on my line. Yes, that was it. I hung up the receiver, then called the funeral home number again. But this time, nobody answered at all. "Francie! Please!" I let it ring fifteen times, and still nobody answered. I hung up, dialed again, let it ring twenty times, but nobody answered the phone. I called the operator, told her I was having trouble with a number, asked her to call it, but still nobody answered the phone in the management offices at the funeral home.

"Oh, God," I murmured, to which the operator replied, "Thank you for calling AT&T."

Once more, I replaced the receiver.

She had just forgotten to pick up the phone again, that's all, and she had gone on home. No, that wasn't likely, if she was as excited as she sounded about the information she had for me. Well, then, she had gone to the rest room and hadn't

241

been able to get to the phone in time. Yes, that was it, and I would just sit here patiently until she got out of the rest room and called me back. Or better yet, maybe I would just drive over there and get her report in person, make sure she wasn't sick or anything, yes, that was the thing to do.

My hands were shaking as I threw on my suit coat. "Oh, Francie, what do you know, and who else knows it, and where are you? Where *are* you?" Ignoring purse and briefcase, I ran out of my office with only my car keys in my hand. If I could have got to my car faster by jumping from my fourth-floor window, I would have done it. But figuring that two broken legs wouldn't help me find Francie, I settled for the elevator, and then for running to my car. All the way over to the funeral home, I told myself I was being ridiculous, there was nothing to worry about, and that when I arrived, I would find Francie very annoyed with me for not staying by the phone so she could call me back. This was only a matter of paperwork, after all, nothing more.

Paperwork . . . sitting on her desk for anyone to see?

How seriously had she taken my rather perfunctory injunctions to guard it carefully and to keep confidential the material she gathered? She was an open, trusting woman, the very traits that made her likable. And vulnerable?

Because of the rush-hour traffic and a sudden downpour of rain, it took me longer than usual to reach the funeral home. By the time I got there, it was 5:45, and there were only two cars in the parking lot. One was a late-model Cadillac. The other, I was overjoyed to see, was a station wagon with a bumper sticker that said, "Happiness Is Being a Grandmother."

"Oh, thank God!" I patted its hood as I trotted past the station wagon. Francie was here, perfectly all right, probably just had an attack of indigestion, couldn't get to the phone, would be right inside the door waiting for me.

Dodging rain puddles, I ran up the steps and pulled at the door, only to find it locked. When pounding on it didn't raise anyone, living or dead, I made binoculars with my hands and peered in. The only light showing was one on Francie's desk. As I turned away and ran back down the steps, I thought: Well, there is bound to be somebody in the public wing, some mourners or some employees working a visitation. I would get in that way, probably find her there. . . .

My breath came in gasps as I ran through the steady rain in the early darkness accompanying the storm. My hose felt like sodden washrags pasted to my legs; my good wool suit hung on me like heavy wet towels, raising a faint odor of dry-cleaning solvent, which I inhaled as I ran. I didn't want to think about what the rain was doing to my silk blouse or calfskin heels. When I reached the front steps of the public wing, I raced up them and jerked at the front door. It, too, was locked. Again, I made binoculars with my hands and peered in, this time seeing nothing in the darkness beyond the lobby. Again, I pounded furiously on the door.

"Stan!" I screamed. "Francie! Freddy! Somebody!"

Where were Freddy and Lennie? Was everybody gone, even the maintenance crew? Business was bad, of course, what with the owner in jail and bodies missing, and extra bodies showing up in caskets.

I leaned my forehead against a wet pane of glass in the door. "Oh God, what have I done to Francie?" Then I realized I wasn't helpless; I could take off a shoe and knock out a window to get to the lock, and then inside to search, and to a phone to call the police. But there were other entrances; surely one of them was open.

"Don't panic," I commanded myself, perhaps a shade late.

I turned from the front door, ready to run back down the steps and to the back of the building.

"Oh!" Coming off the first step, I immediately slammed up against the hard, warm body of a living person. It was a shock tantamount to running blindside into a wall, and it took my breath away. Even so, my first thought was, Thank God, but then I looked up to see that my passage was blocked by a teenager with spiked blond hair and enlarged black pupils. He grasped my arms so that I couldn't back away from him.

"I knew you'd come," the Jackal said.

243

35

"Come with me, come with me. . . ."

He began to back down the steps, hugging me to him, pinning my arms to my sides with his arms, pulling me along like a monstrous, struggling doll. When we reached the bottom step, he began to drag me in the direction of the memorial park.

"Wait, for God's sake, Jack, let me go!"

He tightened his grip on me, kept moving. Every lecture I had ever heard on self-defense flitted through my mind like a slide show gone wild, with all the pictures zipping by too fast, until finally one stuck in the projector: I raised a knee to shove in his groin, but missed, lost my footing completely, so then he was literally dragging me with him. I went limp then, hoping to slow him down. But he seemed unbelievably strong, as if endowed with a supernatural or chemical strength; he hardly lost a step and only dragged me faster, as if I weighed no more than a rag doll. I tried to work my way upright, my feet scrabbling like crabs to find a purchase in the muddy grass, but I stumbled with every step he took. When I could find enough breath, with his tight grip squeezing the air from my chest, I screamed, managing only intermittent, breathless shrieks, like those of a tormented cat. Once when he hoisted me up so that our faces touched, I tried to bite him, only to feel myself slip down and my teeth graze the leather collar of his jacket. We passed through the gate and on through into the memorial park. And all the while he dragged me, all the way down from the top step, he talked to me in a strange, high, tight, staccato voice that overrode my screams, my protests and pleas, his words running together, as if in a stream of consciousness, but in which there was no consciousness, only the mad, roiling stream of senseless words.

"I chose you, Cain, my lady in the graveyard, my lady in the rain, from the beginning I chose you for this moment, and I knew you'd come to me because you'd know it's time for you to come to me, and we'll go together just like we've planned all week, just like we've talked about, you and me, and I'll get the money together and we'll go and they'll never find us, I knew you'd come to me, my lady in the graveyard, my lady of the grave, my lady in the rain, my Cain, my Cain, come to me, come to me. . . ."

As he dragged me, I had barely time enough and sense to wonder where he had been all week when the police had been looking for him; to wonder if he had been swallowing, sniffing, shooting, drinking drugs the whole time; to wonder if he even knew where he was, who I was, what he was doing, where we were going. . . .

"You just have to wait for me now and I'll get the money together, and then I'll come back for you, and then we'll get out of here and go away and they'll never find us among the dead men, in the graveyard, in the rain. . . ."

It was a hyperactive, helium-filled voice from another planet, and it scared the hell out of me. My face bounced against his leather chest. I closed my eyes to protect them from the open, biting edges of the metal zipper on his jacket, but then I couldn't see where he dragged me. He smelled like an animal that has been caged in unchanged straw. Between some words he made low growls and grunts in his throat, as if the animal were hungry, and hunting. I began to hurt all over, from being dragged over the gravel walk, from being pinioned painfully to his body, from having my face jammed up against the ungiving leather and metal of his jacket. Just as I began to groan, low in my own

245

throat like a second animal, but this one the terrified hunted, he stopped suddenly. I scrambled to my feet, twisted violently in his grasp in a last, desperate effort to escape, but he whirled me around, pushed me backward into space, so that I screamed, stumbled, began to tumble a distance that seemed an eternity until I hit my head and elbows on a floor. Through a kaleidoscope of pain, I saw the Jackal standing above me, and beyond him an evergreen tree, and above that a blue-black sky, and rain. Then he shut a door that slammed heavily, and the world went black, except for the spinning colors of pain. Soon, even those points of light receded, leaving me alone in a cold darkness with an odor of must and decay in my nose, on my tongue, in my lungs. The dead have no need of light or warmth: it was a burial vault.

After a few unspeakable moments of comprehension, I raised myself to a sitting position. When I realized I was hunched over—knees pulled to my chin, arms crossed, hands clutching my own shoulders—I forced my body to unravel until I could sit cross-legged with my neck straight and my hands resting in my lap, as if, by forcing my muscles to unclench, I might convince my mind to relax, like a yogi on a bed of nails. I heard a scream begin to rise from the base of my throat and took a deep, shuddering breath to stop it.

The smell, like a damp, foul coldness, frightened me. The thought of what I might touch if I reached out my hands repelled me even more. Did they put bodies into coffins before locking them in vaults? Surely they did. But how many bodies, and what happened to them when the coffins decayed around them? Was I surrounded by rotting wood, rotting flesh, skeletons whose knotty, pitted surfaces crawled with . . . ?

"Stop that," I said aloud, to quell the creeping panic.

Cautiously, I stretched out my left arm—wincing at the pain the movement produced in my scraped, banged elbow—and made a semicircle with it in space. Nothing presented itself to my touch, although I felt as if I were stirring the thick, fetid air like a spoon through spoiled batter. I performed the same act with my other arm, again touching nothing. Whatever or whoever was in there with me was out of reach, at least. I breathed a little easier, if not more deeply, and tried not to think of things imaginary and real that might creep up to touch me in the dark.

The darkness was total. It was a black as deep as permanence, a black as all-encompassing as pain, a black as thick as fear, a black like the darkness in a child's room when the bulb in the night-light burns out, a black like the darkness in a widow's heart the day her husband dies, a black like a black hole, sucking me down, down into it.

"What if you were blind?" I said it aloud, again to staunch the bleeding wound of panic, but the sound of my own terror echoed down long-forgotten, haunted corridors in my brain. "If you were blind, it would always be dark like this."

No, said the voice of panic, if you were blind, you would sense changes of light, there wouldn't be this absolute, final, locked-in, eternal . . .

"Surely, some blind persons live in complete darkness," I argued in a loud, shaking voice I hardly recognized as my own. "And it doesn't frighten them. They're used to it, it's no big deal to them."

They aren't locked in a tomb, the voice of panic whispered.

"But what is a tomb but a small room with a door, and anyway, he said he'd be back for me . . ."

And you believe him? The voice of panic scoffed. There is no reason to think he will ever let you out, no logical reason at all. Even if he intends to, he is too high on drugs to remember what he has done with you. He will forget. Or he will be in a traffic accident and be killed, and nobody will ever know you are in here, and you will die a horrible, agonizing death of thirst and pain and starvation . . .

"Shut up. Shut up. Shut up."

You think it never really happens, the voice of panic said, growing shrill in my head, but think of those young girls they shut up in caves in the Himalayas as sacrifices to gods, think about the people who have fallen down wells and nobody has ever found, think about the miners who are caught in rock slides and slowly suffocate to death, think about people whose cars slide

247

off into rivers and they are locked inside and the water comes in, and think about little kids who get shut up in old refrigerators, and think about people who are kidnapped and locked in closets and nobody finds them until it is too late, and think about what it feels like when their oxygen begins to deplete and how those Irish hunger strikers went blind from starvation, and think about how you have always been slightly claustrophobic, how you can't stand to walk into meat lockers or bank vaults and you don't like walk-in closets or saunas, and how you begin to get a fluttery feeling at the bottom of your intestines and you begin to breathe faster, faster, and . . .

"Think of Francie!" I said.

I began to crawl on my hands and knees toward the door. My left hand struck something soft; at my touch, a foul smell filled the air, as if I had pressed something that released hideous gases. I drew back with a horrified scream and almost lost it. But then my right hand struck something solid. I felt the bottom edge of the door. By crawling on my hands up the door, I was able to stand, to lean against it, to try the handle . . . a handle? That's odd, I managed to think. . . . Why would there be a handle on the *inside* of a burial vault?

The door, which was not locked after all, swung open.

Quickly, I stepped clear of the door, out into the rain, then forced myself to turn around and look back. It wasn't a burial vault at all: my "tomb" of horror was only the maintenance shed that was built to look like a vault. Within, I saw bags of fertilizer—undoubtedly, the source of the decaying, musty smell. One of those bags was the "horrible" soft thing I had touched. I also glimpsed a sleeping bag and other grubby evidence of the Jackal's having taken up residence there for the past week.

"Fool," I pronounced.

But I didn't have time to feel humiliated.

Instead, I took off running again, toward the funeral home, this time in my stocking feet, and thinking of Francie with every pounding step.

36

From the memorial park, I ran to the crematory that was behind the mortuary, near the parking garage for the limousines. When I reached the cremation chamber, I jerked at the door so violently that when it opened, a cloud of fine dust wafted out at me. I crimped my lips shut against the probability that the dust was human ash.

Inside, there was a large gray furnace with a small, closed door at eye level. I opened the door and looked into the fiery chamber. Inside, a wood coffin was burning. I could only pray it didn't contain anybody unscheduled. My fingers, when I lifted them from the door, came away with a thin, grayish white coating of ash. Shuddering, I blew on them, floating ash into the small room, then scraped my fingers roughly against my suit, like Lady Macbeth rubbing out the telltale spot of death. Feeling nauseated with dread and distaste, I abandoned the crematorium, letting its door slam behind me. The rain that rinsed my face felt coldly, promisingly alive.

But it was with a growing and dreadful feeling of certainty about where to find Francie that I raced to the back door of the funeral home, this time heading for the delivery area where ambulances dropped off bodies, and where the morgue was located. If any door remained open, surely it would be this one.

I pulled on it, feeling unutterable relief when it came open easily to my touch. The relief turned quickly to apprehension, however, as I realized how carefully I must proceed from that point on. If the door was still open, it meant somebody was still on the premises, and I didn't know who, besides the Jackal, to be afraid of.

Quietly, I stepped into the delivery area and closed the door behind me. Someone had left the lights on, so for once, I wasn't fumbling in the dark. There were no living persons, besides me, in the delivery area—only a single coffin and a metal gurney with a body under a sheet. The murderer had almost succeeded in hiding Sylvia Davis's body, forever, in a coffin. Mightn't he try it one more time, figuring he would be luckier this time with Francie?

Nearly sick with dread, I padded quickly over to the gurney, leaving a trail of wet footprints behind me. I held my breath and pulled back the sheet: a naked old man lay there. His whiskers stood out on his bloodless skin like creosote posts; his eyelashes curled down over his cheek like a baby's. I re-covered him with the sheet and turned next to the coffin. It took a moment of studying to figure out how to unlock and open it, but finally I lifted the lid on its silent hinges: the coffin was empty.

But there was a black phone on the wall beside it.

Thank God. I reached for it to call the police.

A sudden clattering crash from inside the morgue froze my breath in my mouth, my heart in my chest, and my hand on the receiver. Silence followed the crash, which had sounded like metal striking the tile floor or wall.

I withdrew my hand from the phone and walked silently toward the morgue door, then flattened myself against the wall beside it to wait and listen. But I heard nothing, only a silence full of bloody and terrifying apparitions. Everything horrible that I could imagine in those moments I did imagine; every nightmare I had ever feared took breath and lived behind that closed morgue door. An image of Francie's face came to me— a gray face, slack and dead. And still, there was no further sound from behind the door.

If whatever was in there didn't come out soon, I would have to open that door and look inside. I counted five deep breaths, and then I slid my back along the wall toward the door and reached for the handle. I placed my hand on it, but before I could exert any pressure, it turned in my hand, shooting a lightning bolt of terror up my arm and into my brain. Somehow, I managed not to scream.

I snaked my hand back to my chest, and waited.

The door opened slowly; then Beryl Kamiski came out of the morgue, her head bent, walking like someone with an incalculable weight on her shoulders. Once through the door, she looked slowly to the left, then to the right, and saw me.

"Oh, my God!" she screamed, obviously and equally startled out of her wits. Her hands flew to her heart, her mouth. "Oh, Jenny, oh, you scared me so. Oh, we have to call the police right now. Please, please help me. Jack Smith just tried to kill me. Please . . ."

She staggered toward me, then turned away, then back, as if she were disoriented, confused, unable to know what to do next. Over and over, she moaned, "God, oh God, oh my God. Help me, help me. Oh my God."

I remained pasted to the wall at first, then I inched toward the door again until I could see inside. The Jackal lay on the white tile floor beside an overturned gurney. His arms and legs were spread-eagled, and a silver embalming needle stuck out of the middle of his chest. A river of red ran from his heart, over the white tile, into a drain in the floor.

"You killed him," I said, dumbfounded.

"Oh God." She moaned. "He was high on something, and crazy, and he was going to kill me, I don't know why. I think he killed poor Sylvia, and Muriel. Please, help me. Call the police, Jenny, please do it."

I stared at her.

"Why, Beryl?"

"Why?" She looked stupefied. "Because he's dead, Jenny, can't you see? Because we have to tell them he killed poor Sylvia and Muriel."

"No, I mean, why was he going to kill you, Beryl?"

"Because he was crazy!" She gaped at me as if I were the crazy one. "What's the matter with you? Somebody just tried to kill me and you stand there asking questions. Please, Jenny, call the police."

I backed over to the black phone and picked up the receiver. Its severed cord dangled uselessly from my hand. It would not have done me much good, a few minutes earlier, anyway.

"Look, look what he did," she moaned.

In order to find a working telephone, I would have to leave her alone.

"All right." I hung up the broken phone and walked toward her. "Come with me."

"No!" She screamed it as if in a panic, then said more quietly, "I have to sit down, I simply have to."

She wanted me to leave her there, I thought. Why? Suddenly, a memory of Muriel Rudolph's body came to my mind; I saw her clearly, in her bathrobe—which a woman might have left on, rather than change, if her early-morning surprise visitor was . . . another woman. And what was it the Jackal had said to me? . . . Something about getting some money together so we could leave?

I was stunned by a sudden avalanche of understanding.

"He tried to blackmail you, too, didn't he?"

She had turned away from me to walk toward a bench on the far side of the delivery area, but now she turned back around to face me. "What did you say, Jenny?"

"The Jackal tried to blackmail you, too, and so you killed him." My words came out slowly, but with increasing firmness, as I sorted them into order, as hesitancy evolved into conviction. "It was you who handled John Rudolph's prearrangement plan. Sylvia told the Jackal about the differences between the way Rudolph's funeral was supposed to be and how it really was, didn't she? They were pals, she told him lots of juicy things. And he figured it out, maybe when Muriel died? He's been living here on the grounds all week, and tonight, he saw your car still in the parking lot, and he saw his chance to corner you. He tried to blackmail you over the

252

murders, didn't he? And he was going to take the money and come back for me, and . . .''

"You're crazy, too," she said, wide-eyed.

"You might have paid him," I surmised, "but it takes a lot of money to live the good life you love, and to buy pretty cars for your pretty boy. As you said, sometimes it's hard to keep them happy, isn't it? He's lazy, Beryl, too lazy to be a good enough salesperson to dress the way he does, to drive the car he does. When did you finally decide to kill Sylvia? When she called you from his house, when you thought he'd slept with her?"

"You're out of your mind." She was shaking her head, as if in wonder at my stupidity, but at the same time, she was taking small, casually slow steps in my direction. I backed closer to the morgue door. When I had hung up the phone I had relinquished my only weapon. But I had figured out a way to get my hands on another one . . . if only my timing was better than it had been thus far this day.

"Where's Francie?" I asked her.

This time she didn't bother to reply but just kept coming toward me. I let her seem to force me backward into the morgue. Just inside the door, she reached over to a table and picked up a length of rubber tubing which she drew taut in her fists. Still, she kept coming, and I kept backing, until I felt the Jackal's body against the heels of my feet. I didn't try to suppress the shudder that ran visibly over my face and body, leaving it to her to interpret it as a shiver of fear.

She smiled, and said easily, conversationally:

"John was always bragging to Sylvia about the fine funeral he was going to have one day." She approached to within a couple of feet of me. "That's how she knew. But when she asked me about it, after he died, I said, don't worry about it, honey, I'll take care of it. But I knew eventually she'd tell Spitt, she was so damned conscientious." The cunning, knowing smile abruptly vanished, turned into a sneer; the warm, vibrant voice turned whiny, in cruel imitation. "At the party, she was crying to me about how much she missed him, about how she didn't get to say good-bye to him, and she was crying about how he was even going to be buried in the wrong coffin, and why hadn't I fixed that, like I said I would? And then she calls me from Russell's, from Russell's!—and she's crying on my shoulder like she always did, whining about how nobody loves her, and how much she misses John, and I say, let's go to the funeral home, honey, let's say us a private little good-bye to John. And while she's standing there looking at him, I came up behind her, and I said, "Good-bye, honey . . ."

I ducked, a split second before she lunged at me. I jerked the trocar out of the Jackal's chest, but then my feet, in their torn, wet stockings, slipped on the bloody floor, and I fell on my back on top of his body. Beryl lunged down at me, aiming the rubber tubing for my exposed throat. With all the strength I could manage from that position, I swung the trocar at her like a baseball bat.

It cracked solidly against her skull.

Her eyes rolled back in her head, the tubing fell onto my face, and she collapsed, falling on me, too, pinning me between her body and the Jackal's.

I worked myself free from their embrace, hoping I hadn't killed her. She would never have told me where Francie was, but maybe she would tell the police.

Once I had regained my feet, I started to leave the morgue to find a phone. It was then that I noticed the single bronze coffin at the back of the morgue.

I ran to it and unsealed it: there was Francie inside.

Like Beryl, she had been struck on the head; like Beryl's, her eyes were closed, but she was still breathing. I had guessed right about that much: Beryl had stored her in an empty coffin until it was safe to come back to kill her, which she might have done if the Jackal, and then I, hadn't interrupted her.

As gently as possible, I dragged Francie out of the coffin. I didn't give a damn about tampering with evidence. Once I got her laid out on the floor, I closed the coffin again. If the cops asked me—if Geof asked me—I would tell them that's where I found her, on the floor. With any luck, my mother's old friend would never have to know in what horrible place she had spent an hour of her life, and she would never have to suffer terrible nightmares of being locked in a small, dark, smothering vault. I covered her with a sheet to keep her warm, then kissed her forehead.

Before I left the morgue, I removed my panty hose, twisted them into a tight, wet rope, and used them to bind Beryl Kaminski's hands to her feet.

When I touched her ankles, she moaned and twitched.

I screamed, and nearly panicked again. It took all of my willpower to keep from grabbing the trocar and bashing her head in . . . again, and again, and again. I realized then that I could still kill her. I could take up the embalming needle and strike her another blow and call it self-defense. Standing there above her, contemplating that possibility, I thought of Darryl Davis and of his grief, and of the humiliation she had brought to Stan's decent family, and of the little Rudolph boys and their sister. What a savings it would be for the taxpayers if I killed her, what a vindication for the families she had ruined, what an evil weight off the world.

I lay the trocar down beside her and left the morgue to locate a telephone. I wanted Lewis to be the first reporter to hear the final details of the story that might bring him his journalistic "Glory Days." But first, I had to call the police station.

"Ailey?" I said, when he answered the page. "It's Jenny. Listen, I have a few new ideas about the case. If you're not busy, maybe you'd like to drop by the funeral home to hear them."